ONE LITTLE LIE

THE WESTBROOKS: FAMILY TIES BOOK 2

AVERY MAXWELL

THE BEST OF US LLC

There are 3.9 billion human males on this planet. The world has enough dicks, don't ya think?
Be nice. Be kind. Be genuine. Be honest. Just be a good human because kindness truly does matter!

To everyone who feels like they're always on the outside looking in, this book is for you.
To everyone holding the door closed, don't be a dick!

I think he scoffs, but his voice is so weak now I can't be sure. He knows it, too, and takes a few steps toward me. We're just inches apart.

Placing both hands on my shoulders, he stares into my eyes. An oddly intimate moment for two brothers, but when he attempts to speak, I know he's conveying the conviction he can't force his voice to portray.

"And Dad's death wasn't your fault either. You've damned yourself for all of eternity in a misguided attempt to keep a brotherly code. And you broke a beautiful soul in the process."

His words knock the wind right out of me. I know I hurt her. I know I probably destroyed her for a short time, but broke her? My teeth clench to keep tears at bay, and I shrug off his strange embrace.

"Then I guess we both have work to do." I'm already out of his door before he can respond.

In a blur, I make my way down the hall to my room. I've just turned the corner as GG's blue-haired nuisance of a friend pops out of the room next to mine. She has a crowbar and pliers in hand, and it's not even the weirdest thing she's done today. I'm living in a shitshow of a sitcom here in Vermont, and I need to get the fuck home.

My eyes close, and I breathe out slowly through my nose. I don't have the energy to handle Betty Anne right now.

"Oh! Well, hello, handsome. I was, er, I was just fixin' something for Rosa, ah, GG, ya know?"

I wave her off as I push the old-fashioned, gold key into my door. "I've got a migraine, Betty Anne. Forgive me." Not waiting for a reply, I quickly push through the door and enter my room.

My hands twitch, searching for an outlet I no longer allow myself. My mind is racing and spiraling with discord. The world is spinning, but then I realize it's actually me, turning in place with my head in my hands. My chest tingles, and I squeeze my eyes tight to block out the first signs of spots that appear in my line of sight.

"No. No. No. You did this to yourself, Halt. This is your punishment." My voice is choppy in the empty room, and I know I'm about to cave.

Grabbing the leather satchel my brother, Preston, routinely teases me for, I dig around until I pull out two hardcover journals. One about a year old, and one that hasn't left my side since I was a child. The book of regret. The book of Rylan.

My breath hitches as I open the latter, and it lands on the very first entry. A rudimentary drawing by a guileless seven-year-old.

My fingers trace over the charcoal stick figures of a crying little girl and the boy who fell in love with her that day. The memory assaults my senses savagely. Struggling to catch my breath, I sink to the floor beside the bed as visions play through my mind like an old school film reel.

Walking down the Waverley-Cay Elementary School hallway, I'm taking the long way back to class, even though I might get into trouble. Ash started kindergarten this year, and he's having trouble making friends. I hate it.

God, it's like I can still smell the stale air that permeated the cement block building in the ninety-degree heat. I rub the tip of my nose harshly, attempting to get rid of the scent.

If I hurry, I know I can peek in on Ash and get back to my class before my teacher notices, but as I pass Colton's classroom, I hear someone sniffle.

Glancing around, I wonder if I made it up. Then I see it. Two little, pink shoes are sticking out from under the rows and rows of raincoats that line the hallway. Not knowing what to do, I part the sea of rubber and vinyl and am shocked to see bright green eyes I recognize staring back at me, full of tears and sadness.

Rylan. Colton's best friend. What the heck is she doing out here?

Her little finger goes to her lips, and she silently shakes her head as the tears fall. A funny sensation in my chest has me burrowing into the coats with her.

"Rylan? What are you doing out here?" I whisper. "Are you hurt?"

"Weave me awone, Hatty." Her shaky voice is still thick with a lisp she hasn't been able to shake. I can feel her pain as if it were my own, but her nickname causes that feeling in my chest to happen again. I'm not sure if I like it or not.

For some reason, I feel too warm every time she calls me Hatty. I know she can't say Halton. She can't say Colton either, but Cowty doesn't make me feel funny.

"Rylan, I can't leave you here. Do you need to go to the nurse?"

I'm a year older than Rylan. Dad says that means it's my job to protect her.

The door beside us opens, and I hear her teacher instruct two little girls to search for Rylan.

How long has she been out here?

The door closes again, and the little girls snicker.

"Maybe she's crying in the bathroom because we told her no one could go to her birthday party."

"My mom said they probably wouldn't even have goody bags," the second girl gasps.

"Yeah, Mommy said I couldn't go because that's where bad people live. Can you believe Rylan is bad?"

My hands are curling into fists when I hear a whispered, "Pwease," and I freeze in place.

"Maybe if we just yell into the bathroom, we won't get the bad girl cooties."

It's the last remark I hear before their voices fade down the hall.

I immediately turn to Rylan, but she won't look at me.

"I-I'm not feewing weww. Nurse," Rylan cries before bolting from her hiding place and heading in the other direction.

I don't know how long I sit there before I get up and follow her to the nurse to tell the first lie of my life. Thirty minutes later,

15

Mom picks me up from school with a skeptical expression on her face.

We go through the motions of checking me out in the office, and when we reach the car, my tears flow as I tell her what happened.

My hands shake as I turn the page, knowing full well what I'll find but unable to stop the onslaught of memories.

"Why do we have to go to a little girl's birthday party?" Preston whines.

"Rylan is Colton's best friend, and they're having a hard time." Mom's reaction was swift, and his lip trembles. She glances at me but quickly returns her gaze to Pres. "How would you feel if no one came to your birthday because of where you lived or what Daddy did for work? Would that feel very good?"

"No," we all mumble in shame.

"The one thing you boys will grow up knowing is how privileged you are and how to use that to make other people's lives better. I was just like Rylan when I was a little girl. It broke my heart year after year when no one would play with me because I didn't have the right clothes or couldn't afford the nice shoes. You will never know that pain, but you'll for damn sure be the ones to make sure no one else ever feels that hurt if you can help it. Do you understand me?"

Five sets of eyes, as round as saucers, stare back at our mother. We all know 'damn' is a bad word, and she just said it. To us.

I slam the book shut. I can't handle this right now, but I'm powerless to the force that was Sylvie Westbrook that day. She worked her magic, and within the week, Rylan's mother was working for my father. The additional health insurance eased the burden of Mr. Maroney's cancer.

Even in the middle of my meltdown, I smile at the heart my mother has. Within a year, she had completely turned their lives around. Mona Maroney, working as my father's executive assistant, and two years later, helping Thomas Maroney rebuild his landscaping business by giving him free rein to create the gardens around the home where I grew up.

Colton's voice stirs me from my thoughts, and my nausea returns.

"Oh, good! You're right next door to Halton." As they open the door next to mine, the adjoining door between the two rooms swings open, and Betty Anne's handyman skills suddenly make perfect sense.

Fucking GG.

Colton sticks his head in the open doorway, and I'm frozen to my spot as my eyes connect once again with haunted green ones.

"Huh. Have the hinges on this door always been broken?"

"How the hell am I supposed to know? I-I, ah, I have to piss." I rush to the bathroom, tripping over my running shoes on the way.

"Jesus, Halt. Are you okay? You look like you've seen a ghost," Colton calls through the door.

Yeah. I've seen a ghost, all right. She's haunted my dreams my entire adult life, and I have no one to blame but myself.

I turn on the shower to drown him out, praying he'll just let it drop.

CHAPTER 3

RYLAN

*P*ropping my suitcase against the door, hoping it will stay closed, I turn to find Colton bellyflopping onto my bed. His hair, a few shades lighter than the rest of the Westbrook crew, falls over his forehead in an *I'm a playboy and I like it,* kind of way. Colty always has a smirk that screams sweetly playful, and the combination makes him dangerous to every living female, regardless of their age. Everyone except me.

"I swear, he's getting weirder every day." He chuckles, rolling over and resting his arms behind his head.

I force a laugh, but my insides are shaking so much I can feel my teeth chattering.

"God, it's so good to have you home, Ryguy. Well, in Vermont." His chuckle turns into a full-on laugh. "Can you believe what a shitshow we've stumbled into?"

I've talked to Colton almost every day of my life, even when I was living in London, so I know all about the craziness that happened with Ashton and their adopted brother, Loki. I've heard every detail of the Westbrook brothers' lives, sometimes in real time. It's almost as if I never left.

Except you did.

And then I came face-to-face with the man who doesn't love me but won't let me go either. Halton Westbrook is going to answer my questions whether he wants to or not. I know seeing me was a shock. Seeing him opened that wound I fight so hard to keep hidden, but I can't keep living the way I have.

This time he's gone too far.

"Rylan? Earth to Rylan? You okay?"

"Hm? Oh, yeah. Sorry. Probably jet lag."

Colton bolts from the bed and wraps me in a giant hug. *The Westbrook special.* These damn men and their hugs. They get it from their father. I didn't realize how much I missed them until now.

"I'll let you get some sleep. I have some work to do for Summerfest with GG, but I'll come back and get you for dinner. Sound good?"

I gulp, and he gives me a worried raise of his brow.

"Sure, that sounds good."

Frowning, Colton places his hands on his hips. All five brothers have a similar build and facial features, but they're also each distinctly their own. The likeness is part of the reason I moved to London for college. I didn't think my heart could take a constant Westbrook reminder. ·

"Are you sure you're okay? Do you need something?" He doesn't give me a chance to reply, a common occurrence with Colty. "You know, we are going to talk about Matthew at some point, and you're going to tell me if I have to fly to London to kick his ass."

Colton may never settle down, but he has the heart of a giant.

"Yeah, Colty. I'm fine. Just tired. I'll sleep for a few hours and be ready for dinner."

The smile, so similar to Hatty's, creeps across his face.

Ugh! *No, Rylan. Not Hatty. He's not Hatty anymore.*

"Sounds good. And listen, I've warned you about GG, but

seriously, she's a menace. Be careful around her. Lexi is good peeps. Blunt, straightforward, but she has a big heart under her tough-girl exterior. You'll get to meet Seth and Ari, too. He's Mom's newest addition to the family, and Ari grew up here. She's our age, really nice. I'm liking it here more than I thought I would, and I think it'll be good for whatever's going on with you."

I swallow the lump in my throat. "Can't wait to meet them." I'm surprised to find that I actually mean it.

Colton makes his way to the door. "Get some sleep, Ryguy. I'll round up the troops for a welcome to Vermont dinner."

"Colty, don't ..."

I wanted to tell him not to make a big deal about it, but he's already gone. Colton went into marketing because he loves to throw a party. He instinctively knows what works, and he told me once that if you can make something fun and inviting, you could sell just about anything.

Maybe that's what I need to do. Find the fun and sell the fact that my heart isn't one splinter away from fracturing, knowing Hatty is right next door.

~

"*W*hy the hell does he keep calling you Ryguy?" Lexi yells across the table to be heard over the country singer crooning about lost love. The constant buzz of the bar frazzles my nerves, but her smile is genuine, so I attempt to relax.

True to form, Colton pulled almost everyone together for dinner, but it didn't surprise me when Hatty didn't show up. *Geez, Ry. Stop thinking of him as Hatty. He's been Halton for years. Why has it reverted to Hatty now that he's close?*

I take a deep drink of the local IPA in front of me and damn near swallow my tongue in the process. Lexi stands up and moves to sit next to me as Ari gives her a serious expression, and I swear mouths a 'be nice' while I cough up a lung.

"Ah." I choke, remembering she asked me about Colton's nickname. "We've been best friends since we were six. I was kind of a tomboy back then. I guess it just stuck."

Lexi quirks a well-maintained eyebrow, and my fingers lift to mine self-consciously. *When was the last time I went for a waxing?* She's all kinds of intimidating, with her six-foot stature and model good looks.

Realizing Lexi and Ari are still staring, I take a daintier sip of my beer this time.

"So, you've known all these guys your whole life?" Ari asks, a hint of wonder in her tone.

I get it. The Westbrooks are a freaking force of nature. If I hadn't met Colton when I did, I would have been just another wallflower watching them take over every room with ease.

Laughter barrels through my chest. "Yeah, Preston has always been the cool guy, the leader watching out for the underdog. Easton was the jock without an ounce of ego. Colton's my goofball, and Ash …" My heart shudders, knowing he's a little broken right now. "Ash was always the gentle soul."

Lexi eyes me in a way that has my face flushing hot.

"You forgot someone," she says casually, but a girl can tell when someone's digging.

"D-Did I? I, ah … who?" I scratch my neck, pretending to think.

Lexi and Ari both angle their chairs toward me at the same time, a smirk I definitely don't like on Lexi's face. Before I can think better of it, I blurt, "You're dangerous."

"And I think you need a friend without a dick," she smarts right back.

That wicked flush creeps down my neck now, and my heart races like I've just sprinted six miles.

"No offense, but girlfriends have never really worked out all that well for me."

When Lexi grins, I feel like prey. "Then we're going to get along just fine, chica." She holds up two fingers, and the bartender literally jumps over the bar.

"Hey, Lex. Ya need something?" the young guy dressed in a plaid, button down with sleeves rolled to the elbows asks. He's cute but young. Younger than Lexi anyway, though I'd judge her to be close to my age.

"You're an old soul, Rylan." The memory of Halton's words whisper over my body like a million tiny butterflies kissing my skin. I shiver and want to rage at the same time. *He fooled you once, Ry, don't go there again.*

"Yes," Lexi informs the googly-eyed bartender. "We need tequila. Six shots, please."

My eyes go wide.

"The Westbrooks have welcome to the chaos, I have welcome to the she-pack where leggings are encouraged, make-up is optional, and friendship rules the roost."

The poor bartender is back before I can speak, placing the shots in front of Lexi and failing to catch her eye. She hands Ari and me a shot, then stares me down until I take it. It's like a strange version of peer pressure. You know she'll be fine if you turn it down, yet you desperately want to be included in her craziness.

I take the glass, and she hands me a lime.

"To the she-pack." Clinking our glasses, we shoot them back and come up spluttering in disgust while sucking on a lime.

"Does anyone actually like that taste?" Ari shivers, her words echoing my thoughts.

"No," Lexi states sardonically. "But we've got some bonding to do before our girl Rylan here combusts."

"Wh ... huh? I'm not going to—"

"Incoming," Ari whisper-screeches, nodding her head

frantically toward the door. I didn't know whisper-screeching was even a thing until this very moment.

Lexi and I follow her gaze to the front door where Easton has a hand on a … *Holy shit*. A smiling, laughing, slightly stumbling Hatty. Feeling Lexi's body tense, I shift my eyes to the left.

"Great," she grumbles. "How the hell did he know we were here?"

"Ah, it's like the Westbrook network. Where one goes, they all go," I whisper, shifting my gaze back to the guys.

They're two slightly different versions of their father, and I'm reminded how strong those Westbrook genes are. Easton's scowl eases slightly when his bright blue eyes find Lexi, but Hatty's glassy stare shines with sheer delight and never leaves my face. He zoned in on me the second the door opened, like a moth to a flame, and my insides shiver.

Easton marches through the crowd, dragging Hatty behind him. I drop my eyes to the glass in my hand but am unable to keep it there for long. By the time they reach us, Hatty's still sporting that boyish grin I haven't seen in years.

What the hell is wrong with him?

"Don't even think about it, Locket," Easton growls.

I'm shocked when Lexi doesn't talk back. It doesn't seem like her to take orders from anyone. Then Hatty laughs, and all the air leaves my lungs so quickly I'm lightheaded.

"What got into him?" Lexi scowls.

"GG," Easton replies while searching for Colton.

"No way. No way! Did she give him her wine?"

I turn to the sound of Lexi's concerned voice.

"What do you mean?"

"Beast! Did he drink GG's wine? It's probably not even legal. No one should be drinking GG's wine!"

Beast? Is she calling Easton Beast? That's … interesting.

He cringes in response, then gets defensive. "Don't you

think that's something you should have—I don't know—maybe mentioned?"

"What's up, guys?" Colt asks, finally leaving the dance floor and whatever local he was swinging around.

"Wh—" Burp. "Why didn't you dance with my Rylan?" Hatty slurs.

My Rylan.

I don't think anyone notices until I make eye contact with Lexi, and she crosses her arms, not even trying to conceal a grin that says 'gotcha'.

"Ryguy was having girl time. Plus, the girl on the dance floor is hot, Halt. Like, incinerate my clothes hot."

I never wanted Colton to see me as hot, but being dismissed so easily stings a little.

"But Rylan is … is …"

Lexi jumps forward before Hatty can say another word.

"Holy shit." Colt grins. "Is Halton drunk? I never thought I'd live to see the day."

"Er, not exactly." Lexi grimaces.

We all turn to her.

"He probably only had half a glass, but his lips will be loose for a while." She gives me a knowing glance, and my spine stiffens. "And he won't remember any of this tomorrow, or the next day, but it might come back to him slowly."

"What the hell did he drink?" Colton's shoulders shake with laughter.

"GG's wine. I thought for sure we'd convinced her not to make this shit anymore."

"What in God's name is in it?" Easton barks, dumping Halton in the chair next to me.

Hatty grins, and I attempt to shift my chair away, but Lexi's foot stops me from moving.

She stares straight at me and laughs. "She calls it her truth wine."

My eyes go wide as I feel fingers twirling a strand of my

hair. Slowly, painfully, time stands still as I turn my head to the left.

With ice-blue eyes a little too cloudy, Hatty smiles his hello. "I've missed you, my verity."

My body trembles and I'm frozen to the spot. Tunnel vision erases everything but those two blue eyes, so open and honest right now. I'm transported back in time, almost ten years, and my heart stops. One missing beat. Two missing beats. Three missing beats, and then ten years and one day comes crashing into me like a tsunami, and all the pain he caused is fresh again.

"I …" My gasp for air is so forceful Lexi can hear it over the band. Her face morphs from playful to concerned before I can blink, and her entire persona changes. Gone is the teasing ballbuster, and in her place is a fierce protector.

At this moment, I realize Lexi has more layers than the earth, and she hides them all in self-preservation. Perhaps we're more alike than I gave us credit for.

"Oh, shit." Leaning down, she places two hands on my shoulders and pulls me in close. "I don't know what the fuck is going on with the two of you, but whatever pain just ran through your mind cannot hurt you again. You hear me?"

I nod foolishly. I'm incapable of doing anything else.

Easton stares between the two of us, and everyone scatters, but it's like I'm in slow motion being guided out the door by Lexi with Colton, Seth, and the others ushering Hatty behind us.

"Put him in GG's truck with us, Easton."

He missteps, and I wonder if it's the use of his formal name that causes his pause. East stares between Lexi and me, concern suddenly appearing on his face, but Lexi shoos him to keep moving. She walks me to the front seat and pushes me inside while she climbs in the back with Hatty.

"Halton, I have a feeling you're going to want to keep

your mouth shut. Do you hear me?" she orders just as Easton climbs in the driver's seat.

"Locket, you'd better start explaining this shit right now."

"Whatever, East. Just get us home. We need to dunk Halton in a cold shower and put him to bed."

"I miss our hammock," Hatty slurs, and there goes that goddamn gasp of mine again.

Lexi reaches around the seat and places a gentle squeeze of support on my shoulder. I'm so grateful, tears prick the corners of my eyes.

What the hell is he talking about? Why is he saying this stuff? I mean nothing to him. He made that very clear a long time ago. I just need to get him to let go of his guilt now so he can let me go, too.

Hatty grunts, and I would bet money that Lexi just elbowed him. I know instantly Colton was right about her. She pretends to be a hard ass, but she's got the heart of a Westbrook.

CHAPTER 4

*H*alton, eleven years old.

"Hi, Mom."

"Hey, handsome. What are you doing down here?" she asks, pulling the laundry out of the dryer.

"Nothin'. I'm going outside for a while." I sound sulky, but I'm not unhappy. It's confusing.

"It's hard being in the middle sometimes, huh?"

I shrug my shoulders because she hit the nail on the head. Preston and East just left to do whatever teenagers do. Colton is lost in his 'epic game of Madden' on the X-box, and Ashton is tearing apart a computer in the library with Loki.

I just don't fit in. I tuck my notebook and pencils tighter under my arm.

"You know," my mom continues with a funny lilt to her voice, "I'm pretty sure I saw Rylan head out to the garden earlier."

My gaze snaps to hers as soon as I hear Rylan's name, but I try to play it cool. She's Colton's friend, after all. It's only the first day of summer vacation, and already things are looking up.

"Is she staying with us all summer again?" I try to keep the hopefulness out of my voice, but my mom smiles.

"All summer," she sings. "Mona or Thomas will pick her up at the end of the day, depending on who finishes work first."

My heart rate speeds up like it always does when Rylan is near.

"Cool. Do we have any of the ah ..."

"Cookies?" she finishes with a smile.

My hands get clammy, and I nod. Rylan loves cookies.

"I put a few in the cooler bag by the door with some drinks." Smiling, she nods toward the back door.

"Thanks," I mumble, feeling strange, and I walk outside. As soon as it shuts behind me, I take off running. I know exactly where to find her.

"Give me a word, Hatty?" she calls over her shoulder before I'm even close enough for her to have heard me.

"How do you do that?" I shout.

She shrugs her shoulders as I get closer. "I don't know. I just feel you, I guess."

There goes that funny little flutter again. A few months ago, I started spouting off words I'd learned in English class, trying to come up with a nickname for her. She's called me Hatty for as long as I can remember, but nothing ever sticks for her, and I'm definitely not calling her Ryguy like Colton. That's stupid.

I grin when I notice the way the sun makes pieces of her brown hair sparkle. Hickory, my mom had called the color once, but hickory is wood. Dull. There's nothing dull about Rylan.

"Sunbeam."

Giggles echo across the narrow path as I inch my way closer. "There is no way you're calling me sunbeam, Hatty." She turns, and I frown.

"Why are you sad?"

Ever since the day I found her at school, Rylan and I have had a secret friendship. She's technically Colton's best friend, but I feel like she's also mine.

"Is Colty still playing video games?"

I feel the frown form on my face, but I'm not giving up that easily.

"Rylan. Seriously, why are you sad?"

She huffs out a breath, and her bangs fly high above her head.

"Madelyn Tanner told me not to try out for cheer team because I'm too fat." Her face scrunches up, and my body tenses like when I'm ready to fight Easton for picking on me.

"Madelyn Tanner is a jerk face, Rylan. You're not fat."

She rolls her eyes. "I'm ... pudgy." Before I can argue, she's jumping up from where she was lying in the grass. "Sunbeam, huh?" She grabs the camera at her side and spins in a circle.

This is our game. I give her a word, and I really am trying to find a nickname for her, but she turns them all down, then captures the word with her camera.

I sit down on her towel and watch her spin in place, taking in all the flowers, plants, and bushes around us. I know the second she finds it. A single ray of light landing on a big, pink flower I could never tell you the name of.

Click. Click. Click. She snaps photos of it from every angle, then runs over and flops down beside me. With our heads together under the sun, we view her visions of sunbeams.

Lifting her gaze to mine with a smile that outshines the sun, she grabs my notebook. "Your turn, Hatty. Draw me a sunbeam."

∽

I wake with a start. The morning rays blind me instantly. *Sunbeams.* Sitting on the edge of the bed, I inspect my room. This is my room, right? *Shit.*

"What the hell happened?"

"Well, Fibby. You were hiding for starters."

"GG? What the hell are you doing in here?"

Last night comes back in a montage of fuzzy clips.

"What happened between making the cookies and waking up here?"

A cackle that could wake the dead sounds off the walls of

my head. I didn't have a hangover before, but I sure as fuck do now.

"Nothin' bad, Fibby. Your brothers and that sweet girl next door took care of ya."

That doesn't sound good.

"I don't remember drinking any ..."

GG cackles again, and I turn to find her sitting in the corner at the small table. She's set up there with her coffee, flipping and crossing cards that are absurdly large.

"What did you give me, anyway? Did you drug me or something? And what exactly are you doing in my room? It's fucking weird, GG."

I know she's eccentric, but watching a guest sleep crosses a line, even for her.

"Oh, calm yaself. I wasn't watching ya sleep. But it is almost noon, and my cards weren't working, so I came to check on ya, Fibby. That's all. And it was just a little home-made wine. You must have drunk more after I left you. That's not my fault." She doesn't even hide her grin, and I'm experiencing first-hand the crazy that is GG.

Preston has dealt with her. Easton has, too. However, that was when she was matching them up. Easton may not admit it, but we all know something is going on between him and Lexi. *I'm happy for him.* That's when the first part of her sentence hits me like a kick to the teeth.

My face pales as she sorts her cards and sets them down haphazardly.

Fibby.

Lexi's grandmother is known for giving nicknames to her love matches. Preston was Broken Heart, which was fitting for more than one reason. Easton is Grumpy Growler.

I have to get out of here.

Standing to go, I feel a breeze where there shouldn't be one and pause. Lifting the sheet, I see I'm buck ass naked.

Wonderful.

"That's right, let it all sink in. We've got our work cut out for us this time, Fibby. Wanna start with why ya lied?"

My mind is at war with memories of prom all those years ago, but I fight through it with clenched teeth, and my voice takes on an edge much too harsh to be used on an eighty-year-old woman when I say, "I don't know what you're fucking talking about, GG. I have to get ready for the Summerfest meeting at the lodge."

And just my luck, it doesn't even phase her.

When she raises her eyes, I know she doesn't plan to leave.

"Here's the thing, Fibby—"

"Stop calling me that," I hiss.

GG sets her cards down and gives me a long, stern glare. Her blue eyes that haven't dulled with age pierce me with intent. "You goin' to tell me the truth?"

I glance away, and she continues.

"See, here's the thing, Fibs. I know who your gal is, but I don't have a name for her. I don't like it, but I think I understand why."

"Nicknames never really stuck with her," I grumble, and want to slap a hand over my mouth like a girl in a chick flick.

What in the ever living hell?

GG snickers, and if I didn't know better, I'd think she had something to do with my slip up.

"There's that ..." she pauses, and I tuck my hands beneath my legs like a child, "but my cards are showin' that you're the only one needing help. You've got so much turmoil and heartache goin' on in there, I'm surprised you haven't imploded already. So, tell me, why do ya keep pushing her away?"

"I don't know what you're talking about, but I really need to—"

"I'm not sure. I'll check on him. You think he's still passed out?" Rylan's voice carries through the open door, and I freeze in place.

Her head crosses the threshold by only a couple of inches, and when her eyes land on mine, she bobbles her phone. She never was graceful, but she's still the most beautiful woman I've ever seen.

"Eeep," she squeaks, and jumps back. "S-Sorry, Colton asked me to make sure you were up. After, ah, after last night, I mean."

GG steps out from the corner, and Rylan squeals again.

"He's just fine. So, this is the famous Rylan." I watch in horror as GG goes nose to nose with her and stares into her eyes so long even I fidget. "Yup. I knew it. Time will tell, child. Time will tell."

"T-Tell what?" Rylan gasps.

"If you'll be the truth or the salve that puts Fibby back together."

My verity.

Pinching the bridge of my nose, I pray no one has filled Rylan in on GG's extra-curricular activities yet, because she can be neither of those things. Standing suddenly, I expect the room to swirl, but apparently, this isn't your standard hangover. Wrapping the sheet around my mid-section, I refuse to make eye contact with either of them as I storm past them and slam the bathroom door for good measure.

Just as I'm about to turn the water on in the shower, GG's inability to whisper gives away her words.

"He's going to be a tough nut to crack, that one, but I'm never wrong."

"Uh, wrong about what?" The confusion in Rylan's voice has the muscles in my neck bulging as I strain to hear the rest of their conversation.

"Destiny."

Shaking my head, I pull back the shower curtain and curse under my breath.

Why, in God's name, are my clothes from last night in a puddle at the bottom of my tub?

~

$\mathcal{W}$alking into GG's lodge an hour later, I feel that sense of dread you get when you think you might have done something embarrassing, but you blacked out and can't quite remember. It only gets worse when I stumble on Colton and Lexi.

"Should we tell him?"

"God, why didn't I think to take any pictures. It'll probably never happen again, and now I have no proof," Colton whines.

"How much do you think he remembers?"

I freeze in the small hallway. They have to be talking about me, and my neck gets hot. *Shit.*

"I don't know, but it was fucking amazing seeing him smile for a change."

"I think we should tell him." Lexi sounds resigned in her decision. At least someone is looking out for me.

"I don't know, Lex. I don't want to take any chances on GG coming after me next. If he really doesn't remember anything, I say no harm, no foul. It's not like he streaked through the streets of town or anything. I swear to God, GG is a scary witch. What if she turns those powers on us? I say we ignore it and see how it pans out for him."

So much for the brotherhood. *Mother of God, this can't be happening.*

"You're pretty convinced he's Fibby then?"

"Hell, yes. It's not me, and she's giving Ash a wide berth. It's about time, too. Halton has always been reserved, but I hate seeing him so miserable all the time."

If I wasn't already dying of mortification, I'd probably

laugh at how freaked out Colt sounds. But he's wrong. I'm not miserable. I just like being alone.

Liar.

"You have nothing to worry about, you know?"

Rylan's voice in such tight proximity causes my heart to lurch in my chest. I take a step back to put some space between us, but I hit the wall.

Has this hallway always been so fucking narrow?

I force my eyes to remain open even as her scent—cookies and sunshine—fills my nostrils. It's all I can do not to inhale deeply like it'll be my last breath.

"Halton," she snaps, and what's left of my heart falls to pieces.

She's never called me Halton before. Not ever. To keep from causing a scene, I swallow the emotions that are threatening.

I nod but don't hold eye contact. Instead, I stare through her, keeping my eyes unfocused, and avoid her glare for as long as I can. I don't know what would be worse, finding happiness or the pain I caused still lingering in her gaze, so I refuse to chance it.

"Whatever, Halton. You have nothing to worry about. You didn't do anything too stupid last night. But you kept calling me your verity. I-I need to know why? Why won't you let me go?" she whispers, but it's strangled, and my chest vibrates with the need to hold her.

"I don't know what you're talking about." My voice sounds bitter, the gravely tone painful.

"Who owns Hatty's Heart?"

Shock has my gaze dropping to hers. *She wasn't supposed to know about that.* They promised me it was untraceable. Just a small shelter company within three others, so I could take care of her if she needed me. Hearing it, even in my head, sets off creeper vibes, but I couldn't control myself.

"I know it's not Colton, and my parents would have just given me the damn car, Halton."

Fuck. I know how it sounds, but when I saw on Instagram that her piece of shit car died and she was taking two different buses to get to work through some seedy parts of London, I'd cracked.

"What about the oven? When we had the electrical fire, were you responsible for the team that showed up two hours later?"

"You're sounding crazy, Rylan. I'm sure your fiancé is very capable of taking care of shit like that."

The weasel. I fucking hate the guy, and I've never even met him. The thought of her marrying him causes the bile to rise dangerously high in my throat.

"He probably would have, but that's not his job anymore since he left me." Her brow scrunches, and she glances down. "Or, kicked me out, rather."

For the second time, my eyes lock on hers against my will.

"He broke up with you?" My voice is deadly, and my hands curl into fists so tightly my arms shake. "Why would he do that?"

"He said he couldn't live with my ghosts anymore. I'll admit, I assumed it was Colty for the longest time, stepping in to help whenever I got myself into a jam. But it wasn't adding up. Colton would have admitted it when I cornered him. It took me months to find Hatty's Heart, but I did, and now you need to tell me the truth or let me go ..."

"Ah, hey, guys. Everything okay?" Lexi asks. Neither of us heard her enter the hallway, and she has to turn sideways to slip between us in the narrow space.

Sliding my body along the wall, I ease away from them both. "Just dandy. Rylan here was telling me about her affinity for conspiracy theories."

The gasp that hits the back of my head belongs to Rylan. I

know without turning that her pouty mouth is open in the perfect O, and her face is flaming red. It always happens when she's pissed, and we are all better off if she stays pissed. The more she hates me, the easier this will be for everyone.

～

"*Where did this come from?" Rylan's smile settles something in me. I never feel at peace unless she's near.*

"Dad helped me build it yesterday." I grip the back of my neck, embarrassed, but I've been a nervous wreck over this all day. I hope she likes it.

"Hatty! This is amazing. It's exactly like we talked about."

It really is. I drew the hammock we've talked about for two years, and finally, I found the courage to ask Dad to help me build it. It took the better part of our weekend, but we finished just in time.

Before I can lift my gaze, she's catapulted herself into my arms, and I hold her tight. My fourteen-year-old hormones are wreaking havoc on my lower anatomy.

"Come lay with me. We can watch the clouds."

Together, we climb in and lay side by side. It's the first of many hours we'll spend like this, and the only time I feel completely whole.

"Give me a word, Hatty?" she whispers, resting her head on my shoulder as she holds her camera to the sky.

"Sempiternal," I rasp.

Lowering her camera, Rylan frowns. I chuckle as she pulls out her phone and Googles it.

"Hmm ... lasting forever, huh?"

I grin, nodding like a fool. Out here in nature, she'll never be able to capture that with her camera. I've taken to trying to stump her over the last few months, and so far, I haven't succeeded.

Turning her camera around, she scoots closer so our faces are pressed together.

"Smile, Hatty."

And I do. Big. Toothy. Happy.

"We'll last forever, huh?" My voice is thick with emotion, but when she rests her palm on my chest, I think I might explode.

"We're sempiternal." Her damn smile wraps around my body like a protective shield, eviscerating all my worries, fears, and insecurities.

CHAPTER 5

"*C*heers." Colton clinks his mug with mine.

We're sitting across from each other in a red-and-white checkered booth at The Marinated Mushroom, Burke Hollow's Italian restaurant and pizzeria. My best friend has never grown out of his pizza obsession, so here we are, having a beer and waiting on his spinach and bacon carb addiction. The scents of yeast and marinara drifting from the kitchen are oddly comforting.

Leaning back into the booth, Colton rests one arm along the back and watches me over the top of his glass. My chest pings painfully when he smirks. They all have the same crooked lip that tilts up. I used to love that about Hatty.

"I talked to Preston this morning."

The claw that had my heart in a vice releases its grip. "Yeah? When's he coming?"

Colton chuckles. "As soon as your parents can get packed up?"

"What? I talked to Mom this morning; she didn't mention anything." *Why wouldn't she have told me?*

"I think it was a Preston special."

Preston has always been generous, but when their father

died, he really had to lean on my mom to learn the ropes of The Westbrook Group. He's made sure to repay her tenfold since he found his footing.

"She says she's never allowed to retire."

"Oh, God. The place would burn to the ground. Preston wouldn't be able to function. He counts on her for everything."

I smile because I know she'll work as long as humanly possible. She and Sylvie have become the best of friends over the years, but she will probably always feel indebted to the Westbrooks for their kindness. Our lives would have been very different if they hadn't swooped in and claimed us as their own all those years ago.

My parents are the best examples of love I've ever seen. I know it broke their hearts when I left home and put an ocean between us. My mom's the only person on earth who knows the truth about Hatty and me, and as much as it broke her, she understood my need for space.

"So," Colton prods, "you gonna tell me what the hell happened in London and why you left in such a hurry?"

Worrying my bottom lip, I play with the straw the waitress left for our waters.

"Ryguy? What's going on?" He reaches across the table and stills my hands.

The bell on the door chimes, and we both lift our gaze. The place has been pretty quiet, so the shrill sound catches our attention, and we both watch as Hatty walks through the door, oblivious to his surroundings.

Like a bad 80's movie, time moves in slow motion as Hatty enters the restaurant.

"Halt," Colton calls. "Hey, over here."

Hatty stops mid-stride, then turns, and everything but him fades to the background. His focus locks on Colton's hand that still has a firm grasp on mine. My fingers twitch with the need to pull them away, but Colty holds on tightly.

"Come on, come sit."

His eyes never leave our hands, but they narrow before a pained expression crosses his face.

After all this time, I still want to run to him. To protect him and fix what's wrong. Once upon a time, I would have known before he did. *How can I still long for him after all he's done?* Slowly, he drags his gaze up my arm to meet my eyes. It feels like a lover's kiss. My mouth instantly goes dry. I might even see stars because I'm surely not breathing.

When Hatty's glare takes me prisoner, I'm lost. *I've loved this man for all my life*. Even if my mind won't admit it, my heart recognizes his beat from a thousand miles away. And when his face goes hard, I know that's just how far from me he is.

"Can't. Just picking up some pizza for Ash. See you later," he barks.

"Jesus. I don't know how to get through to him," Colt whispers sadly, finally releasing my hands.

We watch as he picks up two large pizzas and, without glancing our way, raises his hand. "See you later."

As quickly as he came, he's gone, and my heart feels hollow.

"I never wish GG's scary fucking voodoo on anyone, but damn, I hope she sets him right."

"How so?" It falls from my lips so fast, I have to force myself to sit back and relax. Placing my hands in my lap, I clasp them together until my knuckles turn white.

"Oh, lord. Don't tell me you forgot? Remember, I told you about the tarot things and how she matched everyone?"

"Yeah?"

"She dropped a nickname a couple of weeks ago. *Fibby*. Who the hell knows what it means, maybe fibber? I mean, I've never known Halton to lie, but she's scary good when it comes to this shit. As long as I can stay far, far away from those cards, I'm good. But things need to change for Halt. He's turning into something he always hated."

"Wh-What's that?" My voice is two octaves too high, but Colton doesn't notice.

"A sad fucking asshole. Don't get me wrong, I love him. I always will. But he hasn't made it easy, ever, and it's getting worse the older he gets."

"Why do you think he's sad?" I can't help myself. I need to know.

Colton shrugs as something dark crosses his face. Something I've never seen from my happy-go-lucky friend. "Sad, or haunted. Either way, someone or something weighs heavily on his soul, and he doesn't know how to let it go."

We're interrupted when the pizza arrives, and I use the distraction to ruminate on all Colton just said. A niggling feeling of unease has settled in my gut, and I don't know what to make of it.

"You're really good at changing the subject, Ryguy, but seriously, I want to know what happened to send you running home without any of your stuff."

"Th-Things just didn't work out with Matthew."

"You were going to marry him."

I was. It seemed like the right thing to do. I gave him as much of my heart as I could. The piece that was left, but I always knew it might not be enough.

"I was," is all I can admit to Colton, though.

"Don't get me wrong here, Ry. You know I love you, but I've known you a long time. You don't seem all that upset by a broken engagement. Promhole devastated you, but someone you were going to marry suddenly broke things off, and you're just ... eh? Didn't work out? What gives?"

God, if he only knew promhole was his brother, and he did more than devastate me. He shattered me into so many pieces I'm still not whole.

"I think I just liked the idea of it working out between

41

Matthew and me. I wanted what Mom and Dad had so badly that I was willing to settle. When he called me on it, I didn't have an argument. I loved him, I think. But was I in love with him? Soul crushingly in love with him? I don't think I've ever known that feeling."

You, my friend, are a goddamn liar.

"I get the feeling that's not the entire story, but I'll be here when you want to talk. Can I tell you something?"

"Always."

"Matthew was a nut monkey."

My fork drops to my plate with a loud, clattering noise. The couple next to us glances over, and I force a smile.

"Why do you say that?"

Colton shrugs and runs his hands over his five o'clock shadow. "He was a prick to me, so that was strike number one. Whoever you marry has to love me, too. We're a package deal." He winks. "Strike number two? He never noticed you. He never held your hand; he didn't watch your face to see your expression change to know if you were happy or sad. He was just blah. You deserve someone that can't take his eyes off of you. Someone who loves you so much they're convinced you'll always shine brighter than the stars. We had pretty great examples of love growing up, Ryguy. Don't sell yourself short. You deserve the fairytale."

I sit back, stunned. "That's pretty romantic coming from Peter Pan. But why didn't you ever say anything?"

"I don't know. I kept thinking you'd back out. I would have, though, before you walked down the aisle." He smirks.

"Wow. Great! Would you have let me buy the dress, too? Geez, Colt. You're supposed to be my best friend."

He tosses his napkin in my face. "Oh, I would have said something before your bachelorette party. I already planned that as the night I'd kidnap you and make you see reason."

"Pretty confident you'd be at my bachelorette party, huh?"

"Pfft. Please, I'm your best friend. I'll be planning the

damn thing. And it will be epic when it happens. Vegas, strippers, the whole nine yards."

"Just because you treat me like one of the guys doesn't mean I actually am one of the guys. You know that, right?"

His grin rivals the devils. "What? No strippers?"

"Will they have penises?"

Colton grimaces. "Right. No strippers."

"So, you really have no idea what's going on with Hatty?" My chest constricts just saying his name.

"Hatty? Jesus. I haven't heard that name in years. Only you could get away with calling him a girl's name." He laughs, then becomes serious. "No, Ryguy. I don't know what happened to him, but it's like one day, the life, the fun, the light just left him. For a while, I thought it was losing Dad. But now? Now I have no fucking clue."

Emotion clogs my throat as he speaks because I know what happened. It happened to me, too. The light goes out when you lose faith in love.

"You sure you're okay? You look a little pale." Colton reaches across the table to feel my forehead. "Ah, not really sure what I'm supposed to be feeling for here."

Laughing, I swat him away. "You feel someone's forehead to see if they have a fever. Geez, Colty. You really haven't changed. I've missed you, though."

"Ditto, Ryguy. Glad to have you home."

∼

*S*itting on the edge of my bed, I stare at the broken door separating me from Hatty. I should just march over there and demand answers, right? That's what I came home for. It's the least I deserve, but if I'm being honest, I'm worried about him, too.

Colton said he's turning into a sad asshole. Carrying around guilt for ten years will do that to a person. It makes

43

me more determined than ever to get him to let it go. It might be the only way for either of us to move forward.

Remembering the ache I felt when our eyes clashed at the pizza place, I steel my resolve. I can't keep holding back my heart, saving it for a man who can never love me in return. Even if, for the briefest moment, I saw a flash of the love I thought we once had.

Childish ideas about love are what got you hurt in the first place, Rylan. Remember that.

Tears swell in my eyes at the thought, but if he can't love me, he has to let me go. And I'll have to learn to live with half a heart.

Crossing the room, I can see he attempted to barricade the door closed, but the thing is basically just leaning against the frame. Pressing my ear to it, I listen, trying to find out if he's in there. After a few minutes of silence, I shake my head and walk to the shower.

≈

hat am I doing? I'm not adventurous. I'm not this bad girl that sneaks out of the house to catch a bus to ride four hours through the Blue Ridge Mountains. I'm an awkward, sixteen-year-old girl who hides behind walls, but here I am.

Hatty needs you.

I wanted to punch him right in the face when he called me hours ago to tell me he was on his way to Asheville, the art mecca of the southeast, for a small showcase on his charcoals.

"What the hell, Hatty? Why didn't you tell me? I would have come with you."

"I'm not sure I can do it. I-I don't want you to see me fail. I just wanted you to know. I need some of your ..."

"Some of my what?"

"It sounds stupid, never mind."

"Hatty Millhouse Westbrook."

"Jesus, Rylan. I fucking hate that name."

"I know." I laugh. "That's why I said it. Now, tell me before I really pull out the big guns."

His voice is soft, and I can hear the rain hitting the car as he drives. "I-I just ... you're my talisman. You bring me good luck. I need that tonight."

My chest aches for him. Hatty is harder on himself than I ever thought possible. It's almost like he hates himself. Loathes who is he, but I never understood why. He's incredible.

"Well, I'm not sure how good a talisman I can be from four hours away, you jerk. Why didn't you tell anyone? If not me, why not Ash or your mom?"

"You know why. You're the only one I would have told, but I don't want you to see me fail. I'm not like the rest of my family. I don't fit in, and they wouldn't understand. They would have showed up because that's what we do, but they wouldn't get me. Not like you do."

"I don't think you give any of us enough credit," I grumble. "And why are you so sure you're going to fail, Hatty? I've known you my whole life. I know how amazing you are."

"Talisman," he whispers. "The traffic is picking up. I should go. Will you be up for a while? If I make it inside, I probably won't get out until after midnight."

"You know I will." But I already know I'll be there by his side, no matter how much trouble I'm about to get into.

"Thanks. Talk to you soon."

"Yup. See ya, Hatty."

The bus pulls into the station, and I wrap my coat tighter around my shoulders. It's scary as hell out here by myself. By myself. The thought has me pulling up short, and the person behind me barrels into my back.

"Sorry," I mumble and step to the side.

I've always had Colton on one side and Hatty on the other. My protectors, my friends, my family. I love them both, but I also know *that love isn't equal. My love for Hatty has changed, evolved, or maybe I just became acutely aware of it at some point in the last few years. Regardless, I've never acted on it. We're friends, and telling him how I feel would surely ruin my relationship with both Westbrooks. Selfishly, I know I need them both too much to risk it.*

Shaking my head, I pull up the map on my phone and start the quarter-mile walk to the river arts district. I have no idea what gallery he's in, but I'm hoping it won't be hard to find. Thankfully, the rain has subsided, but it's a dreary night for such a special occasion.

I walk faster than usual. Maybe it's nerves doing this alone, or maybe I just sense Hatty's discomfort like it's my own, but I make it to the corner of Lyman Street and River Arts Place in record time.

The streets are busy with people fluttering about. Whispers of grand art and spectacular landscapes drift through the open air, but it all fades as my eyes land on Hatty, sitting on the side of the road with his head in his hands.

He didn't go inside, and my heart plummets for him. I can't help but wonder if he would have gone in if I'd been with him.

Quietly, I make my way down the block until I'm standing right behind him. "Give me a word, Hatty?"

His shoulders tense, but his head springs up, searching to his left, then right, so I step forward and take a seat on the wet pavement beside him. He slumps forward on a sigh.

"Dulcet."

"What is?" I ask.

"Your voice. I-I couldn't go in. They wanted me to speak to the group. There were only about twenty people, but all their eyes would have been on me. I just couldn't do it."

Resting my head on his shoulder, I feel him relax. "If my voice soothes you, why wouldn't you have let me be here for you, Hatty? Make me understand."

"I don't understand myself, Rylan. How am I supposed to make you understand?"

"Try? For me?"

Turning his face, he rests his chin on the top of my head. "My brothers are larger than life. My parents are literally the best people I've ever known, and they expect nothing of us but to give back to the community. To be a good person. My brothers excel at putting on a show, playing the part, but me? God, Rylan. I die inside a little every time I have to put on a suit and smile for the cameras. There are so many of us I can hide behind them, but when it's just me? I-I want nothing more than to run and hideaway on a mountain somewhere so no one can see me. I have every opportunity in the world. My family is richer than sin, and I can't even bring myself to put it to good use by participating in the events my mom plans. How messed up is that?"

I squeeze his arm in encouragement, and he continues.

"I hoped by doing this on my own, I'd prove something, at least to myself. But all it did was confirm my inability to fit in. I don't fit in anywhere."

"You fit with me, Hatty. You always have."

He turns then, and my head falls away from his shoulder. "You are the good moiety of my soul."

"You need to stop reading the dictionary. I can't keep up with these big words anymore." I laugh, but it fades as Hatty stares at my lips. My heart races as the air shifts between us, and I forget to breathe.

"You came," he whispers.

Is it just me, or is his face inching closer to mine?

"I always will, Hatty. If you can't believe in yourself, I'll always be here to do it for you."

"You're the cynosure in my world."

"I don't know—"

He closes the distance between us, effectively cutting off my question when his lips land gently on mine.

I gasp, and his tongue timidly caresses my lip. A feeling deep in my belly I never knew existed rages and roils as I clamber to get closer, but as quickly as it started, he pulls away and smiles.

My eyes search his for meaning. He kissed me. But what does it mean?

"You're the only thing I know to be true, Rylan. The only time I feel whole is with you. You're my talisman, my world, my verity."

"Truth," I gasp. Verity was a vocabulary word in school last year. I remember telling him I thought it was the most beautiful word in the entire English language, and now he's called me his truth.

A shy smile pulls at his lips, and he leans in to kiss me once more. "My verity," he sighs just before I taste his lips for the second time.

~

J gasp for breath as I realize my shower has run cold. The memories of Hatty and I knock the wind from my lungs as I double over, attempting to breathe. It's been years since a memory has assaulted me like this, and it hurts more than I remember.

I can't go back to this dark place.

It took me years to move on from him. I have to be stronger than this. Just because he's next door doesn't change the way he feels. Unrequited love is a real bitch sometimes, but I won't let it shred me to pieces again. I need to make him understand he doesn't have to feel guilty over me anymore. He can forget all about the love we once had, and maybe, just maybe, my heart will learn to move on again, too.

CHAPTER 6

HALTON

*S*eeing my brother hold Rylan's hand is the worst kind of pain. It seals my fate, too. *My father was right*. My life is fucked.

I don't remember the drive back up the mountain, or what Ash said when I threw the pizzas at him and walked away. All I know is I'm a man on the edge, and I don't know how I can survive seeing her every day.

When she first moved to London, my heart forgot to beat, but seeing her now? Now I know I would have lost my mind a long time ago if she'd been close by.

How can I possibly handle seeing her and Colton together? Knowing she was with dingle dick in London was hard. Fuck, it sucked. But part of me was happy I wouldn't have to see my brother start a life with her.

And this confirms what I already knew to be true.

I'm not good enough for her. A good man would be happy for his brother, regardless of the pain, and that's not me. The rage I felt seeing him hold her hand was other-worldly. I'd never experienced a hate, a pain so viscerally as I did today. That makes me a fucking monster.

"You can't do this to him, Halt. Colton loved her first." My

father's words are so clear, I could swear he was standing in front of me again. *"She deserves to be happy, Halton. Someone that lifts her up to shine in a crowd full of strangers. You're—"* I hadn't let him finish. I knew what he would say, and I didn't need to hear my own father telling me I wasn't good enough.

The memory of what comes next has my body in motion, even as my mind stays caught in a nightmare.

~

*T*he swinging door of the old, industrial kitchen jerks me from my thoughts. Everything comes into focus, like waking in the middle of sleepwalking. The commercial mixer whips the butter, sugar, and eggs while I mix the dry ingredients by hand.

"Can't say I'm surprised, Fibby."

A primitive sound grumbles in the back of my throat as GG approaches.

"Tell me what draws you to baking, Fibs."

"The control." There's no hesitation. I know why baking soothes me. "I always know what I'm going to get. Two and a quarter cups flour, perfectly sifted and measured cut into cold butter, will yield the same result every time. It's numbers and measurements. It's exact. It's honest."

"That's true, sometimes," she hedges. My body stiffens as she moves closer, washes her hands, and steps beside me at the mixer. "But sometimes, things in our world change, Halton. Altitude, for instance. You can use the exact same recipe here and again in Denver, Colorado, and you're gonna have a very different experience. You see, while you control what you can control, there's always the potential for that outside force to knock your plans to hell."

She turns the beaters of the mixer off earlier than I would have liked. Glancing at the clock, I know I wanted to whip the butter and sugar for another forty-five seconds.

"And sometimes, you have to learn to adapt." She presses the button on my timer, and I grind my teeth.

I can't be rude to her; this is her fucking kitchen.

"Betty Anne's neighbor churned this butter you're using," she explains. "Homemade butter isn't the same as store-bought, so you adapt." She lifts the arm of the mixer and motions for me to add my dry ingredients.

Begrudgingly, I do.

"When did you start baking, Fibs?"

"In college."

"Any reason you only make cookies?"

"I-I make other things, too," I lie.

She scrutinizes my face as I dump a portion of the flour mixture into the mixer. "Mmhmm. I'm willin' to bet most people in your life have no idea when you're stretchin' the truth. Am I right?"

"I'm not a liar, GG." My words are cold, but she doesn't back down.

"No, I reckon ya ain't. I'm willin' to bet you've only ever told a handful of lies in your entire life, but the ones you did tell? Woo-wee. They broke you in so many ways you haven't been able to recover."

I turn my back on her to grab the peanut butter. I'm not sure what happened to the cookies I made last night, but hopefully, these will make their way to Rylan.

"What did ya do before the baking? What was your outlet?"

"Doesn't matter."

"That's where you're wrong, Fibby. It matters more than ya know. Until ya stop punishin' yaself, everyone's going to hurt."

My nostrils flare, and I have to work to control my breathing. "What the hell is that supposed to mean?"

"Baking's not your passion, Fibby. Your passion is what keeps you alive. It feeds your soul. Ya wanna know why your

51

gal doesn't have a name yet?"

"No." Sweat forms on my hairline, and I wipe it with the sleeve of my shirt.

"'Cause you're so locked away she can't get in, even when she wants to. We've got to fix you before the cards can reveal your truth."

Her words. Today. It all makes me snap, and my fist comes down on the counter with a crack. "I'm not broken, GG."

She raises a silvery eyebrow and stares me down.

My voice is shaky and unsure. "Did you need something, GG?" I quickly bend to grab the cookie sheets so she can't see my eyes. I know there will be no hiding the sadness there tonight.

"Remember when you all ambushed the McDowells' home for Thanksgiving?"

Jesus, how could I forget. Preston's best friend, Dexter, had made it his mission to make GG's other granddaughter *his forever*. We descended on this tiny town like a pack of wild boars.

"I saw you then, you know. Really saw you. Hiding out in the corners of life. When's the last time you were a part of the conversation, Halton? Not just a body that moved with the sea but actually lived in all that life has to offer? You're keeping yaself in black and white while the world moves on in vivid color. Life's happening all around you, yet you lock yourself away in purgatory."

I slam the cookie sheets down just as GG slides a port glass down the long, granite countertop.

"Little dab will do ya."

"I don't think so." I still don't know what the fuck happened last time I drank that shit.

"It will calm your soul, Fibby. Just enough so you can sleep without the dreams. Just don't go helpin' yaself to no

52

more, or you'll end up at the Packing House riding that mechanical bull."

My eyes go wide. "D-Did I?"

GG's scary cackle echoes off the stainless steel in every corner. "Not that I know of. Ya got yaself a good group that loves ya. Let them in, Fibby. It's time. Secrets can kill a lesser man than you. Time to buck up and tell your story."

If only it were that easy. GG knocks back her port glass, and I do the same. If she can handle a little shot of this shit, so can I. *I hope.*

"Make sure ya turn the oven off when you're done. We're gonna fix you right up. All those pieces you broke also have the power to heal your heart if ya let it. Gonna teach ya to love yaself so we can getcha that girl."

My throat is itchy, and I blame the damn wine. "What's in that stuff, anyway?" I finally ask just before she walks out the door.

"Just some herbs … a little elixir, if you will. But don't ya go pulling a Lexi on me, too. A little skullcap and mugwort never hurt anyone."

My mouth drops as she cackles and leaves me alone. I immediately pull out my phone to Google skullcap and mugwort. 'Skullcap can be used as a mild sedative while mugwort is said to have psychotropic side effects.' *Fan-fuck-ing-tastic.*

I stare between the door and the empty port glass. There's nothing I can do about it now, so I finish my cookies, oddly thankful for the distraction. I'm already feeling less murderous.

~

I'm smiling. It is such an odd thought to have while standing in a hallway staring at a closed door, but

53

it feels nice. I feel light, almost … almost happy. I've missed this feeling.

A giggle chokes off in the back of my throat, and I bite my lip to keep from laughing like a loon as I drop the plate of cookies on the floor, knock on Rylan's door, and run into my room to hide.

I'm crouched down beside our connecting door when I hear her open hers and laugh. The sound is like the playlist to my childhood, and since I can't bring myself to care about anything right now, I cross the room and pick up the hotel phone to dial her room number.

Laughter erupts from my belly when I hear it ring through the broken door. I'm watching it like a hawk when I see her face pressing between the six-inch gap.

Raising the phone from my ear, I point to her room. Rolling her eyes, she moves away from the wall, and I hold my breath as she picks up the receiver. Somehow, I feel safer knowing she's tethered to the landline with the old coil of cord that won't allow her to move about the room.

"Hello?" Her voice is hesitant, nervous.

"Verity." Mine is breathless.

I hear her sigh through the phone, and I picture her dropping her head into her hands like she did as a teenager.

"Halton, what are you doing?"

"Please. Please don't call me that." My fist clutches the hollow ache in my chest. Suddenly, my clothes are suffocating, and I strip down to my boxers in an attempt to alleviate the feeling.

"What do you want me to call you?"

"I'll always be your Hatty. Eat a cookie, Rylan."

"I don't eat cookies anymore."

I hate that answer.

"Why?"

"Because they put extra weight right into my ass, Halton."

"Hatty," I growl.

"Why don't you draw anymore?"

How does she know I don't draw?

"Your fingers aren't stained from the charcoal, Hatty. Either you use a different medium, or you don't draw anymore. Why?"

"Fuck, my chest hurts." I claw at it again, anything to make it stop. "I-I don't draw, Rylan, because it's my punishment for hurting you."

"But … I don't understand," she gasps.

"Are you happy, Verity?"

"H-Hatty." Her voice gives away her tears, and I feel my own form. "Why are you calling?"

"I miss you."

"You hate me," she spits. "You made that very clear a long time ago."

"I've never hated you."

"You never loved me either."

"I—" My voice breaks, and I feel the euphoric state I was just in slipping. "We all loved you. That's the problem."

"I forgive you, Halton."

Breathing becomes painful. My heart shatters every time she calls me Halton, but I answer as honestly as I can, "You shouldn't."

There's silence, and I pray to all that's holy she didn't hang up.

"That's why you've spied on me, right? Guilt?"

Guilt, heartache, stupidity, weakness. She can take her pick.

"I didn't spy on you." *I made sure you were taken care of.*

"Listen, I don't know why you took that bet. I spent years wondering, but it … it hurt too much, Halton. I had to let it go. Your words were ugly. Your actions despicable. Regardless, I forgive you. You have to let it go, too. You have to let *me* go. We're not the same kids anymore. That friendship has sailed, and I, I need to live my life."

I bite my tongue so hard I taste blood. It's the only way to ensure I don't tell her I lied. That's a pain that brands my chest every hour of every day.

"I don't know how," I finally concede because it's the truth. I can't love her, and I can't let her go.

She gasps, and I have to close my eyes. I grip the bedsheets in my fist so I don't go to her.

"How?" she whispers. "How did you know everything? Did you have someone following me?"

"Jesus, Rylan. No. I'm not a stalker." My words sound off, and I think I might be slurring at this point.

"But I've never found you on social media. D-Did you block me?"

"Never. *I'm* not on social media."

"But you admit it was you, stepping in every time I fell?"

My eyes close to block out the pain. "I've never been far away," I say softly. "I couldn't. You're my verity. My panacea."

There's a long silence, and I stare up at the ceiling, waiting for her to reply, so I don't notice when she enters the room.

"Why, Hatty?"

So many answers to that one question. Dropping the phone, I sit up in bed to stare at her. She's so fucking beautiful it rips my heart out that she can't be mine. *Why can't she be mine?* She's standing before me in a nightshirt that goes to mid-thigh, and I struggle for words.

"I loved you, Hatty. With everything that I am, I loved you." The floor sways beneath my feet, and I plant them wide to keep from toppling off the bed.

"Did you ever even really care about me? I know you didn't love me—"

"I'm going to hell," I rumble as I jump up, cutting off her words. I cross the room to stand before her in two long strides, and she peers up at me wide-eyed.

"Have you been drinking?"

"I had a shot with GG."

"Of what?"

"Rylan, do you want to talk about GG right now?"

She bites her lip, and I snap. The world is a little fuzzy, but I can't think of one damn reason why I can't have this girl. I know there's a reason. A really fucking big one. But right now, all I can think about is her and me.

I scan her body and feel my dick spring to life. Rylan's hands are clasped in front of her like she's about to pray, but we'll save that for tomorrow. Grasping her hands, I straighten the fingers of her left one and entwine mine over both of hers, then lift them above her head. Stepping into her space, I back her into the wall, crowding her until she's breathless.

"What are you doing, Hatty?"

"I never hated you," I vow just before my lips crash into hers. With both of her arms contained, she can't move. She doesn't have to think, just feel.

Pulling back, I take her swollen bottom lip between my teeth. "Do you want me, Verity?"

"I-I—"

Lowering my lips, I swallow her answer. Before she can think, I spin her, keeping her hands locked in mine. My arm now cages her back into my front, and I walk us backward to the bed. I can barely feel my legs, but when we crash into the plush mattress, my only thought is Rylan.

Holding her tightly, I relish the feel of her body pressing into me as I run my free hand up her thigh, then lean in to kiss her neck.

"Fucking hell, Rylan. Do you know how many dreams I've had about you? How one time with you ruined me for life?"

My hand lands on her bare stomach, and I inch my fingers lower, groaning when I realize she still doesn't sleep in panties.

"Hatty, I—"

Her words cut off as I graze her bundle of nerves, then dip my middle finger deep inside of her channel.

"Fuck, Verity. It's only ever been you, don't you see that?"

I pick up my pace with my palm on her clit, and I can already feel her body tensing.

"Just you. You were always meant for me. Always," I roar, the sound bringing me back to the present, and I pause in my assault, trying to catch my bearings.

But then she moans, long, low, and sweet as fucking honey, and I'm more determined than ever to bring her to orgasm. My name on her lips. My fingers inside of her pussy. *Mine.*

"Feel how you react to me, Rylan? Me. I wanted you more. I needed you more, but I can't have you. I can't give you …"

Her body goes rigid a split second before her harsh words call out, "Stop! Halton, stop."

The room lurches into focus, and I glance around. It's like an out-of-body experience as Rylan jumps off my lap, and I'm forced to let her go.

"Y-You can't do this to me again, Halton. If I'm not good enough for you …"

"You're too good for me, Rylan. Don't you see? I can't love you, but I can't let you go either."

"Why?" she screams, and I wince as her face becomes blurry. "Why, Halton? Why can't you love me? Can't implies that you have a choice. And you do have a choice." Her voice cracks, and it slices through me like a knife. "Have you ever loved me, Halton? Deep down in your bones, cry yourself to sleep at night? Endless, painful days that feel empty and bleak without someone by your side? Have you ever loved anyone that fiercely? Because if you did, you would choose it. You would choose me, but you say you can't?"

I attempt to focus on her face, but I don't need to see it. I can hear her tears, and I drop my head into my hands.

What did I do?

"He loved you first." My words sound like an echo of my former self.

"But who loves me now?"

Words. I hear them all around me, but someone glued my eyes shut, and it sounds like we're underwater. My head floats, and words echo, but I can't open my eyes.

"But who loves me now?"

Soft hands hold my cheeks, and rain falls onto my face as the scent of cookies and sunshine flood my senses. Then my world goes blissfully black.

CHAPTER 7

"*M*aybe you're not heart sick, maybe you're just tired."

Using my palms, I rub the sleep from my eyes. Rolling my head toward the sounds coming from the corner, I find GG propped up at the table again, and I shake my head.

"I'm pretty sure you aren't supposed to enter a guest room whenever you feel like it. Especially not when they're sleeping."

"I didn't come in through your room. I came to check on Rylan and saw the door."

My gaze snaps to the thin wall separating our rooms. That's when I notice the door lying on my floor, and I sit up in a panic, searching the room, but she's not here.

"But who loves me now?" I don't know where that thought comes from, but I get a chill of recognition and have a feeling it isn't good.

I attempt to harden my face as I scrutinize GG, but she doesn't give a shit. She shrugs her shoulders and rolls her eyes like a damn teenager. Shaking my head, I try to make sense of ... well, of everything, but the last thing I remember is dropping the cookies at Rylan's door and making a run for it.

I point my finger accusingly at GG. "There is some other fucking thing in that wine, GG. What is it?"

"Pfft. You're a lightweight, Fibby."

"GG, so help me … What the hell is in it?"

"I told ya, Fibby. Some herbs, and other such things. Nothin that's gonna kill ya. It gets ya out of ya head, so you can live."

"I'm living just fine," I bellow. "Just fine."

"Did ya know your left eye twitches just a hair when you're lyin'?"

Pinching the bridge of my nose, I check to make sure I have clothes on this time before standing.

"The boys have ya all set up for the bachelor auction today. I thought I was gonna have to wake your ass up."

Bile threatens the back of my throat. Colton got it in his head that the way to win over Burke Hollow and save GG's mountain from predatory investors is to bring their summer festival, aptly named Summerfest, back to the classics. Kissing booth, dunk tank, bachelor auction, and other bull shit I want no part of. Since my plan to build homes on the mountain isn't fully in motion yet, we're forced to continue with Summerfest.

My gaze drifts to my watch, and I blanch. Two p.m. *Holy shit*. I don't know that I've ever slept this late.

"No more wine, GG. You hear me? No more."

"I see Rylan got her cookies," she informs me while completely ignoring my decree.

My breath hitches, and I feel the flush creep across my cheeks as I sink back down onto the bed.

What did I do? Think, Halton. I dropped the cookies off and hid like a goddamn pussy. But what next? Everything is blank. I remember laying in bed, staring at the door. Is that it? *"But who loves me now?"* Why the hell do I keep hearing that line in my head. More importantly, why does it sound like Rylan? I rack my brain for even a glimpse into my rattled memory, but I've got nothing, and slowly, I breathe easier when no other memory comes.

Thank fuck.

"Well, my cards are opening, but not enough to get a name. You're makin' progress, Fibby. Keep up the good work. We're all on your side, ya know? But you've got to put in the effort now. I'll see ya at the fields. Don't dilly dally either. You're already late."

She shuffles across the room, cackling at the door on the floor, and is gone a second later. With my elbows on my knees, I hold my head, praying I don't vomit on the old, worn carpet.

I just have to make it through ten minutes on stage. Ten minutes by myself on stage. I can do that. Maybe I can even pay the person off, so I don't have to actually go on the date. That could work. *It's just ten minutes, Halton.* Ten fucking minutes.

In a daze, I make my way to the bathroom, brush my teeth, and say screw it to everything else. Making my way through the Wagon Wheel, I'm thankful I don't run into anyone on the way. I'll walk to the fairgrounds from here. The exercise will do me good.

~

"Jesus Christ, Halton. You look like shit," my brother, Preston, shouts across the field as I arrive. "What the hell happened to you?"

"I think GG drugged me."

His wife, Emory, gasps at his side. "What?" She leans in, giving me a hug, and inspects me up close. She's a heart surgeon, and I suspect she's taking my pulse as she holds onto my wrist.

Running a hand through my hair roughly, I grab my glasses out of my front pocket and put them on. *One more shield against the world.*

"I don't know. She gave me this wine, and I blacked out. Twice. I have no idea what the hell happened."

Preston howls with laughter. "Why the fuck did you drink it the second time?"

I shrug because it's a fair question. "I don't know, Pres. She drank it. I thought a freaking port glass of it would be fine."

"Did you even shower today?"

"No. And I probably slept in these clothes. Any other questions?"

Clapping me on the back, he brings me in for a hug. Preston takes his role as big brother seriously. "Nope. That's it from me, but you'd better make your way to the stage. East is on edge and was ripping everyone to shreds earlier, so you don't want to piss him off."

"I should have stayed in bed," I grumble.

"Too late, little brother."

"Don't worry," Emory whispers. "We'll put in a good bid to get the ball rolling."

Knowing the hell they have been through recently, I give her a sincere smile. She's the best thing that has ever happened to Preston, and I appreciate the love she has for him. "Thanks, Ems."

Trudging forward, I come face-to-face with Colton shortly after.

"Ugh," he groans. "Seriously, Halton? You look like that guy from the movie *Beetlejuice*. Just lose the constipated expression when you get up there on that stage. Women have come from all over the state for a chance at a date with you. Please don't fuck this up with your scowling asshole face."

"I'm not the right guy for this, Colt. I told you that."

"No shit, but who else do we have? You don't think we can put Ash through this right now, do you?"

"Don't be a dick."

"Okay, well, I have to be in the kissing booth." He waggles his eyebrows like a creeper, and I cringe. "I'm happy to switch with you."

"Fuck off. I told you I'm not interested in catching herpes while we're here."

"Well, that leaves you for the auction, then. Suck it up, buttercup. Who knows? Maybe you'll meet your soulmate at this thing."

I spin and stomp off before I punch him in the fucking mouth. I've already met, hurt, and pushed away my soulmate. I'll be whacking off to visions of her for the rest of my life because my father was right about something else, too. Love like that only comes around once in a lifetime.

The closer I get to the stage, the harder the pulse in my neck throbs, and I have to shake out my hands to keep them from trembling. My shoulders are so tight I can already feel a tension headache forming. And as I climb the three steps to find East, sweat rolls down my spine and settles at the top of my boxer briefs.

Great, I have to deal with fucking swamp ass on top of everything else.

"Halton," my brother barks.

I flinch. Christ, I'm not going to survive this. My only consolation is that Easton appears to be as messed up as I am.

His phone chimes, and I slide to the left, so I'm partially blocked from view by his body.

"Holy shit," Easton's voice booms out over the crowd. Turning to me, he says something, but I'm blinking feverishly, attempting to make out the words. He throws his hands in the air and barks out at the audience. "Pres? My phone died …"

Everything happens in slow motion, but my bodily reaction is swift. My tongue sticks to the roof of my mouth, and I can't swallow. If anyone got close enough, they'd see I'm shaking from head to toe. Goosebumps cover my skin, and I'm sweating like a whore in church.

"I-I can't breathe," I whisper, but no one's listening to me as the mayor goes on and on about God only knows what.

"Just look at this sexy, hunka man here. Halton, do a little spin for us, will you?" Mayor Baker's voice cuts through my fear.

My eyes go painfully wide as my body follows his command on autopilot.

I'm going to throw up. I swallow once, twice, three times, and the floor sways below me. My knees shake, and I know I'm going down, so I place my hands on my thighs and bend over at the waist, hoping I can hold myself up for a few more seconds.

"Twenty thousand dollars."

I know that voice. *Rylan. She's saving me.* The world around me sways and shifts as I seek her out in the crowd.

Air enters my lungs as if she breathed it into me herself, a strange sense of déjà vu happening when my eyes catch hers and I see a pain so real, so raw I almost drop to my knees. *Why can't you love me?*

What did I do?

"Ba-uh. Twenty thousand going once," Baker splutters. "Going twice."

The crowd is stunned into silence. Twenty thousand dollars is more than some of these people make in a year.

"It was you," Colton screams from his perch at the kissing booth. "You're the reason she left. You're the reason she wouldn't come back. You fucking bastard."

My head droops, and I know my life is about to be fucked seven ways to Sunday. I don't know if it's Rylan's bid, the expression on her face, or the realization that she's the one to

65

save me when my entire family is here, but I have no doubt Colton just put all the pieces together. I'm the reason he lost his best friend. His love. I'm the asshole he says I am, and so much worse.

Steeling myself, I hear him coming, screaming at me the entire way. I don't blame him, and I won't fight him. It's my fault he's missed out on the love of his life all these years, so when he barrels forward, dropping his shoulder into my gut, I take it.

"How could you do that? How could you use her as a pawn in a sick fucking bet like that, Halton? She's like our sister, for fuck's sake. She's family." He throws a punch that makes my jaw crack, and I welcome the pain. "Fight me, you asshole. How could you use her and push her away like that? Do you have any idea how much she loved you? How badly you broke her? Answer me, goddamn it, Halton."

He gets another punch into my side before someone pulls him off me.

Somewhere in the background, Easton talks to the crowd as Preston and his best friend, Dex, subdue Colton.

"You're a fucking coward, Halt. A piece of shit, you know that?" He thrashes against our brothers' hold, but they don't release him. "Do you have any idea how much you hurt her? How long, huh? How long did you string her along? You broke her fucking heart." He sneers. "I'll never forgive you for this, asshole."

Preston pushes him back as blood trickles down my lip. The metallic taste is a reminder that I deserved this.

"I …" What the hell am I going to say? Placing my hands on my hips, my shoulders slouch in defeat.

Dex hands me a towel and stares long and hard. He's been part of our chaos for as long as I can remember, so it doesn't surprise me to see disgust written all over his face, too. "I don't know what the hell just happened here, but you'd better pray to God it doesn't fuck us over with GG's moun-

66

tain. Get out of here and clean yourself up before Sylvie arrives. We'll meet you at Ashton's after we shut down the booths."

"Don't bother. Go to Colt. He needs you guys right now. I … he's right. I'm a coward and the worst kind of man. J-Just take care of him."

A sharp shove comes from behind. "If you believe that we've failed you, too, fuckwad. We won't do it again. Get your shit together, and then we're having a family meeting," Preston growls.

I nod in understanding, but deep down, I know I won't be attending.

CHAPTER 8

RYLAN

I'm frozen to my spot. My worst fear is happening right before my eyes as Colton and Hatty face off, and my heart races when I realize Hatty won't fight back.

I'm too raw from last night. Too ashamed of myself to think straight. But I couldn't leave him up there like that, even if he did deserve it. He looks like hell, and I have no doubt GG's truth wine did him in again.

I shouldn't have allowed anything to happen between us last night. I feel dirty and used. Again. But I could hear it in his voice. He's hurting, too. I wish I understood why. After last night, I have no doubt he has love for me. He just won't allow himself to feel it, and that might hurt more than anything.

GG interrupts my thoughts by roping her arm through mine. "He doesn't think too highly of himself."

"He never did."

"Mmhmm. Just as I thought. Do ya love him?"

I peer down at her, fear grabbing hold of my throat. She really is scary, but all I see is love and understanding as I search her gaze. "I always have."

My shoulders slump like a thousand-pound weight was just lifted.

"He's gonna tear himself apart before he can be whole, ya know."

I nod because I don't dare argue with her.

"He's hurting, Rylan. Time has made it worse, and somethin' made him believe he isn't worthy of your love. Any idea what that might be?"

"N-No. GG, we happened a long time ago. I don't know him anymore."

Liar. Gah! I'm hearing voices now.

"Time means nothin' when it comes to love, dear. When he was hurting before he pushed you away, could you fix him?"

"He was never broken, GG. He just didn't know how he fit …"

I stumble as a memory goes off like a gun to my chest.

"My moiety. I only fit in when you're with me, Rylan. My world doesn't make sense without you in it. It's like I'm drowning every day of my life, and I can only break the surface when you're with me. You're my life raft. My sun … I rotate around you, seeking your warmth because that's when I'm living. You're my panacea for a dull, lonely life."

≈

"$\mathcal{T}$hat's a lot to throw at a seventeen-year-old girl, huh?" Lexi states as I retell our story. Her words hold judgment, as she glares with pale blue eyes, but I understand why she would think that. Hatty and I were always on another level when we were together.

"Our relationship was different," I explain. "Two old souls that fit together to make the other whole."

I glance away from the girls and take in Ari's home. It's

cozy, with muted gray walls and pale yellow accents. It feels lived in, which puts me at ease.

"So, he was your other half, took your virginity on prom night, then pushed you away? Not only pushed you away, but took a bet with high school assholes to see who could pop your cherry first?"

I cringe at her crass words, and my shoulders shrug even as my heart screams to stand up for him. Visions of his tormented expression last night have haunted me all day.

"We couldn't go to prom together."

"Why not?" Ari asks, refilling my wine glass. After the disaster at Summerfest, they swooped in like a swat team, scooped me up, and brought me back to Ari's while the Westbrooks rounded up the guys. My spine tingles with worry. I hope the two men who have always resided in my heart don't kill each other.

She takes a seat next to me on the couch, and I'm surprised to find I'm incredibly drawn to her. She's a gentle soul with kind eyes and quick with a hug. Her short pixie cut bounces as she sits and it accentuates her delicate features, but it's her soft-spoken voice that causes me to smile. Colton was right about her, too.

"We kept our 'relationship'," I use air quotes because we never labeled it, "a secret. It just seemed like the right thing for us. At one point, Hatty wanted to tell Colton, but I talked him out of it. I didn't want to come between them, and I wasn't sure how Colton would take it."

"Not well, by the looks of things today." Lexi smirks. I don't think she can even help her snarkiness sometimes.

"No, I-I think that had more to do with me leaving and rarely coming home."

"Because it hurt too much to see him?" Ari guesses.

"Yeah." I choke back a sob.

"So, a group of ball sacks made a disgusting bet about who could sleep with you first?"

"Who could sleep with the rich guy's fat friend first was the actual bet, I think."

"Fuckers." Lexi actually looks pissed, and I appreciate her loyalty.

"How did you find out?" Ari asks gently.

"Well, Hatty refused to go to prom if we couldn't go together, but Colton wouldn't go without me. He ended up coercing a friend of his to take me. Our school was on the smaller side, so it was a combined prom for juniors and seniors. I went, and Hatty said he'd meet me at home after. But I left early. Really early because I heard girls in the bathroom talking about the bet."

"I fucking hate girls," Lexi growls.

Swallowing thickly, I force myself to tell the story only my mom knows. "I called Hatty, and he picked me up a few minutes later. I told him what happened, and I thought he was going to set the world on fire. He only calmed down because I asked him to take me to my happy place."

"Where was that?" Ari asks with a dreamy expression on her face.

"My dad created the gardens at the Westbrook house."

"Oh my God, they're beautiful," Lexi gasps, and a sense of pride in my father warms my chest.

"They really are. Anyway, that's where my friendship with Halton grew, evolved, morphed into a love I'd never imagined could be real. A few years before this, he had his dad help him build a hammock. A hammock we had discussed in detail, and it became our place.

"We'd been together for about six months or so. He had an art show that he never made it to. We kissed, and our relationship changed from that point on. The night of the prom, under the stars, I lost my virginity to the boy I thought I would love forever. The next morning …" I take a sip of wine for courage. "The next morning, his dad saw us walking inside, and he asked to speak to Halton.

71

"I waited by the front door, so he could give me a ride home. When he came to find me, he was quiet and agitated. The ride to my house was short and strained, but I just assumed he was embarrassed. I know I was. I mean, there's no way his dad didn't know what we'd been up to. However, when he dropped me off, his tone was hard. Nothing like I'd ever seen from him. He …" I pause to swallow my heartache, and Lexi hands me another glass of wine.

"He told me thanks for the hundred bucks. I was confused at first. Then he said it was the hardest money he'd ever won. He didn't realize I would be such a prude or that he'd have to play the long game to win. He said it was the longest six months of his life and sped off. I don't think I'd even shut the door."

"That asshole," Ari cries.

"Yeah. But then his dad died that day. My mom was on the phone with Sylvie when I walked in. Mr. Westbrook collapsed after we left and died before the paramedics arrived. Sylvie was trying to round up her boys and knew Halton was driving me home. Then he left shortly after the funeral for college. I was supposed to go to the Rhode Island School of Design to be near him the following year, but obviously, I changed my plans. I only saw him a couple of times after that. His mom made him come to London for my twenty-first birthday, and then he made an excuse anytime there was even a chance we'd run into each other after that."

"So, what made you come home?"

"He's been protecting me all these years," I blurt. I feel uneasy as I attempt to explain how he's taken care of me. I know they may not understand, but this is Hatty. Protecting me in secret when he can't be there in person.

Glancing around the room, both of my new friends wait expectantly. I appreciate that they don't rush me, and with a heavy sigh, I continue my story.

"When I was in college, some weirdo followed me home

from a party, and the next day campus security seemed to follow me everywhere. When my oven blew up from an electrical fire, a crew showed up in less than two hours, and initially, my landlord didn't know where they'd come from." I swallow because the next part is harder to explain.

"I was engaged. In London, to a man named Matthew. We had an okay life." Sighing, I stare at the wall to collect my thoughts. "He treated me well enough, but he never understood my relationship with Colton or the Westbrooks. He didn't like how someone always seemed to step in to make my life just a little bit easier whenever something went wrong. But when my car broke down, and a new one showed up the next day, it was the final straw. The delivery man said I'd won it, but we both knew I hadn't entered anything, and there were no taxes to pay. Matthew kicked me out of our flat. He said he didn't want to compete with the ghosts of my past anymore. I packed up the little I had in our apartment and moved in with friends for a couple of months while I hired a private investigator."

"This is all very stalkerish, you know that, right?" Lexi asks, leaning against the counter.

"It is, and it isn't. He's a protector, even if he doesn't know it. At first, I assumed it was Colty, but he would have admitted to the car. When I found out who had bought the car, I knew it was Hatty."

"How?" Ari gasps, thoroughly engrossed in my saga.

"A company named Hatty's Heart purchased it."

"No shit." Lexi chuckles. "He may be a romantic, but he's no super sleuth."

"I came back because I assumed he was doing this out of guilt."

"You were always supposed to be mine." I have to shake away the memory.

"As shitty as he was to me, I knew him. His heart would never have allowed him to move on from hurting me. I came

73

home to tell him I forgave him. After all these years, it seems like a silly thing to do, but if he's been taking care of me, I assumed it was out of guilt. I-I needed him to let me go, but then he …"

"He what?" they both screech.

"He drank GG's wine and told me he never hated me. He said they all loved me too much, and that was the problem." I hesitate, wondering if I should tell them about last night, but ultimately, shame in myself keeps me from saying anything. "I don't know. His dad collapsed right after their fight that morning. Maybe he blames himself and me. I'm not exactly sure what they fought about, but it was a different guy that walked out of that office to bring me home."

Suddenly exhausted, I sink farther into the couch and the tears I've held in for years fall silently down my face.

"Ry? You know their dad had a genetic heart condition, right? It's something he was born with, and that's why he died?"

I sniffle because I've heard this all before. "Yeah, I know. Hatty does, too, but he was the last one to see him alive, and they fought. I remember hearing them yelling on the other side of the house."

The girls flank me on either side but say nothing as we all stare straight ahead for a long moment.

"Man, that's some star-crossed lovers shit if I've ever seen it," Lexi finally says, breaking the silence.

"What happened to your fiancé?"

"After he broke up with me, he started dating someone from his office. Last I heard, they were already engaged."

"Pfft. What a loser," Lexi chides. "Wait. Halton had an art show?"

My stomach turns, remembering his admission last night.

"I don't draw anymore, Rylan. It's my punishment for hurting you."

"He was amazing," I whisper because the truth hurts more than I want to acknowledge.

"I never would have guessed it."

"I have an art studio." Ari nudges my shoulder. "Well, I have an art studio in the works if you needed anything, I mean. Do you think Colton's killed him yet?"

"Geez, I hope not. I never wanted to come between them."

"And after all this, you still love him?"

Turning to Lexi, something like understanding passes between us, and I cave. "I think my heart's loved him since I was six years old. I tried to move on, but my heart has always belonged to him. Is that messed up?"

Sighing, she tosses her blonde hair over her shoulder. "I'm not the one to ask, Ry. I've been fucked up for most of my adult life, but if you asked GG, she'd probably say something about the heart always knowing its mate."

Lexi's phone dings, and she grabs it off the coffee table.

"I don't know where to go from here," I admit.

"Oh, Rylan. I think you've been away too long. Don't you know these Westbrooks always have something up their sleeve?"

Butterflies hit my chest like an angry hive, but I tamp it down. The first flutters of hope threaten my self-preservation, and I can't allow myself to think about what-ifs when Hatty can only talk to me after a crazy, old woman has him drugged.

"Your grandmother is a scary piece of work, you know that, right?"

"Oh, trust me. Truth wine is the least crazy thing she's done this week."

I stare at her in disbelief, but Ari confirms it's true.

"I've known that woman my entire life. Crazy keeps getting crazier. It's best to just clear a path for her and follow her destruction because, so far, she's lit the path for love and happiness for each couple she's set her sights on. Scary as hell, but right on the money."

There goes that hope again. This time, though, I pray they're right because one thing I'm sure of? I won't survive losing Hatty again.

Turning to Lexi, I grin. "So, you and Easton are married, huh?" I'd completely forgotten that in the chaos of the bachelor auction, he outed their Vegas nuptials.

"Jesus," she grumbles. "That's a story for another day."

Holding up my glass, I clink with hers. "I'll hold you to it."

ASHTON

CHAPTER 9

$\mathcal{M}$y head hurts as I close another one of Dad's journals. I'd called Mom and asked her to bring them today. She was curious but didn't push when I told her I couldn't explain why I needed them yet.

I know there has to be something in here that will resonate with Halton. He and Preston picked up the journaling habit from our father, but he's more alike to all of us than he realizes. I just have to find the proof to get him out of the darkness.

I was with my father when he collapsed shortly after his fight with Halt. I was fifteen, but remember the pain in Halton's voice like it was yesterday.

When Halt stormed off, I told my father he was wrong. Colt loved Rylan, yes, but he was never in love with her the way Halton was. I saw it in my father's eyes when we had it out that day. He already knew he'd made a mistake, but he was clutching his chest, trying to write a note, and couldn't hold the pen steady.

"Halt … best man … love her forev—" He fell to the floor and handed me a key that changed my life forever. "We fight for those that can't, Ash. You and Loki now …" His voice faded, and I knew he was gone. Everything happened under a dark cloud after that. I remember trying to talk to Halton, but he shut down every attempt.

Then SIA happened, the Secret Intelligence Agency, and my father's secret I almost lost my life protecting. But I should have pushed Halt to talk.

I should have known he's been hurting, pining over Rylan all this time. I've been so wrapped up in other people's shit, I didn't notice my brother, my best friend, was slowly dying inside.

I failed him once. I won't do it again.

So, when my brothers burst through my door a few hours later, I know we only have one option. It's time for the Westbrook brothers to do what they do best. Meddle.

~

"Where is he?" I ask after Preston fills me in on the Summerfest debacle.

I eye Colton closely as he paces my tiny space like a pent-up tiger. He's ready to pounce, to destroy, to hunt, and I can't say I blame him. He's been hurt in this fucked-up mess, too.

"Ash? Why the hell are you living in a double-wide so far away from us at the lodge?" Preston glances around and grimaces.

I bought a double-wide trailer a couple of days ago and temporarily put it on the lot where my house is being built. It's not the kind of living any of us have experienced before, but I relish the simplicity, the isolation it offers.

"I need my space." I give him no other explanation, and sadness takes over his expression, so I drop my gaze.

"Jesus, Ash."

"Explain it to me again," Colton demands, giving me a reprieve from Preston's interrogation. "You think he fucking broke her on purpose, in a misguided attempt at keeping the brotherly code? Without ever asking me? Talking to me? Having a goddamn conversation that could have saved us all so much pain?"

He spins to glare at me. "And you've known all of this? This entire time you've let us hurt over a lie?"

I shake my head sadly because I know that's the way it appears. "No, Colt. I heard his argument with Dad. I saw Dad's stricken face when he realized he messed up, and there was nothing I could do. I was fifteen and had just lost my dad, too. As time went on, we all changed. I-I admit, I messed up. I failed you all ..." My voice breaks, and Preston hands me a throat lozenge. I eye him curiously. *When the hell did he start carrying these around?* I pop it into my mouth, though, because otherwise, anything I try to say now will come out barely above a whisper.

"Jesus Christ, Ash. You're not our keeper. You're not the glue. We're a family. This is supposed to be a joint effort," Preston curses, pointing at a chair and silently ordering me to sit.

"Did you know?" Colton asks point-blank, and I narrow my eyes because I'm not sure what he's asking. "Did you know he loved her? That she loved him?"

"Shit, I think we all did," Loki chimes in.

We all turn to him. The room is full of brothers by blood and brothers by choice, all connected by a common thread. A family born of trust and love, and I keep breaking their confidence at every turn.

"What?" Colton's voice is shaky as he backs himself into the corner. It's like he needs the wall to hold him up.

My chest constricts. I've caused so much pain, and for once, I don't know how to fix any of it.

"Where do you think she went when you were playing video games? Or when you were outside playing basketball?"

We're all glancing between Loki and Colton as realization hits.

"How long were they close? How did I never know it?"

"Colt, you know we love you, but there's a reason we've always called you Peter Pan. You're the first to step up to help someone, but you're also the first to find the fun. I'd say their friendship started at that first birthday party we all went to." Preston keeps his voice quiet, but I'm worried Colton will feel attacked.

"She's always been your best friend, Colt, but I think she and Halton had a different connection right from the beginning. They were always hanging out in the gardens, and I wondered if things were changing when he and your dad built the hammock," Loki explains.

Sighing, Colton drops his head into his hands. "You're telling me I was a shitty friend."

"Not at all. I'm simply pointing out that while you have love for her, Halton has always been in love with her. I think it probably explains why he's become so bitter over the years, too."

Emotion floods Colton's face, and it's so vivid I can feel his pain.

"So, you expect me to just forgive him for breaking her? For pushing her away from him and me?"

"Try to step back from your anger for just a second and ask yourself, do you want him to be happy? Do you want her to be happy?"

"He's my goddamn brother, Preston. Of course I want him to be fucking happy. And she's my best friend who has spent years building herself back up. Am I just supposed to say, 'have at it,' and hope he has his shit together enough not to hurt her again?"

"No," Easton speaks up. "I think it's something they need to work out for themselves, without our blessings or dissent. Do you guys remember Halton right before Dad died? Stop, and really think about who he was then. He was more emotional, more alive, freer than I'd ever seen him. That all changed overnight. I assumed it was his way of handling death, but thinking back now? Maybe it had more to do with Rylan."

"She was different, too," Colton chokes out.

"Yeah, she was," he agrees.

"I don't think I can give him my blessing."

"And I don't think that's our place. But, as his brother and as her friend, you should want them to rebuild the friendship they once had, if nothing else."

Colton, always the most expressive, stands, and a myriad of emotions flash across his face. "I can't handle this right now. You guys do what you need to."

"Colt—"

He raises his hand to cut Preston off. "I just need some time. Do whatever you think is best." He doesn't give us time to say anything else. He's out the door a second later.

"Fuck," Preston exclaims. "What the hell do we do now?"

"I think Pacen is on Block Island."

All my brothers turn to face me, and I realize I didn't segue into that very well.

"Sorry," I rasp. Jesus, it hurts to talk. "I've been searching for her. It's pretty obvious she's in hiding, but I need to speak with her about … about my attack, about what happened. She'll remember Rylan from when they were kids."

"That's right. She used to tag along with her sister when she would come over. She and Rylan are about the same age." Easton runs a hand roughly through his hair.

Pacen's sister, Vanessa, was once someone East thought he'd grow old with. I know he's still trying to come to terms with all he's learned about her recently. *What would it be like to learn a betrayal you've held in your heart for years, wasn't a betrayal at all?*

My mind immediately shifts to Pacen, but I refuse to be distracted. Not again, anyway. Shaking my head, I return my focus to the conversation happening around me.

"You want to send Halton and Rylan to Block Island," Loki surmises. He crosses his arms with a crooked grin. "It's the height of summer, and there's only one hotel on that little island. There's no way there are any rooms or houses available."

Loki and I have worked together for so long he pieces my plan together before anyone else.

"So, what does that mean?" Preston asks, confused.

I don't fight the twitch of my lip, even as pain shoots through the scar there. "They're going camping."

Every mouth in the room drops to the floor.

A full minute later, the entire trailer buzzes with laughter and conversation.

"At the very least, they'll figure out if their friendship is salvageable. We'll let them work out the rest on their own."

"Yeah, if GG doesn't step in first." Preston's chuckle starts a new round of laughter, and for the first time in months, I almost feel happy.

CHAPTER 10

*T*wo and a quarter cup of flour. One teaspoon of salt. A dash of cinnamon. I measure each one exactly. It's order in the chaos that's my life. With my AirPods in place, I blast Imagine Dragons. I need to drown out the noise and breathe.

I know I'll have to face my brothers soon. Colton will probably take another swing at me, though I can't blame him.

Thwack.

What in the ever living fuck? Turning, I find GG wielding a wooden spoon like a weapon. This crazy old bat just smacked my ass, hard, with that wooden spoon, and she's laughing about it.

There's no mistaking where Lexi gets the mischievous twinkle in her eyes. GG has it in spades. The wrinkles around her mouth also show years of laughter, and it almost pulls me from my foul mood. Almost.

Taking out the AirPods, I glare at her. "What the hell was that for?" My ass is on fire, and I'd really like to rub away the sting, but I won't give her that satisfaction.

"Ya can block out life for a little while, Fibby, but it always catches up with ya. So, talk."

"I have nothing to say."

Her eyes narrow drawing attention to the deep crow's feet at the corners. "You might be more stubborn than all your brothers combined."

I snort because she's probably right.

"So, your brothers know a lot more about ya now, do they?"

I'm never getting rid of her, so I concede to her inquisition. "I suppose they do. I never meant to hurt anyone. I-I was young and stupid."

"I know that, Fibby. And I think they do, too. But how long are you gonna punish yourself and Rylan?"

My gaze flies to her so fast I hear my neck crackle. "I'm not hurting her. I'm protecting her."

"From what? Are you dangerous?"

"What? No, I'd never hurt her physically, but I'm not the boy I was back then, either. I don't have the same capacity to love."

"Hmm."

The way she says it makes me want to bang my head against the wall because I know she's withholding something.

"What, GG? It's not like you to hold back, so just say whatever it is you came down here to say." I try to focus on folding my wet ingredients into my flour mixture, but the motions that usually calm me appear to be useless right now.

"It's funny, ya know? I just had the same exact conversation with Verity."

My bowl goes crashing to the floor. The sound echoes off the stainless steel of the industrial-grade kitchen.

"Wh-What did you just say?"

"Ya heard me. Your gal's got a name. It hit me watching you up on that stage. The moment you heard her voice. She pulled you from the dark, even if only briefly. She's your fundamental truth, Fibby. You're whole when she's near."

I can't swallow past the lump in my throat, and sweat rolls down my spine, sending a chill throughout my entire body.

"Did she tell you that word?" My voice doesn't sound like my own. I'm completely thrown off by this scary, tarot reading granny in front of me.

"Pfft, Fibby. I'm eighty-two years old. I know lots of words."

"That's not, ah, that's not what I meant."

She winks, and my eyes widen in alarm. "I know it ain't. Wanna know how I know?"

I shake my head because it's too much of a coincidence that she's given Rylan a name I gave her years ago.

"Well, I'll tell ya anyway. I know because it's the truth. I know it, you know it, and I think deep down, so does everyone else. The question is, what are you gonna do about it?"

"Nothing. I hurt her once. I won't do it again."

"What if pushing her away hurts worse than any lie you've ever told her?"

Her words seize the air in my lungs, and my palm involuntarily rubs the hollow spot in my aching chest. It's becoming a habit I can't break. Bowing my head, I squeeze my eyes tight as I attempt to regain control.

What if she's hurting, too?

"Lovin' someone the way you love that girl doesn't have time limits, and the beautiful thing about love is it can heal all wounds. Even yours. Don't ya think it's time to stop punishing yourself?"

My head shakes no on its own accord. Apparently, I have no control over my body while in the throes of panic.

"If ya can't do it for yourself, Fibby, maybe consider doin' it for her. You might be surprised what you'll get in return."

"What does that mean?" I choke out.

"It means, if you start your day giving love, forgiveness,

85

and kindness, you just might be shocked to see how quickly it boomerangs." She pauses as she inspects me for so long I feel hot under her intense gaze. "If you knew she was suffering, what would you do to fix it?"

"Anything." The answer is out of my mouth before I can think better of it.

"That's what I thought, Fibby. Maybe the best thing you can do is forgive yourself enough to repair the friendship you once had. She's worth the fight you're battling within yourself, and if you're honest, you'll find your way."

Her phone rings louder than any ringtone I've ever heard, and she pulls it from her pocket.

"Hello."

Turning my back, I try to calm down before the heart palpitations I'm having give me a heart attack. Who knew one overactive organ could hurt so badly?

"Oh, yes. I have everything you'll need. Betty Anne and I will pull it all together now. I knew ya boys would step up." She cackles, and the hairs on the back of my neck stand on end.

Daring a peek in her direction, I watch as she puts the phone back in her pocket with a troubling smile on her face.

"Well, Fibby. You have a family that loves you, a girl with a fractured heart, and a soul that needs mending. Trust your gut, and let the love in. I have to go call Betty Anne about … well, about some supplies." She laughs again, and I get the feeling my world is about to be turned upside down.

Twenty minutes later, I find out why.

Preston, East, Dexter, Loki, and Ashton invade my sanctuary like a bunch of linebackers. I cross my arms over my chest in a protective stance. For some reason, I feel like I'll need to guard myself.

"For crying out loud, Halt. We've been looking everywhere for you," East barks.

All eyes are on the Betty Boop apron I'm wearing. "It was

the only goddamn one I could find, okay?"

"What are you doing in here?" Preston glances around, and I'd bet money he's never baked a cookie in his life. "Have you been making the cookies that keep turning up in the lounge?"

I shrug my shoulders because after GG's damn truth wine, I'm not entirely sure where my creations went.

"Holy hell, Halton. You can bake, man. How come we never knew this?" Preston asks with disappointment in his voice. It's a sentiment I'm becoming familiar with.

"Because I do it for myself. I do it because I like the exact-ness of it. I ... sometimes I—"

"Sometimes you need an escape," Easton finishes sagely.

I nod because I'm at my emotional limit.

"Halt?" Ashton's voice is barely a whisper, but I hear the plea and raise my gaze to his. "I need you."

And there it is. A battle cry none of us ever walk away from. We were raised to drop everything for the family. It doesn't matter if they're family by blood or by choice ... you drop everything to help.

"What is it, Ash? What's the matter?"

His face is stricken, and I realize this is the first time I have ever heard him ask for help. Ever. Even as a child, he would work on something until he figured it out. At first, we thought he was just stubborn, but now we know it's more than that. He's a fixer, a problem solver, and I know I'll do whatever he asks.

He glances at Preston and makes a continue motion with his hands. It's like a sucker punch to witness him struggling so much.

"Ash thinks Pacen is hiding out on Block Island. He no longer believes she's the reason for his attack, but she has information he needs to move on."

Glancing around the room, I begin to understand what he needs. Dexter and Preston have families they need to take care of. Easton just dropped the marriage bomb, and knowing Lexi, he's got his work cut out for him. Loki will need to return to North Carolina soon for the business he, Seth, and Ash have started. Staring at Ash, I also know why he can't go. He's been shying away from people more and more as the months go on.

It doesn't escape me that Colton's not here for this powwow. I know I'm going to have to work to repair that relationship, but for now, getting away from everyone will help me clear my head and figure out the best way to go about reconciling. With everyone.

"So, you need me to go."

"Yes," Ash whispers.

"What is it I need to do?"

Again, Ash points to Preston.

"Ash believes she's hiding on her own. No one's forcing her, but he doesn't know why. If that's true, she's going to spook easy. You'll have to spend some time there observing, getting to know the locals, and when you find her, bring her home."

My eyebrows pinch together. "What if she doesn't want to come?"

"Tell her she owes me at least that much," Ash rasps.

"Ah, there's something else, too."

Turning to Preston, I wait for him to continue.

"Well," he pinches the back of his neck. It's a gesture that tells me he's uncomfortable. "You remember how small that island is?"

I think back to the few weekends we spent there when East was in college. He had a friend who grew up there, and we visited a few times.

"Yeah, really fucking small. There's not even a grocery store, is there?"

"Not like we're used to, no. So, you know there's only one hotel?" East asks, and I nod for him to continue, not sure I like where this is going. "Well, it's booked solid, and there aren't any rentals available either. But Ash is pretty adamant that you need to stay on the island."

"Ohhkay. What are you getting at?"

"You'll have to camp out. Allie's family still lives there, and they have a lean-to that's pretty private on the edge of their land. There's an outhouse and an outdoor shower, but it'll be pretty rustic living for a while."

"A lean-to? Do you mean those buildings that only have three sides and are wide open to the elements on the other?"

Easton grimaces, and I laugh because this is ridiculous. But maybe some time alone in the wilderness will be just what I need.

"Okay, I can handle it. How long are we talking?"

All eyes land on Ash, but it's Preston who speaks. "Not sure. It could be a couple of days or a couple of weeks. It depends on how intent she is on staying hidden."

My eyes nearly bug out of my head. Two weeks in a lean-to? I mean, our parents always made sure we experienced everything in life. They didn't want us growing up only knowing the privilege we were born into, but to fully understand how other people lived. Living in a lean-to for two weeks exceeds anything they ever had us do, though.

"Jesus." Now it's my turn to pull at the back of my neck. "You're sure she's there? That island can't be bigger than ten miles across. You still think it could take weeks?"

"It's actually seven miles long and three miles wide," Easton corrects. "But yes, she's there, and it could take weeks. If she's been there a while, she'll be thought of as a local, and they take protecting their own to a whole other level."

"All right. When do you want me to leave?"

"Tomorrow. GG's pulling together all the supplies you'll need now." Preston smiles.

I sigh, and my shoulders finally relax. Some time alone

actually sounds pretty fucking perfect right now.

East leans over me and sticks his finger into my batter. If I had GG's wooden spoon, I would have smacked him.

"Cut the shit, East. You're contaminating my dough."

"You really are good, Halt. The peanut butter cookies were off the chain amazing. I probably ate ten of them," Preston confesses.

At least someone ate them.

"Great," I grumble. "Anything else I need to know for tomorrow? Or can everyone leave me alone now?"

"Ash is putting it all together for you. You'll have everything you need in the morning."

I nod, and one by one, they give me one-armed man hugs. Everyone except Preston, who spins me around and wraps both of his massive arms around my shoulders. I swear he's trying to squeeze the life out of me.

"Thought you could use a Westbrook special," he says with a wink after finally releasing me.

I don't admit it, but he's right. I needed a Westbrook special more than I knew. I clap him on the back, and it's all he needs.

"We're always here for you, Halt. We know you've been miserable for the last few years. Some of us were just too dense to realize why. If you can get your life back, if you can be happy, do it. Colton will come around, I promise. But really think about what would make you enjoy life again. If it's what I think it is, don't waste any more time. I know better than anyone that another day isn't always guaranteed."

Emotions overwhelm me, so I nod as his words ring loudly in my head.

What would make me enjoy life again? Images of Rylan assault me, but I just don't know if I deserve to even try.

Turning back to my dough, I fold in the coconut and chocolate chips. These are Rylan's favorite. I'll make sure she gets them before I take off tomorrow.

CHAPTER 11

RYLAN

"*A*re you going to tell me what we're doing here?" Stepping back on the sidewalk, I glance up at the sign over the store. *Peace of Your Soul-Army Supply Store.* "The name's a pretty big contradiction, huh?"

Lexi peers up and laughs. "Yeah, army supply is used very loosely here. It's more like our version of the Bass Pro Shops. It's a one-stop shop for work clothes, outdoor gear, and surprisingly, no military supplies."

Shaking my head, I enter after Lexi. Ari pulls up the rear.

"You still haven't answered me, though. What could I possibly need here?"

"Camping gear."

My face must match my shock because Lexi laughs.

"Yup. You and Halton are heading to Block Island to search for the girl that's missing." Ari's explanation has my stomach dropping even more.

"Ah, what? Hatty runs in the other direction anytime he sees me." *Unless he's on truth wine!* "You're telling me suddenly he's willing to go camping. With me?"

"Well …" Lexi hedges, and my insides twist up in knots.

"Listen, do you want to repair your friendship, if nothing else?"

More than anything, my traitorous heart sings, but I need to lead with my head this time.

"Of course, but—"

"Well, then you have to trust us. The Westbrook boys of bad decisions actually came up with a pretty good plan. And it's one he won't be able to say no to because Ash asked him for help."

"What does that mean?"

"Do you know the girl that's missing? Pacen?"

"Yeah, we used to play together at the Westbrooks' house."

"Well, Ash needs to talk to her, and he found her on Block Island. He believes she's hiding on purpose, so you two have to go there and get cozy with the locals to find her. Ash thinks if you go along, she'll be more willing to come home."

"I haven't talked to her in years." My voice raises an octave as panic sets in. "Why does he think she'll talk to me?"

"He's just covering his bases. Unfortunately, there are no rooms or rentals available because it's such a small island, so you'll be camping on the property of an old friend of Easton's."

Suddenly, something dawns on me, and I shake my head, my chestnut hair grazing the tops of my shoulders. "And Hatty has no idea I'm going, I take it?"

"Nope, you'll be a surprise, and with all of us standing there, he'll have to get in touch with his feelings."

"Or he could slam the door in my face and make things worse."

"What would you rather do? Take the risk and try to heal, or keep living knowing you can never fully give yourself to anyone else because he still has your heart in his grasp?"

Geez. I hate that Lexi is so good with words.

"Why are you so invested? You're the one that was just calling him a stalker and giving attitude about it all."

Lexi places her hands on her hips, and Ari backs up nervously.

Freaking great.

But then, Lexi does the most un-Lexi-like thing ever. Her beautiful, baby blue eyes fill with tears.

"Sometimes, your heart knows what you need before your brain will allow it." Her hands drop to her side, and she worries her fingers. "Listen, until recently, I didn't believe in love. Once bitten, twice shy and all that, but these damn Westbrooks have a way of weaseling their way into your life and never letting go."

I feel my face scrunch into a frown as I regard her.

She shrugs. "I saw something in you I recognized, okay? I don't want you to go through all this pain if it was all a misunderstanding …"

"A misunderstanding?" I scoff. "He was very clear that night, Lexi. And the fact that he won't stay in the same room with me now is pretty telling, don't you think?"

"The Westbrooks are men of honor, even if it kills me to say that. I just think … I don't know. After talking to Easton, I think there might be more to this story. I guess it's up to you if you want to find out what that is. Do you want to try to salvage something that smells suspiciously like forever?"

"What if it's not, though?" My voice is barely audible, fear gripping my throat tightly. "What if he meant all the nasty things he said? It's not like he's made any attempt at all to reach out. Wh-What if I get hurt again?"

Ari propels herself forward like a slingshot and wraps me in a hug that nearly knocks me over. Lexi sighs but steps forward and wraps her long arms around the both of us.

"He may not have reached out directly, but it sure seems like he's been doing everything he can to hang on to you. And if you get hurt again, we'll kill him. Then we'll all help you pick up the pieces. But it's your decision. Do you want to corner him for answers, or live the rest of your life with a broken heart?"

Closing my eyes, I force back the tears. He hurt me so badly. Can I willingly put myself out there again? Can I handle any more rejection?

"Rylan?" My eyes fly open at Ari's soft voice. "You said he's been keeping tabs on you. Protecting you from afar all this time? That doesn't sound like a man who hates you. It sounds like a man so in love he can't let go."

If my heart beats any harder, I think I'll pass out.

"Geez, girl! You get super sweaty when you're nervous." Lexi grimaces and steps back.

Yeah, it's not pretty. It was fine when I was younger; I was a tomboy. But now? Not cute.

"Sorry." My voice is strained as emotions, thoughts, and worries all vie for my attention.

"It's okay. I sweat when I'm nervous, too." Ari winks.

"What's it going to be, Rylan?" Lexi is back in control with her arms folded over her chest. She's all business.

Ari has a point. If he really hated me, that emotion would have overridden his guilt long ago. *Right?*

"I admit, I don't know Halton all that well, but I know that family. As much as it kills me to admit it, they're good people. Halton is an asshole sometimes, but I find it hard to believe he's so different from the rest of them. What he did to you is very un-Westbrook-like."

I nod because she's making sense. If I'm being honest with myself, I knew it even as it was happening. Hatty's words were vicious, but his eyes told a different story, and that's what makes the decision for me.

"Will one of you come to get me if he leaves me on the island?"

The girls laugh, but I see mischief forming on Lexi's face.

"If he leaves you there, we'll all take turns beating some

sense into him. Then we'll come get you." Lexi's damn grin is as scary as her grandmother sometimes.

"All right, what do I need?"

Their faces light up like Christmas morning, and a groan escapes my lips. Shopping has never been fun. The emergence of online shopping has been a godsend, but they have all of our arms overloaded with supplies in less than an hour. I'm suddenly regretting this decision.

～

*E*aston knocked on my door far too early this morning and ushered me out to a waiting SUV with tinted windows. It was all very clandestine, but I sit and watch as Hatty walks toward me twenty minutes later, bag in hand and surrounded by his brothers.

Everyone except Colton.

Colton hasn't taken my calls since Summerfest. I'll need to fix this when we get back.

My jaw is so tight as he talks to Preston that I can hear the bones grinding. What's he going to say when he opens this door? *Oh, God. Maybe this was a mistake.*

Gah! They're getting closer, so I grab my phone to text Lexi.

Rylan: Where are you? I thought you were going to be here? What if he kicks me out?

Lexi: Jesus. Tuck it forward, would ya?

Rylan: Tuck what forward? What are you talking about? Where are you? I might need an escape plan.

Lexi: Tuck it forward, show your lady balls, your courage. You've got this.

Lexi: And we're on the porch. Easton and Pres wanted to get him to the car on their own.

Rylan: What the hell? (forehead palm emoji)

Ari: Oh! They're on the move again. Show time, lady!

I drop my phone into my lap, and my hands immediately clasp together. I shouldn't be this nervous. I didn't do anything wrong. However, when he opens the door and finds me sitting in the passenger seat, my heart plummets.

This is going to be a disaster.

CHAPTER 12

HALTON

"*J*ust stick to Ashton's plan, and you'll be fine. It's all laid out for you in the file." Preston continues to usher me forward. With Easton on the other side, I feel as if I'm being escorted straight to hell.

"Okay, I've got it, guys. Have either of you spoken to Colton?" I hate the idea of leaving Vermont on bad terms with him.

They exchange a glance that makes my stomach clench. I've never really been in a fight with my brothers. We would go at each other sometimes, but we always hugged it out after. I'm not sure what to do, but I know I hate this.

"He's hurt, too. Not just because of whatever happened between you and Rylan, but because neither of you ever told him. He'll come around. He just needs some time," East promises.

We reach the car, and they each lean in for a hug, but they flank me like I'm about to run.

"Ah, everything okay?"

"Yup." Preston grins. "Just seeing you off. Ash has planned every detail of this trip for you. So, even if something seems … unexpected, know that it's not. It's his doing."

"Oh-kay. You get stranger by the day, big brother."

They're both smiling now, and it's really making me uncomfortable, so I figure it's time to get out of here.

"I'll let you know when I get there." Opening the door to climb in, I stop mid-stride when I'm greeted by two misty green eyes.

"When you both arrive," Easton says, shoving me into a seated position.

I spin toward them, but they are already closing the door on me, so I roll down the window. The scent of Rylan in this fucking hot box is too much.

"What the fuck?" I growl.

"Ash thinks Pacen might be more willing to talk if Rylan is with you. It isn't negotiable, and you need to get moving so you don't miss your ferry to the island." Preston uses his big brother tone, but I barely register his words.

Fuck my life. A lean-to with Rylan, possibly for weeks? This will ruin me.

I place my hands on the steering wheel at ten and two and bow my head while taking a few deep breaths.

"Halton?"

My name is like a dagger through the heart when Rylan uses it. My hands are so tight on the steering wheel I'm surprised it doesn't crack.

"Halt, you need to breathe."

Tilting my head toward her, I realize I'm holding my breath, and I release it with a loud whoosh.

"Halton?" She places a hand on my forearm, and I wince.

"Stop fucking calling me that." My words sound vicious, but they mask my pain. Rolling my shoulders, I try again more gently. "Please, I'd rather you call me nothing at all than Halton." I don't know why this matters so much to me, but it does.

Rylan releases my arm, and it feels like she's taken all the air with her, too.

Someone knocks on the door, and I turn to find Ash. I think this is the first time he's come out of hiding this week. He makes a 'let's get this show on the road' motion with his hands, and I turn the key that sits in the ignition.

"Did you know about this?" I rasp, rolling up the window again, and pull onto the road.

I glance in her direction but refuse eye contact. I can see just enough to watch her neck work while swallowing, and the basest of instincts to lick her wash over me.

Get your head on straight, asshole.

"I did." Her voice is strong, resolute, and it throws me off.

My little wild child has certainly grown up.

"Why?"

I've done nothing but hurt her for years. Why the hell would she agree to be trapped in a car with me for five hours? *Oh, shit. And we're camping.*

"Hatty?" The plea in her voice cracks my armor, and I lift my gaze to hers. "I've missed you, too."

Fuzzy visions of me sitting on the floor outside of her room flood my head while my admission becomes clear.

"I'm sorry I hurt you, Verity. I'll miss you every day for the rest of my life."

"Desultory," I grumble under my breath.

"Well, you've certainly gotten good at our game, Hatty. Just a sec." Out of the corner of my eye, I watch as she pulls up Google. "Hmm." She turns in her seat to stare at me, and my neck gets hot under her perusal. "Without a plan, huh? That was always how we worked best, so yup! I think it works."

"What do you—"

I'm cut off when she unbuckles and leans over the console.

"Jesus, Rylan. Put your goddamn seatbelt back on."

"Have you suddenly become a drag racer?"

"What? No, but you never know what other people are

doing on the road. Put. On. Your. Seatbelt." My words are strained until her scent is right under my nose. Involuntarily, my muscles relax as she pushes her lithe body into the side of mine and holds up a camera.

She smiles prettily, but I can't erase my scowl. I can't let my guard down. I've already lost my dad because I loved her too much. I can't lose Colton, too.

Rylan jabs me hard in the chest with her thumb, and I feel the warmth radiating in my chest long after she removes her hand.

"We're going to fix that, you know."

I peek to my right to find her leaning against her door, with a leg folded up under her, staring straight at me.

"Fix what?" *Jesus, Halton. You need to keep her at bay, but you don't have to be a nut monkey about it.*

"Your smile." She shrugs and faces forward, finally buckling her seatbelt again.

"My smiles not broken, Ver— Rylan, it's …" *What? It's what, Halton?*

"It's on punishment, just like when we were kids. Except instead of taking your charcoal away for a few days, you've taken away everything you love for years."

"GG and her fucking truth wine," I mumble under my breath.

"It's time to let it all go, Hatty. I'm gonna be your sunbeam again."

I nearly crash the car when I snap my gaze to hers. She winks, and I wonder what the hell else I said while doped up on truth wine.

"Can you put on some music or something?" I feel her smile but can't return it. Apparently, I haven't punished myself enough. Now everyone in my life is piling it on, too. This is going to be a special kind of hell. Camping with her? Living with her? Seeing her twenty-four-seven is going to break me. I always considered myself a strong man, but Jesus. This is too much.

A melancholy sound filters through the speakers. Rylan sings along, off-key, and I'm transported back in time to when life was good. My breathing becomes a little less labored with each passing note, and my chest doesn't feel like a razor's edge.

This will either send me over the brink of sanity or bring me back from the dark. I wish it could be the latter with every fiber of my soul, but Colton has to come first. *I also can't forget that it was my fight with Dad over Rylan that killed him.* That thought alone sends the darkness crashing in like a tsunami.

"What the hell is this music? I always pictured you as a lifelong Taylor Swift fan."

When she doesn't answer me, I dare a peek in her direction. Rylan sits with a sad smile on her face, her fingers tapping out the beat on her thigh. Her bare thigh. I swallow hard and tear my gaze away. *Did she always wear such short shorts?*

Rylan still doesn't answer, so I'm forced to make eye contact again, and finally, she answers.

"I am forever a Swifty. This is Taylor."

My brows furrow in confusion. "This is Taylor Swift? Taylor's music is sunshine and moonbeams. Teenybopper ballads. This is … this is sad."

The sigh that escapes sends her scent rushing toward me, and I can't control the full-body shiver it evokes.

"No, this is Taylor. She grew up, Hatty. We all did."

Don't I fucking know it? Rylan was always beautiful but never felt comfortable in her body. There was an innocence about her, something magnetic, entrancing, that no one else ever got to see. It was just for me. But now? Now she's a goddess dressed like the girl next door. Her hair is fuller somehow. It shimmers more in the sun, and she has grown into a woman that could eviscerate a man with a single glance. I'd be lying if I said I hadn't noticed how shapely her long legs have become or the tits that must have developed after I left for college. *God, her fucking tits are amazing.*

Shifting my weight, I attempt to tamp down the raging hard-on just the thought of her tits causes. Shaking off my teenage fantasies, I stare straight ahead as I speak. "I don't like it. What the hell is it?"

"It's called 'Exile'."

I'm shaking my head, wondering why the hell this song, this Taylor Swift song no less, is putting me on the verge of a full-on panic attack.

"Change it." My tone is harsh. More vitriolic than I intended, so I try to backtrack. "Please. Put on something … just anything else. Something that makes you happy. Please."

Out of the corner of my eye, I see her scroll through her phone and the music changes. I press a button on the steering wheel and glance at the console. Seeing it's more Taylor, I relax. Then the words start, and goosebumps appear all over my body. *'All You Had to Do Was Stay'*. The song's namesake is sung over and over again. Taylor's voice blends with Rylan's off-key version, and I know when this trip is over, for better or worse, we'll never be the same.

CHAPTER 13

RYLAN

*L*exi: How's it going?

Rylan: We just got to the ferry dock.

Rylan: Except for the initial conversation, all I've gotten out of him are grunts, and a few mumbled words when I had to pee.

Rylan: And he kept shifting in his seat like he was so uncomfortable he was trying to climb out of his skin.

Lexi: Or he was trying to hide a boner. That seems more likely to me.

I burst out laughing. She is seriously ridiculous. Hatty frowns and glances at me, so I shrug apologetically. What am I going to say? We're talking about your dick? Another wave of laughter rolls through me, but I bite my lip to keep quiet.

Rylan: Pretty sure that's not the issue.

Lexi: Listen, I won't pretend to know what kind of relationship you guys had or have, but what were you guys like when you were younger? I know you said old souls, yada yada. But what I mean is Halt seems so reserved. I can't imagine that's completely new?

I examine her words for a long time with hunched shoulders before I finally answer.

Rylan: No, I was a free spirit, and he liked order, rules. I guess you could say we balanced each other.

Lexi: Have you changed?

Have I?

Rylan: I guess a little. Matthew wanted everything a certain way. It was just easier to go along with it.

Lexi: That's not what I asked. Have YOU changed?

Rylan: ...

Rylan: Without the expectations of others? Probably not. I would still stay up all night watching the stars. Go buy ice cream at 3 a.m. because I couldn't sleep. Lose days because everything looks better through the lens of my camera.

I press send, then sit back and scrutinize my words. *How had I lost myself so completely?*

Lexi: Well, this seems like the perfect opportunity for you to dance in the rain. Maybe getting in touch with yourself will also bring Halt back to life?

I shift my gaze to the man sitting next to me. Beside me, but miles away. My stomach flutters with nerves. Those damn feelings of hope are taking over my body again.

Rylan: Or he could shatter me beyond repair.

Lexi: Only you can decide if it's worth the risk.

Lexi: I swore to never let love in again. I can tell you firsthand that's a worse pain than the rocky road love sometimes puts you on.

Lexi: I know Colton is pissed off right now, but he's also starting to understand what you and Halt meant to each other. He wouldn't let you suffer alone this time.

Lexi: None of us would. But let me remind you, GG hasn't been wrong yet.

Exhaling deeply, I bow my head, suddenly feeling a headache coming on.

"Are you okay?" Hatty's voice cuts through my inner turmoil.

Glancing up at him, I see he's fighting a war, too. He wants to stay away from me, but he's drawn to me in a way he can't control when he thinks I'm upset.

"Yeah, sorry. It's just been a long day."

He narrows his eyes and gives a curt nod. Even after all these years, I can tell he doesn't believe me, but he doesn't push either, so I turn my attention back to my phone.

Rylan: I'm not sure where to go from here.

Lexi: Dance in the rain, Rylan, and let him fall in love with you all over again.

Rylan: What if it doesn't work?

Lexi: What if it does?

"Ah, we're here. We have to head down to the golf cart." Hatty's voice is rough, and I'm shocked when he holds out his hand to help me up. Judging by his expression and shaking hands, he is, too. I'm expecting him to snatch it back, but I grab ahold before he can. Skin to skin, our bodies remember the connection we once shared.

Hatty hauls me up with such force my body slams into his, and we're stuck in time, staring at each other for what feels like hours, but it's really only a few seconds. Clearing his throat, he drops my hand and takes a step back. It feels like being dunked in an ice bath and unable to surface. I long for his touch, his gentleness, his love.

Dance in the rain, Rylan.

Wrapping my arms around my body, I make a decision. Even if I can't ever have Hatty as my own, I am going to dance in the rain and fight for a friendship that once made me whole.

"Ready?" His throaty voice is full of the emotion swirling around my heart.

Sucking in a fortifying breath, I steel myself for this journey. "Always. Lead the way, Hatty."

Please don't break me again, my seventeen-year-old self screams in my head, but I push her back. Seventeen-year-old me didn't know how to fight for what she wanted, for what was right. I'm not that girl anymore, and it's time Hatty grew up, too.

~

*H*atty and I stand side by side, staring at our new home ... if you can call it that. A half shelter, no bigger than twelve by ten feet in size, seems to laugh at us from its perch overlooking the Atlantic Ocean.

"What do we do when it rains?"

He shakes his head and climbs up onto the lean-to platform. I stay put, gaping at him while he inspects the structure. "Ah, it looks like there's a tarp that rolls down."

He stares at the ceiling, and I move closer to take a peek.

"At least it looks like the roof will hold." He pinches the back of his neck, steps forward and jumps down off the platform. "Let's unpack the golf cart, then I'll head back to get the rest of our stuff from the docks."

Something Ash conveniently forgot to mention was that he couldn't get a reservation to bring the SUV across on the ferry. Instead, he had a golf cart waiting for us. Apparently, that's the way most people move around this island.

His phone dings, and he pulls it from his pocket. Sighing, he pushes his glasses off his face to pinch the bridge of his nose. This is his exasperated stance. I smile, realizing how much I still know about him.

"What's wrong?"

Hatty glances up, as if he forgot I was here, and slides his phone back into his pocket.

"Ash had someone pick up the SUV. It's registered to him, so he didn't want it turning up any red flags for Pacen or her father."

"So ... we're stranded?" I find this funny and don't even try to keep the humor out of my voice.

Narrowing his eyes, Hatty points a finger at me. "Did you know about this, too?"

I laugh, full belly shaking laughter that causes tears to roll down my face. He's fighting it, but I see the curl of his lip.

"No, Hatty. I didn't know they would strand us on an island. I wonder what else he has up his sleeve?"

This time, he does chuckle, and my heart nearly bursts.

There's my Hatty.

"He was always a sneaky little shit."

We stand across from each other, smiling like fools. The tension that has followed us since I returned evaporating for the briefest of moments. I see the instant he reins himself in and puts the mask back on. I feel his pain as he shuts down.

"Well, we should ... ah, get unloaded so I can go back for the rest." His voice falls flat, and his shoulders slump forward. He steps around me, and the wall he just constructed nearly knocks me over.

Am I cut out for this?

Yes, you idiot. It's either try or spend your life knowing you're not whole.

Forcing a cheery expression, I turn with him. "Sounds good, Hatty. What do you want me to do?"

He stops abruptly and studies me. I'm sure he was expecting sullen, maybe even hurt, but I'm done letting him run from me.

Here's to the new Rylan. The one who's after answers, love, and a happily ever after.

"You can run, Hatty, but you can't hide anymore. What do you want me to do first?"

"Ah, um," he splutters. "I'm not hiding."

"We'll see about that. How about if I grab the groceries? Good?"

He nods, and I see his cheeks have turned the slightest shade of pink. I also don't miss the fact that his eyes are on my ass as I bend over the golf cart. Or the way he noncha-lantly adjusts himself as he walks away.

At least it's proof he's still attracted to me, even without GG's truth wine. Score one for team Rylan!

I climb up into the lean-to, and it's no small effort. I'm not exactly short, but this thing could use a step or two. I'm sweating and sticky when I finally pull myself up onto the platform. Turning toward the edge, I find Hatty standing with one leg in the golf cart. His eyes are stuck on me, and the lopsided grin I haven't seen in years completely trans-forms his face.

"You think that was funny?" I ask, placing both hands on my hips, and watch as his gaze follows the movement, then glides down my exposed legs. They're more toned than he's used to. Running helped me shed the baby fat I couldn't shake in my teens, and the bonus is my legs are killer.

As his eyes slide slowly up my body, my eyebrow hitches in amusement. Suddenly realizing where he is, his gaze snaps to mine. Seeing my gotcha face, he pulls at his collar and surveys the ground.

"Umm." He clears his throat and tries again. "Are you okay here while I go get the supplies? I can pack more in if I can load up the passenger seat, too."

"And it gives you a break from me."

It slips out, but if I'm going to find the Rylan he fell in love with once, I have to stop censoring myself.

"Listen, Ry …"

"It's okay. This is a lot. I get it. Being forced into an awkward situation with someone you hate would take a herculean effort for anyone. Go get the stuff. I'll start unpacking." I turn so I don't have to see his reaction, and nearly jump out of my skin when his voice is right behind me.

"I've never hated you, Verity. Not even once. But you have to hate me. You have to." His whispered words cause my hair to flutter beside my ear. He's so close I can feel his body heat radiating off him. If I took half a step, my back would be flush with his front. By the time I build up the courage to do just that, he's gone.

Spinning around, I see him climb into the golf cart and drive away without ever peering back.

Holy geez. This is going to test the limits of what I can handle. If I don't break, I certainly won't ever be the same.

Needing to burn off some nervous energy, I dig around in the bag Lexi helped me pack and find my running gear. As I glance around to see if anyone can see me, I almost laugh. There isn't a neighbor in sight, and the lean-to faces the ocean, so I strip where I am, pulling on a sports bra and running shorts. Then I plop down and lace up my sneakers.

I open the running app on my watch, hop down, and turn in a circle. Making sure I sync the GPS, I mark my current position so I can find my way back and take off toward the road that runs along the coastline.

I hope a few miles will be enough to clear my head.

CHAPTER 14

HALTON

I'm just over a small hill when I stop the golf cart and glance back at the lean-to. I shouldn't have gotten so close to her or left the way I did. My brain doesn't seem to work when she's around.

Craning my neck, so the structure comes into view, I nearly swallow my tongue when Rylan rips off her shirt. I can't blink, and I can't turn away, even though I know I should. First, I'm a creepy stalker, and now I'm a creepy Peeping Tom. There're two things I never thought I'd be.

She turns her back to me and falls out of view. I'm sure she thought no one could see her. The lean-to faces the ocean for Christ's sake, but the road veers enough to the right that I can see everything. Rylan pops back up and drops her pants. I can almost feel the silky skin of her ass on my fingertips, and my cock stands at attention, painfully pressing against the zipper of my shorts.

Shaking my head, I'm relieved to see she's put on some sort of crop top, but fuck me. If she's going to wear shit like that every day, I'll need to run ten miles just to function.

Forcing my gaze forward, I hit the accelerator before I do something incredibly stupid.

The ride to the dock doesn't take long, but strapping all our shit into an open golf cart takes almost an hour. *What the hell did they pack in here?*

I'm about to head back when I see a small grab n'go stand. Knowing it will take a few hours to set up camp, I jog across the street. While I'm staring at the coffee menu, a thought occurs to me. *Does Rylan still like hers with more cream than coffee?* The realization that I no longer know something so simple hurts. There was a time when I knew everything about her. Everything from the first time she got her period to when there was a spider in her room.

You don't have that right anymore, Halton. You burned that bridge a long time ago.

"What can I get for you, young man?"

"May I have two large, iced coffees, please? One black, and one with extra cream."

"Anything else?" the older gentleman asks.

"Ah, yeah. Maybe two BLTs, please."

"You got it."

He attempts to make small talk that I'm sure most vacationers enjoy, but I can't stop thinking about Rylan and how we're practically strangers now. Aside from what I can glean from Instagram, I don't know her. And that causes the acidic sensation to form in my throat again.

Walking back to the golf cart with a lot less enthusiasm, I place the coffees in the cup holders and slowly take the winding road back to camp. I can't make any sharp turns or go too fast, or all our shit will end up on the side of the road.

The closer I get to camp, the higher my anxiety rises. I have to sleep next to her, for lord only knows how many days, and I can't touch her under any circumstances. *Why, hello, blue ball city! What a fucking nightmare it is to be here.*

As I pull into the "driveway"—and I use that term loosely —the Atlantic Ocean comes into view, and I pause. It's beautiful here.

Not as beautiful as your gal.

How the hell I can hear GG's voice in my head right now is beyond me. Maybe her truth wine is more potent than I thought.

That makes me chuckle, and I go in search of Rylan to give her the cream with a splash of coffee. Only, she's not in the lean-to. I scan our surroundings but don't see her. Knowing she must be in the outhouse, I set the coffees down and head in that direction in case there isn't any toilet paper. *Girls need toilet paper, right?* Except, as I get closer, I notice the door is wide open, and I pick up my pace.

"Rylan?"

Silence.

Fear takes hold, and I run to the other side of the lean-to where the 'shower' is, but that's empty, too.

"Rylan?" I yell, a little hysterically. "Rylan?" I try again but get no response. I've never felt a true sense of dread until now. It sits heavy and ferocious in my gut.

I don't even realize I'm running until I take a flying leap into the lean-to. *Maybe she left a note.* I scan the space frantically, searching for anything that will give me a clue to where she's gone. When I spot her phone on top of her clothes, I sink to my knees.

Calm down. Take deep breaths. She's probably just gone for a walk.

Why didn't she take her phone?

"Fuck!"

We're here, searching for a girl whose father was mixed up with the mob Loki and Ashton spent years taking down. What are the chances we're in danger? Why didn't that ever cross my mind?

Because it didn't matter when it was just you!

I can't panic. She always enjoyed being outside, and I was gone longer than expected. *She's just out exploring. She's fine*, I tell myself repeatedly until I almost believe it.

Pep talk complete, I drop the sandwiches and her iced coffee into the cooler and get to work unpacking some of the shit my brothers sent with us. I'll avoid setting up the beds, because there aren't any and because I want Rylan to choose how we situate ourselves for the night.

It takes about an hour to unload most of the bags and set up camp, but it feels much longer because I'm compulsively checking my watch.

Where the hell are you, Rylan?

When thirty more minutes pass, and I can't sit still any longer, I grab my satchel and rip out a piece of paper.

Rylan, I've gone out searching for you. If you return before I do, please call my cell.

~~Hal~~

Hatty

I can't shake the feeling that something's wrong, but I do my best to tamp it down. Colton is the drama queen of the family, not me. Ash wouldn't have sent us here unprepared if he thought we were in danger. He's too thorough.

Calm the fuck down, Hatty.

Rylan's voice echoes in my head and settles a little of the chaos, at least slightly, but staring up at the sky, I know a storm is rolling in, so I pick up my pace. Hopefully, she'll show up, or I'll find her on the beach somewhere before the rain starts.

I'm almost at the golf cart when I remember Rylan had grabbed a bunch of flyers on the ferry. Jogging back to where she'd dropped her bag, I hesitate for half a second. *Is it wrong to go through her stuff?* If it is, I'll deal with that later.

Sifting through her things, I find the brochures tucked into a book I remember. It's our scrapbook. I freeze. If I open the cover, I know I'll see her photos on one page, with my drawing of the same thing on the other. We did this for years, and she kept them all safe.

She still carries this with her?

113

Tears prick my eyes, and my breaths are too shallow. Closing my eyes, I shake my head, trying to rid the feelings fighting their way to the surface. I can't allow them space in my head or my heart. Feelings like this are dangerous. But my hands move on their own, causing my eyes to fly open as memories crash into me like a brick wall.

"Give me a word, Hatty?"

"Languor."

I flip the page because I can't stop myself.

"Give me a word, Hatty?"

"Sprightly."

And another.

"Give me a word, Hatty?"

"Ethereal."

I grab the stack of papers she stuck inside and slam it shut between my open palms. The snap it makes sounds eerie in the silence. Using the sleeve of my T-shirt, I wipe the sweat from my brow. I think of nothing but breathing in and out. In and out until I'm calm enough to search for the information I need.

Locating the Old Harbor Walking Tour map, I stick it into my pocket and move to the golf cart on autopilot.

She carries our love with her.

"Cut the shit, Halton. You don't get to keep her," I grumble under my breath even as a small kernel of hope tries to break through my heart.

Turning left at the end of the drive, I come to a fork in the road a half-mile from camp. Referring to the map, I turn right, following the coast. If she went for a walk, she'd want to see the ocean. *Right?*

It doesn't take long to make the two-mile loop. But a mile in, the sky turns black with storm clouds and unleashes God's fury. The panic I've fought to keep at bay explodes.

The golf cart slips and slides through the dirt roads. It's a pain in the ass, but I finally make it back to camp. Just as I make the turn onto the driveway, the damn cart splutters to a stop and dies.

"Just fucking great," I bellow to the swirling sea, then take off up the path to see if Rylan's back.

A fear I've never known grips me when I realize she hasn't returned to me. *No, not me, numbnuts. She hasn't returned to camp.*

CHAPTER 15

HALTON

*O*ut of options, my stomach revolts as I grab my phone and stab at it until Ashton's face appears on the screen. Staring into the empty lean-to I know I'm jumping to conclusions, but after my family's year and the danger they've faced, I worry my fear is valid.

"She's gone." My voice alternates between hysterical and venomous, but my shaking hands make it impossible for Ash to get a good look at me.

"Who? Who's gone?" he whispers.

"Rylan," I bellow. "Are we in danger here, Ash? Would someone have taken her?"

His phone shifts, and Loki's face comes into view. "Halt? Calm down, brother. Tell me what happened."

"What happened is I dropped her off at the lean-to and went back to grab our supplies because you only left us with a mother fucking golf cart. When I got back, she was gone. Her clothes are in a pile on the ground, and her phone was tossed on top of them. Would someone have taken her?" All the rage I'm feeling flies out with my words.

Loki glances at someone off screen, and I know he's talking to Ash.

"Answer me," I scream.

Preston enters the frame next. His face close to the screen somehow allows me to think clearly. "Preston," I choke out. "D-Did someone take her? She doesn't even know. She doesn't know I lied. I— Fuck! Pres, please tell me she's not in danger. Tell me what to do! I can't lose her like this."

My voice cracks, and I don't even care if I break down and sob right here in front of them. I can't lose her like this, I won't recover. Loki almost lost his wife. Emory almost lost Preston. They have to understand. They have to.

"Get out of the rain, Halton."

I stare between him and the open sky and realize I never took cover. The rain feels ice cold after the smothering heat we'd suffered all day, but I nod and jump up into the lean-to.

"Do you love her?" Preston asks calmly once I'm under shelter, and if he were here, I'd punch the guy right in the face.

All the reasons I have for pushing her away are meaningless as the worry for her safety takes center stage.

"Of course I fucking love her. I've always loved her. What the hell does that have to do with anything? Tell me how to find her. Can Ash put a stop on the ferry? If she's still on the island, I'll search every inch until I find her. Just tell me."

"How long has she been gone?" Ash asks so softly I almost missed it.

"Ah," I spin in a circle. "I-I don't know. Maybe three or four hours."

"Is anything out of place? Were her clothes torn, or do they look like she left them there?"

Images of her naked body flash before my eyes, and are suddenly replaced with my worst nightmare. Her naked body beaten and bruised in a ditch somewhere.

"Halton. Focus. Is anything out of place?"

Pulling at my hair, I take in my surroundings. I've moved

so much stuff around it's hard to remember, but I didn't find anything that caused me to worry more than I already was.

"It doesn't look like it, no. But she doesn't have her phone," I say meekly. The first sign of tears threatens the back of my eyes.

"Okay, that's good, Halt. That's really good. If someone had taken her, there would have been a struggle. Your girl wouldn't go down without a fight," Loki chimes in.

Your girl. Fuck if those two words don't feel right all the way down to my soul.

"Are we in danger here, Loki? Is it possible that Pacen's father is out for revenge? Could someone have taken her?"

Preston lowers the phone, and I hear whispers but can't make out words.

"Answer me, goddamn it."

"No," Ash crackles.

"I have no reason to believe Patrick Macomb would be after you or even have any clue you're there. He has his own shit to dig out of right now," Loki explains from the background.

"I wouldn't put you in danger, Halt."

Ashton's words are so sincere, guilt slaps me in the face. I know he wouldn't.

"I know, Ash. I'm sorry. I-I'm just scared. Really fucking scared. It's like a tropical hailstorm of shit here right now, and I don't know where she is. The rain is so cold, Ash. What if she didn't find shelter?"

"She's a smart girl, Halt. But we'll find her, okay?"

Staring into Preston's eyes, for the first time I realize how similar he is to our dad, and I give a jerky nod of my head. Words hurt too much right now.

"Does she wear any smart devices?" Loki asks, shaking me from my thoughts.

Fuck. Does she? Closing my eyes, I picture her in the car

today and can almost feel her hand on my forearm again. That's when I see it.

"She has an Apple watch."

"Okay, that's good," Loki soothes. "That's probably why she didn't take her phone. If it's one with its own service, she wouldn't need her phone."

"I'll call it," Preston informs us as he hands Ashton's phone over to Loki.

"Ash is already on his computer. He'll use her watch to track her down, but it will take some time because the infrastructure there is so old. Just hang tight. We'll find her," Loki promises.

The Chainsmokers song, "Family", pierces the quiet, and it takes me a minute to realize it's coming from Rylan's phone in my hand. Glancing down, I see Preston's name, and my chest warms. A crooked smile forming even in the midst of an all-out crisis because she still considers us family. Or at least some of us.

Does she have a song for me? Do I want to know? Of course you want to know, asshole.

I'm so tempted to see what song she has for me, if anything, but I force my focus to stay on finding her first.

"She didn't answer," I finally mumble.

"It's a small island, Halt. Her service may have cut out, but Ash will track her to the last known location, and we'll go from there. Just be patient."

Be patient? I want to scream. Is he fucking kidding me?

"Would you be patient if it were Sloane that was missing?"

Loki holds the phone closer to his face. I know he'd do anything to save his wife, Sloane, and I need him to understand how serious I am, but Preston takes the phone.

"Are you ready to admit it?"

"Admit what?"

"That whatever you did to push her away was a mistake?" His cocky grin is in place, but his eyes are full of love.

"Easton is the one with mistakes. I just have lies. Call me back when you have an answer for me. I need to conserve my battery until I can get the generator running."

Preston opens his mouth to say something, but I end the call and sit on the floor. Resting my head on my knees, I hold both our phones in my hands at my sides. I'm wet and cold, but I fear Rylan might be in worse shape. The rain is way too fucking cold for summer. I guess that happens in the middle of the ocean.

Staring at our phones, I let my curiosity get the better of me, and I search my contacts for a name I thought I'd never call again. Rylan's face appears, and I hold my breath while it connects.

Dermot Kennedy's "Better Days" starts softly and crescendos as I take in the words, silently hating myself more than I ever thought possible.

"What did you do?" My words cut through the sound of summer rain as the wind whips all around, causing the tarp to flap wildly.

I must listen to that song at least a dozen times before my phone rings again and Preston's face appears on the screen.

"We think she's about three-quarters of a mile up the shore. Her watch pinged steadily until she hit that point, and then it went silent. How fast can you get there?"

I appreciate he gets straight to the point, but my mind is already processing the next steps.

"The golf cart is dead. I'll have to run," I bark. Preston cringes with guilt, and it gives me a small amount of satisfaction. "Which way do I go?"

Preston gives me directions as I put in my AirPods and place my phone in the pocket of a raincoat I unpacked earlier.

"Just tell me when I'm getting close," I tell them as I take off sprinting. My feet hit the dirt road and I nearly fall flat on my face as my shoes slosh around in the muddy mess. "Fucking hell. The road's a mess."

"Okay, we're tracking you. I'll let you know when you arrive at her last known location."

I grunt, but no words come. Rylan's song for me plays on a loop in my head, and before I know it, Preston is yelling at me to stop.

"She cut out here. Search the area and then backtrack. Do you see anywhere she could take cover?"

Glancing around, I hold my hand to my head, attempting to shield my eyes from the heavy rain that's falling in thick sheets all around me.

"I-I can barely see anything out here."

"I'm scanning Google maps now. If you face camp, I think there's a crop of trees at two o'clock. Do you see them?"

Turning in place, I squint, trying to make out my two o'clock. "Yeah. Yeah, I think I see them."

"I would check there first. I don't see anywhere else she could take cover."

"Got it."

I have to run back about twenty yards, but just before I get to the spot, my foot hits a crumbling patch of road, and my leg slides out from under me.

"Fuck me," I scream as I go down.

"What? What happened?" Preston's concerned voice comes through my AirPod.

"The goddamn road crumbled beneath me, and I pulled something. I'm fine."

"Jesus."

Standing, I wince as pain soars through my groin down into my hamstring. But then I see it. A flash of hot pink, just like the crop top Rylan was wearing, huddled beneath the tree, and I run toward her. The pain in my leg is forgotten as adrenaline takes over.

"Oh, God. I-I found her."

Ripping the AirPods from my ears, I collapse next to Rylan. "Sweetheart? Are you okay? What happened?"

She raises her head to mine. Her tears mingle with rain, and she gives me a half smile.

All the air leaves my lungs as relief floods my veins. A need I've never experienced roars through my body so fast and fierce I don't have time to think of the repercussions. I take her face in my hands, staring into her eyes where forever lives, and I do the worst thing I could do. I kiss her with every ounce of life I have left.

A kiss that says I'm so fucking sorry. A kiss that says I don't know what I'm doing, but I need you more than air. A kiss that says this is the second biggest mistake I've ever made in my life, and I immediately know I'm lying to myself again because there is no way in hell a mistake could ever feel this right.

Rylan gasps, and I use the opportunity to explore her sweet mouth. She tastes just as I remembered. She tastes like home, and I growl as a possessive streak zings through me, screaming, *She's mine.*

My tongue wars with Rylan's as I demand submission. The need to control this kiss is so overwhelming I almost climb on top of her. But when her icy hand cups the back of my neck, reality smacks me in the face.

She's fucking frozen, asshole. You can't maul her out here in a tropical storm. Pulling back, I scan her body for injuries and notice one ankle is bigger than the other.

"I-I knew you'd find me, Hatty." Rylan's teeth chatter in between words.

I stare at her for a moment as I realize her entire body has a blueish tint to it. She's trembling from head to toe and covered in mud. As the sun set, the temperature dropped close to twenty degrees, and every first aid course I've ever taken kicks in.

Wrapping her in my arms, I lift her and start the long walk home.

CHAPTER 16

RYLAN

*H*atty cradles my shivering body to his chest and walks us through the rain. I've never felt more stupid or more relieved in all my life. *I knew he'd find me, though.*

We're both silent as he trudges through the muddy swamp that used to be a dirt road. He slips a couple of times but keeps his balance, and we stay upright. I shouldn't love the comfort of his arms as much as I do, but I can't help it. I snuggle in for as long as he'll let me because I know he'll shut down soon enough.

He veers to the right, and I know we're almost back to camp. I clench my teeth to keep them from chattering as he marches us to the side of the lean-to, opens the gate, and turns on the open-air shower.

"Wh-What are you doing?"

"We're covered in mud, sweetheart. We need to rinse off, then I'll get you warm."

Sweetheart. That one word has the power to destroy me, so I attempt to block it out.

He doesn't set me down as he stands us under the warm spray that mixes with ice cold rainwater. He just turns in place, allowing the water to run all over my body, then leans in, balancing me with one hand while he turns it off, and carries me into the lean-to.

Once inside, he gingerly sets me down on the ground and frowns when he notices me favoring one foot. It morphs into a scowl as he turns away, leaving me standing in the center of our makeshift home dripping water while he straps down the tarp with the buckles and snaps already in place.

Satisfied the tarp is secure, he turns and presses the buttons on two lanterns he must have set up earlier before finally coming back and handing me a towel. I'm not sure why I just stood here instead of helping. I guess I'm in shock, but even as he wraps a towel around my frozen body, something crackles to life between us.

His large palms come to rest on either side of my face. We stare at each other for a long moment before he leans in and rests his forehead against mine.

"What happened, my verity? You scared the shit out of me." His voice is whisper-soft, but he's so close, the air he exhales fans across my face, and I shiver as if he touched me intimately.

With chattering teeth, I attempt to speak. "It started to r-rain, and I slipped when the road got muddy. I th-think I sprained my ankle. I couldn't put much w-weight on it, then the rain got heavier, s-so I hobbled to the trees to wait it out, but it just kept raining harder and harder. My watch lost a signal, I guess. I-I tried to call Colton, but it wouldn't connect."

He rears back as if I struck him.

"Colton?" he whispers with a touch of sadness and closes his eyes like he's trying to block a bad memory.

"I …" My body shivers as wave after wave of icy cold washes through me. "I wasn't sure you'd care," I admit, laying all my insecurities at his feet.

His gaze finds mine, pleading for something I don't understand.

"I've always cared, Verity. Always. Possibly too much."

I shake my head no, but he silences me with a kiss. A gentle kiss that speaks of forgiveness and hope, and my body heats from within. He pulls away far too quickly, and a whimper escapes my lips.

He moves his hands to my upper arms and curses. "Jesus, Rylan. You're freezing."

"Really? You just set fire to all the parts that matter."

His eyes darken, but he doesn't say anything. Instead, he turns and opens my bag. I begin to protest but realize there's no point. He's going to do whatever he thinks needs to be done at this point. And secretly, I love it.

When he returns, he hands me a pair of lacey pink panties and one of his T-shirts. I lift my gaze to his, and he shrugs.

"Turn around and get dressed. I'll do the same, then I'll tend to your ankle."

He either forgot that I don't sleep in panties, or he's ignoring it. I stand frozen to my spot, and when he turns to check on me, the lopsided grin I love so much appears.

"Still not good at listening to directions I see?"

"Some things never change, Hatty."

His smile fades as he scratches the side of his head. "I think I like that."

A big, toothy grin appears on my face. "Me too," I whisper, then do as he asks.

Hobbling in place, I remove my wet clothing and throw on his shirt, then slide my panties up my legs, attempting to place as little weight as possible on my sore ankle.

When I turn around, Halton is dressed in dry boxer briefs and nothing else. He's staring straight at me with his muscled arms crossed over his chest.

"You're a lot bigger than you used to be."

His eyes go wide, and he adjusts his stance, causing my gaze to roam lower, and I gasp.

"Holy shit."

An incessant buzzing sounds cuts through the tension in the air, and Halton steps forward with a curse. That's when I notice he's limping, too.

"What the hell, Hatty? Are you hurt?" I go to step forward, but he stops me with a single word.

"Don't."

I still, but watch him intently.

"Don't move. I'm fine," he clarifies.

Reaching down, Hatty pulls his phone from a pile of clothes.

"Jesus Christ, Halton. What the fuck? You can't say 'Oh, God, I've found her,' then hang up on us and not answer for almost forty-five minutes."

I try not to giggle, but I can hear Preston's reprimand through the phone. Hatty's eyes find mine in the dim light.

"I have her. We're safe, but get us a goddamn car immediately. And someplace safe to stay. This is bullshit, Pres, and you know it."

"Honestly, the ferries are all booked—"

"Then rent one of our own. For fuck's sake, Preston. This isn't rocket science. You would do it if it were for you, so get it done."

"Fine," he acquiesces, "but there isn't much we can do about accommodations. I swear everything is full."

"Then we'll stay on the mainland and take day trips here."

"No," Ash interrupts.

"Staying there is important. The locals are a lot like they are here in Burke Hollow. They won't give up information easily. You have to get to know everyone," Preston finishes.

"Hatty?" I ask softly. "We'll be fine here. A car will be good in case we run into an emergency, but we can tough it out."

"Is she okay?" Preston asks quietly.

"She has a sprained ankle. I haven't had a chance to see how serious it is yet."

"Great. So, you're telling me you have matching injuries?"

I gasp when my eyes dart to his legs as he rubs and pinches his thigh muscle.

"What the hell, Hatty?" My voice is harsher than I've ever heard it. "You carried me for a mile when you're hurt, too?" I drop to my knees and crawl across the small space to get a better look. When I fall back onto my heels to stare up at him, I see a man hanging on by a thread.

His eyes roam from my face, down my neck, and stop at my breasts. Sneaking a peek, I notice my hair has dripped down the front of his shirt, and it's now see-through. My nipples stand at attention, the rosy buds on full display through the thin cotton.

"We're fine," Hatty grinds out. "Just get us a car."

After tossing the phone onto a nearby cooler, Hatty crosses his arms again, then steps forward and offers me his hand. I'm about to take it when he thinks better of it and places both hands under my arms and lifts me to standing.

The sensation of my nipples rubbing against his muscular chest causes a hiss of pleasure to escape, and I feel his erection pressing into my belly.

He speaks with a hoarse voice, but my brain has turned to mush.

"Ah, what?"

That Westbrook smirk sneaks past his serious expression.

"I said, I'm going to make up our beds so you can sit down, and I'll tend to your ankle."

"What about your—"

"Don't argue with me right now, sweetheart. Today is not the day. I'm a hairsbreadth away from losing my shit here, okay?"

My eyes go wide, and I give an exaggerated nod.

"Good. Just give me five minutes."

I stand in the center of the room, watching as he moves around me with the grace of a tiger stalking its prey. He frowns when he opens the first sleeping bag.

"What's the matter?" I ask, hobbling closer.

"Who packed this shit?"

"Er ... Lexi and I shopped for some of it yesterday, and the rest, I think GG packed up from the lodge. Why?" Peering around him, I try to see what's causing him distress.

"Is there another sleeping bag somewhere?"

"What?" I screech, glancing around.

He opens the first sack that should hold a sleeping bag and unrolls a big, thick mat. A black bottle slides across the floor as it lies flat.

Dropping to my knees, I crawl past him to see what it is.

"Jesus. Rylan, for fuck's sake. Stop crawling," he groans.

Glancing over my shoulder, I catch him adjusting his dick, and I snicker. *Score two for team Rylan!* I lean forward and reach for the bottle. Turning my head, I find his gaze firmly on my ass, and I shimmy it a little for him.

"Get a good show, did ya?"

His head snaps to attention, but he ignores my comment.

"If that's what I think it is, just toss it outside right now. I mean it."

Holding up the glass, I inspect it but don't find any markings on the strangely shaped bottle.

"What is it?"

Hatty storms over—well, as much as he can while favoring one leg—and rips it from my hands.

"GG's damn truth wine. Do not drink this. Do you understand? It's the devil's juice."

Laughter starts in my belly and finally forces its way out. Even Hatty can't keep a straight face.

"I'm being serious here, Rylan. I don't know what she puts in it, but just a sip will knock you off your ass."

"So I've seen." I'm gasping for breath now, and he shakes his head.

Rolling his eyes, he goes back to work.

"Hatty, you're limping more than me. Sit down, and we can figure this out together."

"Not a chance," he mumbles. "I'll always take care of you."

I gasp, and he looks faint. I don't think he meant to say that out loud. He turns his back quickly and opens up the second bag. It's bigger than the first, and he unrolls an awkwardly large sleeping bag.

"What the hell is this?" He holds up a sleeping bag big enough for …

"Oh, shit."

"What? What am I missing?" he demands.

"Ah, well …" I try really hard to suppress my laughter, but it's nearly impossible. GG is a crazy matchmaking magician.

"What, Rylan? My patience is running thin here. Are we supposed to split this up somehow?" He shakes it out, then inspects the zipper.

"No," I giggle. "That's a double sleeping bag, Hatty."

He drops it like it's on fire and places his hands on his hips.

"Just what does that mean?"

"It means it's for two people."

He gives me a blank expression, and I laugh hysterically.

"It means," gasp, "we're supposed to sleep in it." Gasp. "Together."

Hatty's body goes ramrod straight, and I see his throat working to swallow.

I bite my bottom lip to keep from laughing at his expression, but he glances away quickly and picks up the mat. Spreading it out evenly on the raised platform that reminds me of a small trampoline, he lays the sleeping bag on top of it.

"Go ahead, climb on, and I'll tend to your foot."

"No."

"Rylan, I swear to God …"

"Not unless you let me look after yours, too."

He sucks in a long hiss of air through his teeth and holds it.

"Breathe, Hatty. Just breathe. We have to take care of each other out here, okay?"

CHAPTER 17

*R*ylan finally gets on the mat, and if she doesn't stop crawling, I'm going to blow my load like a horny teenager.

"Don't move."

She raises her eyebrow with a sexy grin, and I turn away as quickly as I can. I don't know when she turned into such a freaking temptress, but I have to keep my wits.

"Colton loved her first." My spine stiffens at the memory. Well, that's one way to deflate a boner.

"Hatty? Are you all right?"

"Hmm?" I can't turn and look at her yet. Not until I can put a lid on whatever this feeling is I'm having.

"Look at me."

"Hold on, I just—"

"Hatty? Look at me." Her voice is more demanding this time.

Shaking my head, I do as she asks. The determination in her expression is almost my undoing.

"What were you just thinking about?"

"How unfair life can be sometimes. Nothing to worry about."

I bend down to hide my face and dig through the sack I know holds the first aid kit. I spend more time than necessary, so I can calm my bodily reaction to her.

She's not just 'her,' Halton. She's 'the one'. My spine tingles hearing GG's voice. Now I'm convinced she hexed me with that wine. After rolling my tense shoulders a few times, I pick up the first aid kit and hobble back to Rylan.

My damn hamstring is sorer than I thought.

Sitting next to her, I point to her foot, which she lifts and sets in my lap. My hand rests on her shin like it's the most natural thing in the world. In another life, it would have been.

As gently as possible, I feel around her delicate bones, noting the inflammation around her ankle.

"Can you flex your foot, sweetheart?"

Fuck. I need to stop calling her that.

"Yeah, it only hurts a little. Honestly, I think I was more scared than anything."

My chest tightens. I hate that she was scared, but I'm thankful she isn't in too much pain.

"That's good. It doesn't look too bad, actually. We'll put some ice on it, and it should be good to go in a couple of days."

Reaching into the kit, I grab an ice pack that I crack open, then shake to activate. I roll the ace bandage around her ankle once, place the icepack on the swollen area, and secure it with the remaining bandage.

"That should be good for a bit. Climb into the sleeping bag, and I'll get you some Advil. I think it's all we have in the kit, but it should help."

"Hatty! You said I could look at your leg."

"I never agreed. I'm fine. I'll take some Advil, too. Oh, but we should eat. Otherwise, you might get an upset stomach. I bought some BLTs for lunch, but they're probably a little soggy now. Let me see what else I can find."

She stops me with a delicate hand on my wrist. My gaze stays locked on the connection. How can a simple touch light up my body like this? Her damn sunbeam shoots straight through her fingertips and warms my chest.

A once in a lifetime connection.

"Soggy BLTs are my favorite, Hatty." Her melodic voice draws my soul to her, but I slowly drag my body away anyway.

Still, I grin because I know her words are true. Not the soggy part, but BLTs were always our thing. Or one of them.

At least I still know something about her.

"Okay. Get inside of the sleeping bag. You still need to warm up, and I'll get the sandwiches and chips."

"Salt and vinegar?" The hopefulness in her voice unlocks a little of the bitterness I carry.

"Yeah, Ver— ah, Rylan. Salt and vinegar." I move away quickly, hoping she doesn't call me out on the fiftieth slip of the night.

When I return, she's slid into the sleeping bag. She also folded down the outside corner like she expected me to climb in next to her.

"Ah." I choke on the words and have to try again. "I'll just sleep on the floor."

Frowning, she crosses her arms. I really wish she wouldn't do that. It pushes her tits up and forces them out. My shirt is already transparent, but the vision she's thrusting at me now has me thinking with the wrong head.

"You will not. Hatty, we slept in that damn ham—" She falters over her words, and I know she's reliving the night that ruined us. I hate myself even more when I see her face fall, so I move without thinking.

"Okay, fine." I climb in next to her and pull the sleeping bag over my lap, but I can feel her deflated presence beside me.

After unwrapping one BLT, I place half on the paper bag and set it in her lap.

"Eat, Rylan. It'll make you feel better."

She pulls it toward her, but I drop mine when I see her dig a fork out of the bag. Glancing over, I watch as she eats the ingredients like a salad.

"What are you doing?"

She jumps as if I startled her. "Eating," she says without glancing up.

"Eating what?"

She huffs and gazes up at me with annoyance. "I love BLTs, Hatty, but I don't eat bread anymore."

"Why the fuck not?"

Rylan drops her head back and stares at the ceiling while exhaling loudly. "Because I didn't want to be fat anymore, Halton."

Now it's my turn to jump. She's called me Hatty all day. Now I'm back to Halton? Obviously, I said something wrong.

"You've never been fat, Rylan." I say it softly, but my conviction is clear.

"I ... whatever. I don't want to talk about it right now."

Unable to take the hurt in her voice, I reach over and pull her chin up to look at me. "You've always been perfect." I hope she can hear the sincerity in my voice, but when her eyes well, I'm gutted.

"Ah, you know what? I'm not really all that hungry," she says pulling her face from my grasp. "I think I just want to go to sleep."

"Please, Rylan."

"Please what?" she snaps. "Please eat? Please leave? Please what, Halton?" She stuffs her uneaten sandwich back into the paper bag and I take it from her.

"Please don't call me Halton. I know I have no right to ask anything of you, but I'm doing it anyway."

I toss our soggy sandwiches into the trash bag I hung up

earlier and tie it off. The last thing we need tonight is to attract any wild animals.

When I turn, she's staring at me expectantly. "Why do you care, Hatty? After all this time, why do you care what I call you?"

I hit the switch on the first lantern, and it catapults half the space into darkness.

"I told you, I've always cared, but sometimes it's not enough. Sometimes, other people's happiness has to come before your own."

I quickly hit the switch on the remaining lantern, and she gasps. It's so dark I can't see my own hand until it smacks me in the face. Shuffling along the floor, I use my toe to feel for the raised cot with my hands outstretched in case I fall.

"Rylan?"

"I can't see you."

"I know. Just keep talking so I can find you."

"Give me a word, Hatty?"

My toe snags on the cot, and I lower myself to the ground, feeling my way up toward the pillows. Finally settling in beside her, I zip up the side of the sleeping bag and roll to my side.

"Dissemble," I sigh.

"You never used to do that with me, Hatty. I wouldn't have liked it when we were younger, and I don't like it now."

"I …"

Rylan squirms, and in the confined space of this fucking sleeping bag, she's wreaking havoc on my manhood. My hand clamps down on her hip, and she freezes.

"You can't move on me like that, sweetheart. Not when we're zippered into a fucking sleeping bag that can barely hold the both of us."

"I was just taking off the ice pack," she breathes.

"Don't. Move," I hiss.

She leans into me, probably to ask a question, but her ass

planted on my cock, followed by a sharp intake of breath, tells me she knows exactly what's happening.

"Oh ..."

"Yeah. Oh."

"Umm ..."

"Just stay still and I'll take off the ice pack."

She nods against my chest, and I pull away to undo the zipper a little. Sliding my hands down into the bag, I hold back a groan as my fingers accidentally skim the curve of her ass. Finally reaching the bottom of the bag, I unwrap the ace bandage as gently as I can, then toss it on the floor beside us.

Falling back into place beside her, I attempt to roll to my other side, and she makes a choking noise.

"What the hell is that?" I ask, sitting up, worried I've hurt her.

"You can't roll that way, Hatty. You nearly choked me out with the edge of the sleeping bag. It isn't big enough for us to face away from each other."

"Well, I told you I should sleep on the floor."

"You're not sleeping on the floor. You just have to spoon me, which was probably GG's plan all along." She laughs.

"Fucking GG." Rubbing my temples in the dark, I try to think of sweaty balls. Old, wrinkly, sweaty balls. Then I recite math facts like I'm fourteen again. Nothing works to tame the wood that is lodged between my legs right now. "I can't spoon you, Rylan."

"Hatty Westbrook," she scolds, "get over here and spoon me. We're adults. I'm tired and freezing, so stop being a big fucking baby and spoon me."

She has no idea what she's asking of me, but her admission of being cold sets off that protective streak again. I'm also pissed off that she can still affect me like this, so I roll over with more gusto than necessary and pull her tightly into my body.

"Oh!" Her shocked gasp does nothing to tame the little

fucker trying to play hide and seek in my boxer briefs.

"Yeah," I growl. "Oh. Go to sleep, Rylan."

"Ah, what about …"

"Don't say a thing. I swear to God, Rylan, just go to sleep."

Her little body shakes against mine, and I know she's laughing. A full-body laugh she won't be able to keep contained for much longer. My eyes have begun to adjust to the darkness, and I can just make out the shape of her beside me.

A man has boundaries. Brothers always come first, but fucking hell, there's only so much I can take. When her little body shakes against mine again, instinct overrules rational thought.

I roll her onto her back in one quick move, so I'm partially on top of her. *What the fuck are you doing, Westbrook?* For the first time in a long time, I ignore the angry voice in my head.

"You think this is funny, do you?"

Her laughter falls free, and the sound soothes my frazzled nerves. It feels like coming home. It feels like forever.

A song I don't recognize plays somewhere to my right, and I see the blue screen of her phone light up. Rylan cringes beneath me.

"I'll get it for you."

She swallows and nods, so I roll away and grab her phone just in time to see Colton's face appear.

"Fuck." It slips past my lips without warning as I hand her the phone. "What song is that?" I ask before she answers.

"It's Kelsea Ballerini's 'Peter Pan.'"

Even in my pain, I have to laugh. "Fitting."

"Yeah. I-I'll just be a minute."

"No, you're good. Goodnight, Rylan."

Closing my eyes, I pretend to drift off as she speaks with my brother. And now, I have to attempt sleep with guilt and longing playing emotional warfare with my soul.

CHAPTER 18

RYLAN

J have no idea what time we went to bed last night, but I think it was early. My phone call with Colton halted any conversation or other things that might have happened.

Colty was just calling to check on me, but our conversation was stilted for the first time since I've known him. When I hung up, Hatty pretended to be asleep, and I sunk into a fit of unease. At some point, he couldn't take my unrest because he grabbed hold of my arm and turned me to my side, then wrapped one heavy arm around my middle and told me to go to sleep.

As soon as he cocooned me in his body, I drifted off and didn't move until I woke up a little while ago on fire. *How can one man effuse such freaking heat?* He has one leg draped over mine, and his arm nestled between my breasts holds me close to his chest. You couldn't slip a piece of paper between us, and I kind of hate myself for loving it so much.

It's hot as hell in here, but I don't dare move. I know as soon as I do, he'll pull away again, so instead, I lay here, listening to the sounds of an angry storm and swirling ocean.

My fingers draw a line on Hatty's arm as I daydream, and he snuggles into my hair, inhaling deeply.

"Morning, sweetheart," he growls, then jumps back like I electrocuted him. "Fuck, sorry. I-I forgot where I was."

I give him a sad smile. "Think I was someone else?"

He frowns, and his eyes darken as he stares at me. There's so much that happens when he's focused solely on me like this. A world apart, yet he feels like a piece of me. It's the sadness in his voice when he speaks that does me in, though. "It's only ever been you in my dreams, Rylan. That's the only place I can have you."

My heart stops beating at his admission, and I forget how to blink. I stare at him in shock until he pulls back even farther and climbs out of bed. He's limping a lot as he pulls on a raincoat, and I feel like an ass.

"Where are you going?" He doesn't answer, just moves toward the tarp covering the entrance. "Hatty, you're limping. What can I do?"

He glances down and winces. Pressing his heel out in front of him, he attempts to stretch out the sore muscle. "It's just a sprain or something. I have to piss, then I'll come back and help you to the outhouse."

I roll my eyes. "I can make it to the outhouse just fine."

"I'll be back in three minutes. Don't move." His voice is so protective it catches me off guard.

"When did you become so bossy?"

"When I thought I lost you for a second time, and there was nothing I could do about it."

I cock my head as I watch him. "Is there something you can do about the first time?"

Sadness punches me in the gut with his expression.

"Nothing that wouldn't hurt everyone I love even more." He shakes his head, and I see the moment he shuts down. "I'll be right back."

Tears threaten as he exits the lean-to, and I rub my eyes

with my palms. I should be happy he's opening up, but it's so cryptic I don't have a clue what any of it means. His hot and cold attitude is giving me whiplash.

Less than two minutes later, Hatty scares the shit out of me when he jumps into the shelter. "Good. You didn't move."

"Jesus, Hatty. I didn't have a chance. Did you even pee?"

"Of course. Let's go." He trudges over and lifts me over his shoulder like a rag doll.

"What the hell are you doing? I can walk. You don't need all this weight on your injury."

He smacks my ass so hard I know I'll have a handprint there.

"What the hell, Halton?"

Smack.

"For crying out loud, stop spanking me," I screech.

"I will stop when you stop thinking you're fat, and when you stop calling me fucking Halton."

"It's your *name*."

"Not for you, it's not. Hold this."

He hands me an umbrella, and I open it as he pulls back the tarp. Seconds later, he plops me down in the most foul-smelling bathroom I've ever been in.

"Yeah, it's a permanent porta-John," he says with a scrunched nose. "Try not to breathe too much in here."

I think I might actually growl at him as the door shuts. Then I almost throw up, so I push the door open again.

"Hatty?" I bark, and he pokes his head around the corner.

"What? Don't you have to go?"

"Yes, actually, I have to shit. But I cannot sit in here with the door closed. You're going to have to hold it open for me."

He stares at me blankly as rain pours down around him.

"You want me to stand here and listen to you shit?"

"Oh, please. When you were ten, you called me into the bathroom to see the massive dump you took. This is payback."

"Rylan, that's when you were a-a tom-boy."

Crossing my arms, I stare him down. "I'm still the same person, Hatty."

His gaze roams slowly down my body, and I feel the flush creep over every inch. He swallows an audible gulp before raising his gaze to mine again.

"You are most definitely not the same tom-boy."

I drop my arms to my sides with balled-up fists. "Hatty. Hold the door open. The longer you argue with me, the longer you're going to stand in the rain."

"For fuck's sake, Verity. Jesus. Fine. Just, don't, ah, I don't know, grunt or anything."

"Grunt? Who the hell grunts when they shit?"

He mumbles something unintelligible but finally turns around with the door in his hand. I grin, drop my panties, stare into the abyss, and almost throw up again while wiping down the seat. Finally, I plant my ass on the cold plastic and try not to laugh as Hatty fidgets on the other side of the door.

If I could stand the smell in here, I would mess with him a little. But as it is, I'm pushing my own limits, so I do my business and wipe. I'm surprised there's a sink with running water in here.

"Why the heck would they have a sink but not a toilet that flushes?"

"I don't know, Rylan." He groans, and it's mixed with a childish whine. "Probably something to do with septic or some shit. I'm not a damn plumber. Just hurry up, okay? This is one of the weirdest things you've ever made me do."

I walk up behind him. Even as the rain pelts my body, I'm on fire for this man.

"It feels good, though, doesn't it?"

He jumps when he realizes I'm out. Turning, he stares at me with an unreadable expression. "I don't think I can say holding a bathroom door open while you shit is something I'd call feeling good."

"No, but being together again does. You can fight it all you want; I feel it enough for the both of us." A cheesy, sweet smile makes its way from ear to ear.

I'm not sure what possessed me to admit that, but it's the truth. Something about standing here in the rain with him tells me if I want my friend back, I'm going to have to push him. Lexi was right, and it makes me smile.

"What do you think of Lexi?" I ask as he hands me the umbrella and lifts me over his shoulder like a sack of potatoes.

Hatty grunts as he navigates the mud back to the lean-to. "She's good for Easton, even if she's pricklier than he is."

"I don't think she's really prickly. I think it's a cover for pain. Just like some people turn into assholes to cover up what really bothers them."

Once we're inside of our ramshackle, temporary home, he slides me down his body. He fingers a lock of my hair, much like he did in the bar after his first experience with GG's wine.

"You're wet," he whispers.

"I am. So, so wet." I emphasize the t and point to the sleeping bag.

His eyes go hard, and his jaw sets, but he doesn't move.

"Sit. I'm going to look at your leg now."

I see the relief flow off him, and I fight to keep my expression neutral. I know I'm not imagining the sexual tension between us, but I don't know where to go from here. He meets me halfway, only to shove me back ten paces every time.

"It looks like the storm is going to blow over by tomorrow." His voice jars me from my reverie, and I turn to find him lying back on his forearms, watching me.

"That's good. So, do we have a plan while we're here, or are we free balling it?"

The harsh sounding laughter that erupts from Hatty's belly is more fitting for an ogre than a human man, and I think it startles him as much as me.

"Free balling, Rylan? Seriously?"

Knowing I made him laugh, I grin. What I wouldn't give to hear that sound every day. "Hey, I don't know what you've been up to. You could be a big baller around town for all I know."

His head drops back between his shoulders, and I get an unobstructed view of his Adam's apple as he laughs. It's not something I've ever found particularly sexy before, but everything about Hatty has always been enchanting. While he laughs—full, throaty, sexy—I imagine running my tongue up his neck. Remembering his salty flavor, I unconsciously lick my lips just as he raises his head.

"Rylan?" His voice is gruff as he follows the tip of my tongue, darting out to wet my lips.

"Hmm?"

The way he stares at me ignites my core. No one has ever seen me the way he has, the way he does, and this proves I'm not imagining it. His eyes hold all the love and longing of a starving man, but I also see conviction and a war I don't know how to win.

"You're everything good and pure in this world. My sunbeam in the darkest sky. I'm sorry if I dimmed that for even the briefest of time."

CHAPTER 19

*H*er shocked gasp has me regretting the words before they're even fully formed. *Why the fuck am I admitting this shit?*

"Wh-Why, Hatty?"

I can't take that pained expression on her face, knowing I put it there, so I direct my gaze at the floor. God, every inch of my skin burns like four million fire ants are crawling all over my body.

Forcing my hands through my hair, I tug on the ends until my scalp prickles and the edge of pain makes me focus. Cradling my head in both hands, I shake it back and forth. I can't admit why I'm falling apart. I can't tell her my biggest lie.

Her touch nearly makes me jump out of my skin. Two soft hands encapsulate my own on either side of my head, and my eyes flutter open. Rylan is on her knees between mine, gently pulling my hands away from my face. I watch in a daze as she holds them in her lap.

We're inches away from each other, and the pain I've caused swirls around our bodies like a tornado of frenetic energy. Ever so slowly, she leans forward until our foreheads touch.

"Hatty, what did you do?" she whispers.

When we're connected like this, I swear I can read her mind. *Why am I so in tune with someone who can't be my forever?* It's not fair, and it makes me want to rage against the world, but she senses that and raises one hand to place it over my heart.

"I did what I had to do, Verity. What I have to do."

Her eyes close, and I hold my breath, awaiting her next move. Her thumb mindlessly caresses the skin on my inner wrist, and I focus my attention there so I don't lose it.

I've already fucked up by kissing her. *I can't do this to Colton.* He's my brother, my family. I don't want to do this to him, not if Rylan is his forever, but I'm only human. I know if she makes a move now, I won't be able to deny her. Or myself. And it scares the hell out of me.

"Do you like yourself, Hatty? The man you've become?"

I'm so shocked by her question, my brain shuts down. My body tenses with years of frustration, pain, and longing until I can't hold it in anymore.

"No," I croak, unable to stop the honesty in this intimate situation.

"Why?"

Her eyelids flicker with moistened lashes as she struggles to focus on my eyes, but I won't let her pull away from me yet. Not when this is the most alive I've felt in years.

"Because you were the best parts of me, Rylan. The only happiness I've ever felt …" I snap my mouth closed. Going down this road with her can only lead to more pain, but she pulls away enough to see my entire face.

"You hurt me, Hatty." Her voice is barely audible. It comes out in a whisper of a breath, but somehow, I feel her strength behind it. "You made me question everything and everyone for a really long time. You put me through hell. I lost my best friend, my life. The life I thought I would have. You took that all away with no explanation."

I swallow hard and bite the inside of my cheek. I owe her a lot of words, but I can't say them without betraying Colton, so I glance away, and she continues.

"But after all this time, do you feel this? This connection we have? Even after all the shit you've put me through, I feel your pain. Here …" She points to her chest, and I'm forced to lift my gaze. Her damp eyelashes are overflowing with tears now, and my nostrils flare as I breathe in and out, trying to rein in my own emotions. "You can deny it all you want, Hatty, but I know. I know you need me as much as I need you. You're not this asshole everyone thinks you've become. You're hiding, and I see you. I'm calling you out on your shit right now. If all I can have of you is friendship, then I'll take it because I think you need it more than me. I love you enough to give that to you because even if you deny it, I know you need me." Her voice breaks, and my hands tighten on hers. I squeeze her fingers in recognition, even if I can't bring my pansy ass to say the words yet. "You will tell me why you hurt me, though."

My head shakes almost violently, but her single finger crosses the space between us and lands on my lips. It takes every ounce of decency I have not to suck on it, but she effectively silences me.

"You will tell me, and soon. But, for now, I'll be your friend. And you'll be mine. We'll start over because at least while we're here, we're all we have. I'll be your friend, Hatty, but don't ever hurt me again. I'm telling you right now, I wouldn't survive it. My heart can't take it. You broke me once, please, please don't do it again."

"I … Fuck, Rylan." I sniffle because emotions are coming out one way or another, and right now, they're choosing my damn nose. Sucking in, I hope I can get through this conversation with some semblance of my manhood intact, but when she raises her dimmed eyes to mine, all pretense falls away. Tears, snot, choked back sobs all escape at once. "I never wanted to hurt you, sweetheart. Never. I-I had to. You'll never understand. I can't make you, but I won't do it again. I promise. I ..." These next words already feel bitter on my tongue, but I force them out, anyway. "I can be your friend. We'll just be friends."

"You want to be like Colton?" There's hurt and resignation in her voice. It guts me.

I don't know how long I search her face or what I'm hoping to find there, but finally, I seal my fate. "No, but I'll be your Hatty."

Her eyes close, and she nods but doesn't pull away. Leaning forward, I place a gentle kiss to her temple, and pull her body into mine. I hug her with all the love I have, because even if she can't be mine, I know my heart will always belong to her. My verity.

"Friends."

"Friends."

We both sound as if we're trying to convince ourselves, or maybe that's wishful thinking on my part.

"Okay, Hatty. Well, as your friend, tell me why you're such an asshole to everyone?"

I scoot back and eye her curiously. "I'm not an asshole." Pausing, I pinch the back of my neck to stall for time. *How do I explain this?* "I guess I can see why people might think I'm an asshole, but I just don't enjoy the same things. That hasn't changed, Rylan. It's hard to pretend you're happily part of the chaos when you're always on the outside looking in. I don't fit."

"You've always felt that way, but you used to handle it better."

That's because I had you. It almost slips out, but I clench my jaw to keep dangerous words from ruining this fragile new beginning.

"Maybe I did," I say instead.

"You know what I think?"

Just hearing the teasing lilt in her voice makes my soul lighter. "I'm sure you'll tell me." An honest to goodness grin appears on my face, and for once, it isn't forced.

"You're right. I think it's a good thing you've been stalking me all these years. You need me."

"I've always needed you," I mumble, and she quirks a brow, but doesn't say anything. "I never stalked you, though. Jesus. Is that what you think?"

"Yes."

That's it. Just yes. She smiles placatingly, then stands and crosses the small room. Thankfully, my injury is forgotten. I'm not sure I could handle her soft hands on my upper thigh right now.

"Do you think this is really the only place they could find for us to stay?" I ask, glancing around, hoping she'll accept the topic change easily.

I know the island is small, but that question has been running through my mind since we arrived, and I'm not sure I trust my brothers with this.

"I have no idea. Ash is pretty adamant that we stay on the island, though. Do you know what's really going on with him?" she asks over her shoulder.

The million-dollar question. I shake my head as she pulls out an electric griddle.

"Please tell me you know how to turn on the generator because I could eat a freaking pig snout right now."

I stare at her in disbelief. How did we just go from the most emotionally raw conversation I've ever had, to pig snouts? But this is what she does to me. What she's always done. Where I see everything as black or white, she finds the gray. She's the wildflower in a garden of daisies. Taller. Brighter. More beautiful than the rest because she stands out. She stands on her own. *My verity.*

Clutching my chest, I force a chuckle as I stand. "Yeah, sweetheart. I know how to turn on the generator."

Rylan stares at me with a spatula in hand.

Wondering if my fly is unzipped, I peer down. "What? Do I have something on me?"

Something dangerously naughty crosses her face, and I feel my skin heat.

"If you keep calling me sweetheart, I'm not going to believe your 'just friends' spiel for long."

My mouth drops open as she regards me, but I gather my wits and set my jaw.

"We are friends."

"We are," she agrees. "You want us to be 'just friends'?"

"Yes."

Her eyes set into narrow slits before she laughs. Loudly. Then steps into my personal space. "Okay, Hatty. I'll let you have that one."

Staring down into those emerald depths, I see heat, love, and honesty, and my voice turns husky. "What are you talking about?"

I cannot sound husky when talking to my friend. *She doesn't have to be ya friend, Fibby.* Startled, I flinch, and Rylan places her hands on her hips, drawing my gaze lower.

"Are you okay?"

"Me?" It comes out like a pre-hormonal squeak.

"Yeah, you just cringed like I spit on you or something."

Grabbing the back of my neck, I take a step back to put some distance between us and grumble under my breath. "Yeah, I'm fine. I think GG hexed me, though. My conscience seems to sound an awful fucking lot like her these days."

Rylan's laughter is somehow even sexier in the small confines, and has me turning my attention back to her. "She is a little scary, but she's not wrong."

"Wrong about what?" *Did she hear it, too?* I'm losing my

goddamn mind. Glancing around, I search for the wine. *I need to get rid of that shit.*

"She said your left eye still twitches when you fib. She's right."

Rylan turns to the cooler and pulls out a carton of eggbeaters and precooked bacon.

"At least they sent actual food," she sing-songs.

I'm standing, unable to move a muscle, wondering what the hell I lied about now. Rylan is a force of nature that is twisting me up tighter than a hurricane. It makes me fear what the damage will be when we finally touch down in the real world.

CHAPTER 20

"*H*ow's your ankle?"

"Better than your hamstring by the looks of things." Nodding at the strange stretch Hatty is doing against the wall, I'm pretty sure he's still in pain. Luckily, a couple of icepacks were all my ankle needed, but he hasn't been as fortunate. "I knew you shouldn't have carried me, you big ape."

"I'm an ape now, am I?" Hatty turns away from the wall and beats on his chest while I sit on the cot with my mouth hanging open.

Laughter spills out of me at the sight. "You're really coming out of your shell over there."

"You've always had that effect on me, princess. It's either that or almost three days trapped in a lean-to is eating away at my mental faculties."

"Princess? Never once has that name fit me."

His face drops for a second as he examines my body. The soft flutters of butterflies that reside in my stomach whenever he's near turn into a damn hornet's nest the longer his gaze lingers.

"Did I say that?"

I give my best 'duh' expression, and he grins.

"You've always been a princess, Rylan. But you fit the description more now than you ever have."

My throat goes so dry I can't speak, and his grin turns into a lecherous smile. "Yeah, princess. It fits."

"I wish I could still tell what was going on inside of that head of yours," I finally admit.

Hatty takes a step back. His voice is low, dangerous, and does wicked things to my panties. "No, you don't, princess."

"I'm not sure I like that name." My voice gives away my need.

"No one likes their nicknames. That's why they stick." He winks and turns back to his stretching.

"Ugh, I need a shower."

Hatty glances over his shoulder and gulps. It sounds like a strange kind of frog, and we both laugh.

Rising from the cot that is doing some serious damage to my back, I stretch like a cat and catch Hatty's gaze on the sliver of skin my raised arms expose on my stomach.

"Friends, Hatty."

He turns around so fast he nearly smacks his face on the wall. "Right," he growls.

Opening the tarp, I see it's still drizzling out. "Well, nothing like a little rain shower." Grabbing my shampoo, conditioner, and body wash, I tell Hatty to turn around so I can strip.

Like a gentleman, he faces the wall, but I can tell every muscle in his body is wound tight. He's mumbling under his breath, and I almost laugh but decide not to tease him. Until he's willing to tell me why he's so adamant about being just friends, there isn't much I can do.

After placing a towel on the edge of the platform, I jump down and make a mad dash for the outdoor shower, completely naked. At least the stall offers a little coverage. I'm short enough that the teak wall will cover the important things, but running back and forth, knowing anyone could pull up, is an adrenaline rush I could do without.

The storm is finally on its last legs, so it's just a light drizzle mixing with the shower water, but it does nothing to cool my overheated body. Freaking Hatty has my lower anatomy throbbing every second of the freaking day, so I spend a little more time than necessary soaping up. It's the only space we have from each other, and I need the distance to get my head on right.

"Friends," I grumble. "How the hell can I be friends with the only man who has ever owned my heart?" Placing my face in the spray of the showerhead, I let out my frustration. It feels good to yell. To get out this energy I have no other outlet for. I didn't think about what Hatty would think of it, though, and before I know it, he's standing on the other side of the shower. Fear in his bright blue eyes. Bright blue eyes that cloud with lust as they drift down over the top of the shower walls.

"Aggh," I screech when I notice him.

Our eyes plead with each other, and he finally forces out words. "What's wrong? Why did you scream?"

The drizzle has stopped or slowed so much it's just a light mist now as he stands there, staring at me. Unadulterated lust exposed in his open expression.

Realizing why he's standing there, my face heats in embarrassment.

"Rylan." His voice is harsh. Demanding. Sexy. He takes a step forward, and I see his throat working. "Are you hurt?"

My eyes are wide and unblinking as I shake my head. In the recesses of my mind, I hear someone telling me I should be covering my naked body, but the directive doesn't quite register as I stand there staring at the man I want more than my next breath.

"Why did you yell?"

"Ah." A nervous giggle escapes, and I'm suddenly that

seventeen-year-old girl about to get naked with the boy I love for the first time. Except I'm naked. He's standing there confused, but when I glance down, I see his erection pressing firmly against his shorts, and it's my turn to gulp. "Umm, frustration?" *Was that squeaky voice mine?* The urge to look behind me is so great I have to physically force my eyes to stay on him. "I, ah …" Yup. That's my voice, all right.

"Frustration?" he moans, staring at the sky. He plants one hand low on his hips and another at the back of his neck. "Frustration is a fucker. I'll, well, I'll let you finish."

He backs away without looking at me.

"Hatty?"

He pauses, and glances down at me, but my focus is on his crotch. *Get your shit together, Rylan.*

"Rylan." My name is a plea, and I snap my attention to his face. "Friends."

One word that has me whimpering in protest.

"Mhm. Friends."

"Okay. I'll see you inside."

I nod because if I speak, there will be no hiding the hurt in my voice. Turning my back, I put my face to the shower spray again and let my tears mix with the water until it runs cold.

~

"*I*'m so fucking bored."

Hatty's voice startles me out of the book I'm reading on my phone. I really shouldn't be reading romance novels when I'm so sexually frustrated I could combust, but freaking Melanie Moreland just had to go and release her next book today. Her stories are like my own personal crack, and I'm powerless to avoid them.

"What are you reading?"

"Ahh." My voice is unsteady. Melanie's freaking hero is

doing a number on me, and I can't think straight. "Umm, it's called *Age of Ava*."

"Is it good?"

"Really good." Jesus. Could I sound any more wanton? This is why you read Melanie's books in private. A sexy as sin audience will not end well for me.

"Can I read it?"

"Nope."

Hatty opens his phone, and I know he's googling it.

"You read romance?"

"Don't you?"

His chuckle bounces off the walls. "No, I can't say that I do. But Loki's wife, Sloane, writes romance. Colton read a few paragraphs to us on the plane heading to Vermont. It's, ah …" He blushes and glances away. "It gets pretty hot, huh?"

"Mhm."

"I need some water. Do you want something to drink?"

I shake my head as I watch him.

"Let's play a game, Hatty."

He turns in slow motion like he doesn't entirely trust what I'm about to say.

"What kind of game?"

"Strip poker," I deadpan, and laugh when he sprays water all over the floor. "Just kidding. How about twenty questions? You know, catch up on what we've missed while I was … away."

"Twenty questions?"

"Are you a parrot? Yes. Twenty questions. I'll go first. Do you like working at The WB?"

"Jesus. You've been hanging out with Lexi too much. It's The Westbrook Group, and yes, I do. I love it, actually. I love working with numbers, finding solutions, keeping our legacy on the straight and narrow, and skyrocketing it toward our future."

"You always liked routine."

"And math."

I laugh, crossing my legs and patting the spot across from me. "And math. You like to find solutions. You're a fixer, Hatty."

He whispers, but I don't catch it as he crosses the room and sits across from me. "My turn. I'm happy you followed your dreams."

"Me too, but that's not a question."

Smirking, he pulls at the beard that's filling in along his jaw. "What do you have planned for work now that you're home?"

"Colton put in a call with his friend, Lochlan, for me."

"Lochlan?" Hatty grunts. "What for? Doesn't he own a bunch of hotels or something?"

"He does, but his sister, Nova, is planning a show in New York in September."

"What kind of show?" His voice softens slightly, but his body language keeps its edge.

"She's a designer. She's creating a moving life exhibit and wants her clothing showcased with nature. Colty has been trying to get me to put in my portfolio for over a year, so when I moved back, it seemed like the right time. Her photographer backed out over creative differences, and he thinks it'll be a good opportunity for me."

"It sounds like it," he grumbles.

"What's the matter?"

"Nothing," he says too quickly. "I'm glad Colton could help."

"Well, I haven't gotten it yet. All he could do was put in a good word. The rest is up to me."

"You'll get it." He's so adamant, I sit back to take him in.

"How are you so sure?"

He studies me, love and wonder in his eyes. "Because you're you, princess. I've always believed in you. You're the best."

His honesty is too much. This back and forth is killing me.

"Give me a word, Hatty?"

His eyes go wide and worried. He knows where I'm going with this. He relaxes slightly when he glances around and thinks he'll be safe, but he doesn't know what Ari slipped me before we left.

We're sitting facing each other with less than three feet between us. His gaze never leaves mine, and the yearning that passes between us makes my heart hurt.

"Letch," he finally mutters.

Leaning to my left, I drag my bag closer and pull out my small Nikon, never once breaking eye contact with this frustrating man in front of me.

After removing the lens cap, I lower my gaze to the camera to check the settings, then bring it to my eye. With his face in the finder, I snap pictures. The click, click, click of the shutter going off is like birds taking flight.

"What are you doing?" Hatty's husky voice assaults my body, and my nipples peak beneath the thin fabric of my tank top.

"Letch," I whisper. Too afraid to lower the camera, I watch his expression darken through the lens. "A strong desire for something." I swallow a painful pit in my throat. "Or someone."

Hatty's knuckles turn white on his knees, and I lower the lens to catch the reaction.

"Friends," he chants under his breath, but whether he's convincing himself or me, I'm not sure. His body is so tense, I'm surprised he isn't shaking from the effort.

"Rylan," he groans, and I know I'm about to lose this round, so I reach into my bag again and pull out the small tin Ari had given me.

Out of the corner of my eye, I see Hatty's hands tremble, but I reach into the bag again anyway and pull out the sketch

158

pad. Leaning forward on my knees, I place the pad of paper and tin full of charcoal in his lap.

"Your turn, Hatty. Draw for me," I whisper, just inches from his mouth.

His gaze follows the movement of my teeth sinking into my bottom lip from nerves. It's the final straw for him as he sucks in a harsh breath. Then another. And another.

Nostrils flaring, his voice is gruff. "I don't draw anymore, princess."

"I know."

He staggers back, using his hands to hold him up, and putting space between us. Shock is the only description for his expression.

"It's your punishment, but we're starting over, Hatty. No more punishments. No more rules. No more lies. Draw. For me. Please."

CHAPTER 21

"*D*raw. For me. Please."

"How?" My words sound like they're catching on sandpaper as they escape my lips, and I can't finish my sentence.

Rylan shrugs impishly. "GG's truth wine."

"Fuck." Dropping my head, I let the air hiss through my teeth.

"You want to be friends, right?"

Lifting my gaze, I know I would do anything for this girl. "Yeah, friends."

Fucking friends. The words are like acid on my tongue, but I force myself not to make a face.

"Well, we built our friendship once upon a time on our mutual love of all things beautiful. That's our foundation, Hatty. A lot of crap has changed, but our foundation was always solid. Learn to see the beautiful things again. Learn to love them. Open your eyes, and your heart will follow. It's in there. I know it. I see your fingers itching to feel the charcoal. I feel the energy coming off you. Open your eyes and see the beauty in all the colors. Just let yourself feel it, Hatty. Find the beautiful parts of life again."

Staring into her pools of emerald green as her words drift over me, all I see is beauty. All I see is perfection. Love. Light. All I see is *her*.

GG was right. I've been living in black and white, and Rylan just smashed through in vivid color. I'm blinded by it. By her.

Rylan leans forward, takes my trembling hand in hers, and points my palm toward the sky. She rests hers on top of mine for a few seconds. Her breathing is as labored as mine. But when our eyes connect, I'm transported back to the night of my would-be art show. The very first time we ever kissed, and I'm powerless to the force of her.

Moving a few inches, I place my palm flat on the ground next to her thigh and close the distance between us. "There's nothing worse than not getting to keep what you want most in life," I admit, right before my lips land on hers.

Kissing her is a sin. It's wrong on every level, but nothing has ever felt more right. My body moves her forward, and she glides across the room with me. Our lips never part as her back hits the cot, and I hover over her.

My mind screams at me to stop, begs me not to betray my brother, but every inch of my heart and soul blocks them out. Lowering my hand, I skim the bare skin of her taut stomach, and she gasps into my mouth. I swallow her sounds, longing to make her scream my name.

The need to mark her as mine is overwhelming. My teeth sink into the sensitive skin just below her earlobe, and we both groan.

"Hatty."

My dick grinds into her, and the primal need for skin on skin has my body ready to explode. How can one embrace bring me back to the days when loving her was so easy, so simple? With one touch, the pit of self-hatred I dwell in melts away. She's still my sunbeam even after all this time. She

161

holds my happiness in her palm, and my soul pleads with my brain to hold her tight and never let her go.

"Fuck, Rylan. Fucking hell," I groan as my hand ghosts over her ribs before settling under the curve of her tit. My thumb flicks rapidly as her nipple hardens beneath my ministrations, and I roughly pull the cup of her bra down to roll the perfect little nub between my thumb and forefinger.

Happiness.

That's what she is for me, and my heart weeps with it when she's in my arms.

It's impossible for me not to feel happy when she's near. She chases away the darkness with her smile, and I'm a fool for ever thinking I could forget her.

"I-I need you, Hatty."

Four little words are my undoing, and I'm suddenly frantic for us to be joined. My other hand lowers to the button of her denim shorts, and I flick it open. With one hand on her nipple, and one sliding into her panties, I lower my lips to hers, but she stiffens.

"Oh, shit." She's scrambling away before I know what the fuck is going on. "Someone's here," she screeches, adjusting her top and attempting to button her jeans.

That's when I hear it. The click of a car door.

"Hello?"

Dropping my gaze, I shake my head. I have a raging hard-on in gym shorts. There's no hiding this shit.

"Who's here?"

"I have no idea," I grumble, adjust myself, then stand to kill the motherfucker.

Poking my head out of the tarp, I see two men walking toward us skeptically.

"Ah, Mr. Westbrook?"

Pushing Rylan behind me, I step out in front of the tarp. "Yes. That's me. How can I help you?"

"Ah, Mr. Colton Westbrook sent us with a car for you."

Colton. It's like a slap across the face. He's fifteen hours away thinking of me, and I'm here trying to fuck his forever. Self-loathing crashes over me like hot lava.

"Thank you," I force out.

One of the men steps forward to hand me the keys. "You can just leave it at the ferry when you leave, and someone will come over to grab it. Otherwise, your brother has taken care of everything."

Of course he has. He's the good one.

I nod, and they head back to the second car just as Rylan pokes her head outside.

"Everything okay?"

"Yeah," I say without glancing back. "Colton sent the car for us. I'm just going to use the bathroom. I'll be back in a bit."

She doesn't say anything, but I feel her eyes on me as I round the corner. I have no self-control with her, and I fear I never will. Pulling out my phone, I text Preston.

Halton: It might be time to set up the overseas office.

Preston: No.

Halton: No? You're the one who has been pushing this. I think you're right. It's time.

Preston: It is. But not for you. You have shit to work out.

Preston: And until we find the mole at the WB, we need you here.

Fuck. It's like my world is crumbling around me. There's a mole in our company that's costing us millions. Pacen's father has been dicking around with GG's mountain, and now Rylan is back, destroying all my resolve with a single glance.

Halton: It's not really your choice. And what shit do I have to work out?

Preston: If you have to ask, with your current situation as it is, you have more to work out than I thought.

163

Preston: And it is my choice. I'm CEO, and your big brother. Get your head out of your ass and find your happy.

Halton: Wtf is that supposed to mean.

Preston added Ashton at 4:14 p.m.

Preston: How does Halt find his happy?

Ashton: (Picture sent)

I gape at my phone in disbelief. Staring back at me are tiny faces. A lot of them. All my brothers, their friends, me, and Rylan. Everyone is smiling into the camera, but my eyes are on Rylan. Happiness explodes from this picture in every twinkling eye, every toothy grin. I'm probably sixteen here, and while everyone smiles for my dad, I'm smiling at my future, my forever. Or so I thought.

Halton: What the fuck is this supposed to mean?

Ashton: When you figure out why you were so happy in this picture, you'll find your way back to the life you were meant to have.

Preston: Find that happiness and hang onto it with both hands. Don't fuck it up again, Halt. This picture is you. The very best version of you, and we all know it. Find this boy again and fix your mistakes.

Halton: I don't know what you're talking about.

Preston: Yes, you fucking do. Don't miss out on happiness because you're too stubborn to accept it or too arrogant to admit your faults. We all have them. We all fuck up. But we're Westbrooks, and we fix shit. Fix your shit, Halton.

Ashton: Fix your shit.

Halton: What if my shit can't be fixed?

Preston: Then you're not looking at the whole picture. You, of all people, know you need to try all the equations.

Preston: Luv you, little brother. Welcome to the chaos ... but fix your shit.

Ashton: Welcome to the chaos.

Ashton: Any updates?

Jesus. I'd almost forgotten why we were even here.

Halton: No. The storm just passed. We'll be able to head into town and start exploring tomorrow.

Ashton: Okay. Thanks, Halton. For everything.

Halton: It's what we do, right?

Preston: Yes. We fix shit. Get it done. ALL of it.

Tucking my phone into my back pocket, I stare at the sky. What the hell am I supposed to do? Find my happy? Do they have any idea what that means or what it will do to Colton if I do?

Jesus. If the car hadn't showed up, I would have slept with her. Again. Tugging on the ends of my hair, I blow out a loud breath. There is no happy for me in this situation, so I steel my resolve and stomp back toward Rylan. I have to apologize and hope she doesn't try to knee me in the nuts.

The rain has let up, so as I hop back onto the platform, I roll up the heavy tarp and release the mesh net meant to keep bugs out. At least this way, we'll get some air into the space.

Rylan is sitting cross legged against the back wall with her phone propped up on her knees. I assume she's reading again, and I wonder if I've been gone longer than I thought.

Tying off the other side of the tarp, I turn to find Rylan watching me. A mix of want and apprehension on her face.

"Are you okay?" she asks, dropping her phone to her side.

"Yeah. Um, listen. I'm sorry."

"You're sorry? For what?" she asks, surprise and a hint of annoyance flickering across her face.

I can't make eye contact, so my eyes dart around the small space. "Well, we're ... ah, we're friends. I shouldn't have kissed you or, well, anything."

"Are you?"

Now I'm forced to look at her. "Am I what?"

"Are you sorry? Or do you just think you shouldn't have kissed me?"

"Both. It's the same thing, isn't it?" I have to ball my fists to keep my fingers from fidgeting.

"No. It's not."

My leg bounces nervously on my toes as she stands and crosses the room. She notices but walks to stand right in front of me, anyway.

"Did you want to kiss me, Hatty?"

"I shouldn't have."

"That's not what I asked. Did you want to kiss me?"

With her so close, I know I can't lie, so I avoid. "I got carried away."

Narrowing her eyes, Rylan takes a step closer. "This new friendship, Hatty? That you wanted, by the way, won't work if you keep lying to me. Or to yourself. Figure out your shit."

I nearly gasp as she says the same thing Preston and Ash just scolded me for. Thankfully, I hold it in until she crosses the room and rips open the mesh netting.

"Where are you going?"

"Out." Her words are biting, and my heart sinks. I seem incapable of not hurting her.

CHAPTER 22

RYLAN

Ari: How's it going? The Weather Channel says you got pounded.

Lexi: Did you? Get pounded, Rylan? (Winking devil emoji)

Rylan: I think you might be worse than Colty.

Ari: She is. She totally is.

Lexi: (Middle finger emoji)

Lexi: Well, did you?

Rylan: No, I did not get "pounded".

Rylan: We came to a sort of truce, though. I think.

Rylan: We're friends. Again. Or still?

Lexi: Friends? (Crying, laughing emoji)

Ari: I mean, friends are good ...

Rylan: ...

Ari: But ...

Rylan: But what?

Ari: There's enough sexual tension between you two to light up the entire East Coast. Not sure how long "friends" will work.

Lexi: It's also not what she wants.

Rylan: Who, me?

Rylan: No offense, Lexi, but you don't really know me. And this is what he can offer.

Ari: Why?

Lexi: Why is that what he can offer?

Rylan: ...

Rylan: He didn't say.

Lexi: Okay. So, you think he's just not into you? That he pulled that bull shit prom move because he really is an asshole?

Rylan: He's not an asshole.

Ari: He's totally into her.

Lexi: What do you think, Rylan?

Rylan: ...

"You ready?"

Hatty's words have me pulling my phone guiltily into my chest to hide the screen.

"Ah, yeah. Yup. All set with the car?"

The cock blocking car.

When I catch Hatty's expression, I know we're both thinking about it.

He eyes me, then my phone, and grins like he knows we're talking about him. "All set, but if we're going to hang out at the National to watch for Pacen, we should probably walk. There isn't much to do there but eat and drink."

The National, I learned, is the only hotel on the island, and they have the best view of the docks and, by proxy, the action on the island.

After our first morning where we had the "friends" talk, and then again when Cocky, the name I'm giving our car, interrupted us, things have been strained between us. Thankfully, someone thought to pack cards, and we've passed the time playing blackjack.

"Walking it is. Are you sure your hamstring is up to it?"

morning.

"It'll be fine. It's only a quarter of a mile to the National if we take the path."

He jumps off the platform, then turns and helps me down. Every time we do this—my body sliding down his—the air between us becomes thick, but he always glances away as soon as he can.

Maybe he isn't into me? Could I be making this all up? Did I always make it up?

Hatty turns around when he realizes I'm not following him.

Just ask him, my heart screams, but when he opens his mouth, I shake my head and fall in step beside him.

"What's on your mind, Rylan?"

"Hmm?"

I'm staring at the ground as we walk. It's been a long time since I've questioned myself like this. The reason slams into me with the force of ten men, and I stop in my tracks. I let Matthew make all the decisions so I wouldn't be wrong again. It was easier to let him direct my life and tell me how I felt about everything because then I couldn't get hurt.

"Sweetheart?"

I hear his words, but the chaos inside of my head is louder.

"I'm okay," I mumble and move forward.

I haven't been living any better than Hatty has. Sure, I thought I loved Matthew, but now I know he never stood a chance, no matter how good a man he was. I never opened myself up, even a fraction of the way I have with Hatty. I let Matthew dictate every aspect of our lives because I wasn't being me.

"I think I was lost."

His shoulders tense, but he keeps walking. "When?"

camera do I prefer?"

He stares at me like I've lost my mind, but I know I haven't. I've just found myself.

"Ah, Rylan. It's been a long time. You could like anything now," he says apologetically.

"No. You know me, Hatty. Answer the question."

Sticking his hands in his back pockets, he kicks at a rock in the road. He seems so young like this, and this is the Hatty my heart knows. Not the hardened man, drowning in fear and lies, but the boy who knows me better than I know myself.

"You probably like the ease of digital because it's instant gratification, but you'll always be an old school film girl. You like the process of controlling the lighting before the shot is taken, not using filters after the fact. You like watching the portraits come to life in the darkroom and manipulating them into your vision."

He pauses, and I see his cheeks tinge pink beneath the scruff that is moving to full-on beard territory.

"Ah, or at least that's what I would guess," he confesses with the shyness of the boy I fell in love with.

"Yeah." Reaching out, I take his hand in mine and keep walking.

He stares at our joined hands, and emotions I can't identify play across his face, but he keeps moving.

"Matthew never knew that. Come to think of it, he really didn't know me at all. It's not all his fault. I never allowed him in. I didn't have room for him in my heart, and if I had? I don't think he would have liked what he found there, anyway."

"Why do you say that, Rylan? You were going to marry him. Surely you must have lov—liked him." He chokes on his words, and I can't help but smirk.

"Matthew wanted someone who fit his world. Someone that conformed to his way of life, how he did things. How he liked things. What's my favorite color?"

"Aqua."

"He would have said navy."

Hatty's hand squeezes my fingers so tightly I wince and have to wiggle my fingers to get him to loosen his grip.

"Wh-Why are you telling me this?"

I tug his hand to force him to stop and look at me. "Because you know me better than anyone ever has. Something happened that morning with your dad."

He pulls his hand free and starts walking again, but I don't let up.

"It's fine if you don't love me anymore, Hatty. We've grown apart, but do you know why I never had room for Matthew in my heart?"

"Don't push this, Rylan."

"Don't push what? The truth? Guess what? I'm done living with the consequences of your lies. I never made room for Matthew in my heart or my life because it was so full loving you. Even after you were a fucking tool, my heart still had space for you. You want to be friends now? Fine. But you can't tell me you never loved me. I know you did. I felt it. It's why I know what it feels like to be truly, wholly loved, and when I'm honest with myself, I never felt that from Matthew. But you know who I do feel it from? You, Hatty."

When I glance up, I see we've made it to The National. Peering up the steep steps that lead to the large porch, I huff out a breath.

"Hatty?" My voice is harsh, and I hold my ground until he glances down at me.

"Fine. I did love you, Rylan, but sometimes love isn't enough, and family has to come first. I'll get us a table."

He stomps up the steps, and I'm left gaping at him. He did love me. Past tense. And now I'm angry and confused, so I march up the steps with steam escaping my ears. Removing the hair elastic from my wrist, I angrily tug all my hair up into a high, messy bun. It's hot as hell, and if I'm going to fight, I need my hair out of the way.

At the top of the stairs, I find him watching me with amusement and maybe a bit of fear. He knows I'm not letting this go.

"Was it your dad?" I ask as he sits down at a table overlooking the ocean. "Did he not like me? Did he think I wasn't good enough for you?"

Hatty's jaw sets, and even over the din of the restaurant, I can hear his teeth grinding.

"It wasn't you he was worried about. Drop this, Rylan. I mean it. Nothing good will come of us heading down this road. Let's have dinner, ask around about Pacen, and go home."

I'm so frazzled I don't know how to respond. Instead, I order a glass of white wine with my dinner and text the only people I can think of.

Rylan: I need help.

Lexi: Kiss him.

Rylan: He admitted that he loved me. Past tense. When I asked what could have happened, if maybe his dad didn't think I was good enough, he said I wasn't the problem.

Rylan: I'm so confused.

Ari: You love him.

Rylan: I do. But he said love isn't enough.

Lexi: Then make it enough. Show him it's enough.

Rylan: How?

Lexi: Every Westbrook on this mountain knows he's in love with you, but they don't know why he's being a fucking idiot. Force him to acknowledge his love for you.

Ari: How does she do that?

Lexi: Nothing makes a Westbrook snap faster than jealousy.

Rylan: That sounds ... underhanded.

Lexi: Listen, he's been dicking around for years. Everyone is worried about him. Force his hand a little. He'll either break through whatever's holding him back, or ...

Rylan: Or?

Lexi: Or you'll know you've done everything you can. You can't fix someone that's not ready to fix themself.

Rylan: So, your advice is to make him jealous?

Lexi: Westbrooks don't like to lose. Especially their women. And they hate to share. They're good men, but they protect what's theirs. Make him acknowledge that you're meant to be his.

Rylan: You're scary. And mean.

Lexi: And amazing and usually right. It's your call, Ry, but that's my advice.

Lexi: (Eye rolling emoji) Easton agrees.

We eat and stew in near silence. Except for the occasional question from our waiter, we haven't exchanged a single word.

"Can I offer you any dessert?"

Hatty's head whips to mine, and I see a hopeful glimmer in his eye, but I shake my head no.

"Have you seen this girl?" he asks instead, pulling up a photo on his phone.

Recognition hits first, and we both see it in the waiter's expression.

"Ah, no. Sorry. Never seen her."

He scurries away, and I watch as a frown appears on Hatty's face.

"He was lying," I offer.

Hatty scrubs a hand roughly over his face. It's a new habit I hadn't noticed before, and it's sexy as hell. My second glass of wine is giving me the courage to peruse his handsome face more openly. His strong jaw twitches as he follows my gaze. His perfectly straight nose leads to full, sexy lips.

"I know," he grinds out through clenched teeth. "Are you talking to me again?"

"We have nothing to say to each other until you start being honest with me, Hatty."

"I'm being as honest as I can."

"And I'm telling you it isn't good enough."

The waiter drops off the check, and I catch his arm. Hatty stiffens in his chair, his gaze laser focused on my hand holding the stranger's arm.

Holy crap, Lexi was right.

"Is there a bar around here? Somewhere we can see the ocean? With music and dancing?"

"That's kind of two different things around here. The Beach Bar will have music on the beach, but it's not really dancing. If you want to dance, you have to go to Captain Nicks."

His smile toward me turns lecherous, and Hatty growls his disapproval.

"Sounds great. Which way is Captain Nicks?"

The waiter glances between Hatty and me, then shrugs and gives me directions.

"What are you doing?" Hatty's manners are so engrained he rises with me as I stand, even though every feature on his face says he wants to stay right where he is.

"Come on, *friend*. I'm going dancing. We're here to scope out the place, right? Pacen is young and beautiful. If she's on this island, every red-blooded local would have noticed her."

He glares at me. He's skeptical, and he should be. I'm about to test his limits, and I guess I'll have my answer one way or another after tonight. I grab my glass of wine and drain the rest of its contents, needing a little liquid courage for what I have in mind. Turning, I head down the stairs, not bothering to see if Hatty follows.

"Exactly what is your plan here, Rylan?"

"Oh, I'm back to Rylan now? Geez, sweetheart rolls off your tongue so much more smoothly."

"Rylan." His voice carries a warning I ignore.

Instead, I walk along the coastal road that will take us to Captain Nicks. It doesn't take long, and as we round the bend in the road, the music filters over the ocean breeze.

"That's it?" he grumbles.

Glancing ahead, I see the colorful sign on the outside of a two-story building better suited as a home than a bar, but the laughter and music filtering our way has a smile gliding across my face. My grin only grows as we make our way inside. The dance floor is smaller, which means you can't dance without getting very *friendly*.

Hatty falls in step behind me but guides us with a hand pressed to the small of my back. The heat from his touch sears my skin, and when he leans in to speak close to my ear, I shiver.

"What do you want to drink?"

He's pissed off. I can hear it in his tone, but I ignore it.

Turning to him, I place my cheek on his, and he stiffens. "Sex," I whisper, allowing my lips to graze his ear, "on the Beach."

Pulling back, I see a hint of hunger in his eyes as his nostrils flare.

"This is a dangerous game you're playing, sweetheart."

"I don't know what you're talking about, *friend*."

CHAPTER 23

HALTON

I'm on my third beer, and I've already committed seven murders in my head. I'm thankful for the bar at my back as strangers invade my senses on three sides. The alcohol they're consuming erases all etiquette for personal space, and I have to fight to keep my snarls in check.

I've never liked crowds, but I could handle them so long as I wasn't the main attraction. Tonight, though, I'm ready to burn down the world as every eye in the place lands on my girl.

Fuck. She isn't my girl, but every red-blooded male cell in my body fights that notion as she sways to the music.

"You sure you don't want to dance, Hatty?"

I shake my head with my jaw clamped shut. She's tempting me, teasing me, and even after all these years, she still knows how to goad me.

"Your loss." Rylan tosses her hair over her shoulder and heads back to the dance floor. At some point in the last hour, she let her long tresses loose of her pissed-off bun, and everyone noticed. Everyone notices everything about her. I've lost track of the number of assholes that have tried to pick her up already. The second her hips started swaying, they surrounded her.

They wouldn't be all over her if you'd get your head out of your ass.

My eyes are dry from not blinking by the time the band takes a break. There's a brief lull before the DJ pipes in new music over the speakers. A song I don't recognize comes on, and Rylan's sexy, little body shimmies and sways to the beat. From my perch at the bar, I watch as two guys grind up on her, but her eyes are locked on me.

In slow motion, she lifts her arms to wrap them around dickhead's neck, and they move as one. I feel like a voyeur. I'm hanging on to my bottle so tightly I'm surprised it doesn't shatter, but even as she dances, her gaze never leaves mine.

She's fucking with me, and I'm completely powerless to stop her.

If I don't get out of here soon, I'm going to end up in jail. The guy behind her wraps an arm around her belly. He splays his hand low on her stomach, pulling her back into his front, and a feral growl escapes from deep in my throat. I'm crossing the dance floor without a thought of my next move. Parting the sea of people to get to her pisses me off. If it had taken one second longer, I might have started throwing elbows.

"Get your hands off her." Anger radiates out of my every pore.

"Listen, man. We're just dancing," he smartly replies while putting some distance between us. I never give him a second look.

"We're leaving. Now," I growl.

"Have fun. I'll see you at home."

I gape at her. Does she seriously think I'm going to leave her here alone?

"I'm not leaving you here."

Out of the corner of my eye, I notice both men fading into the crowd.

"Then dance with me."

I take a step back.

"Dance with me, or I'm going to find someone who will."

My body shifts, reaching for her before I can think better of it.

"Are you threatening me, sweetheart?"

"A threat would imply you have something to lose. Do you have something to lose, Hatty?"

Bastille's "Distorted Light Beam" filters through the overhead speakers as the lights dim low. It's a dark and dangerous beat, but it's the words that obliterate my resolve.

Stepping into her space until our bodies collide, I place my hands on her hips and position her flush against me. Soft curves meld into hard planes, and my hips gyrate in time to the angry beat pulsing through my veins.

The tightness in my body ratchets up to near unbearable levels, tension radiating from every muscle. But my mind, so used to the looming chaos and anxiety, quiets as our bodies fuse together. The near constant war inside of my head bleeds into my heart when I have her in my arms. The fear, the panic? It all subsides and rolls into a most basic need to claim her. That's the only explanation I have for the words that fall from my lips next.

"I've already lost everything that made me whole. Forcing my hand like this will leave me a shell of a man. Is that what you want?"

Her shocked gasp hits the crook of my neck as I part her legs with my thigh. The closer I get to her, the calmer my body and soul become. I swear, the cure for my weakness resides within her. Snaking my hand to her lower back, I hold her ass tightly against my leg as we move to the song that feels as if it were written for this one moment in time.

"You haven't lost anything, Hatty."

"You're wrong." I groan when her belly shifts and it presses against my erection. "I'm in hell. That's what this is. Are you trying to punish me, Rylan? I hurt you, so you're hurting me back by forcing me to watch other guys put their hands all over you?"

I move us roughly to the music, and I almost come in my pants.

"No, Hatty. Not at all. I just want you to open your eyes and see." Her tongue darts out and gently caresses my ear.

"See what? What I can't have? How fucking miserable—"

Rylan's hands weave into my hair, and she pulls me down. Our lips crash together almost violently. When she nips my bottom lip, I open to her. She wastes no time entering my mouth as my hands tighten on her hips. I have no thoughts of consequences or our surroundings. Not when she fucks me with her tongue until a little whimper escapes her throat and she pulls back.

"No. I want you to see me, Hatty. Us. I want you." She grinds against my cock to prove her point. "Tell me you don't want me. Tell me you don't feel this." She rubs against me again, and I have to still her hips before I rip off all her clothes in front of everyone.

I've never hurt so much in my life. It's like my heart is being ripped out of my chest, and I'm just standing here watching it bleed out. "It's not about what I want, Rylan. I've always wanted you. I can't have you. You're not mine to keep."

Tears well in her eyes. Fear that I've finally pushed her away for the final time, and relief that I may have pushed her away for the final time, take turns punching me in the nutsack. "I'm so sorry—"

She holds up a hand to stop me. "Do you love me?"

I can't hear her over the music, but her words are written plain as day on her swollen lips.

"I always will," I finally admit. "But it isn't enough, and it isn't right."

Standing on her tiptoes, she pulls me in closer so I can hear her.

"Love is a choice you make, Hatty, and you chose wrong." Using both hands, she shoves me back with tears flowing down her face.

People around us have noticed and separate to give her room to escape.

I watch in shock as she forces her way toward the exit. I blink away the surprise, then follow in her wake. She may hate me, but I have to make sure she gets home safely. I'll sleep in the car and send her home tomorrow.

Hanging my head in shame, I exit the bar. The tightness in my chest is overwhelming as panic crashes in, taking center stage once again. Glancing around, I see Rylan up ahead, so I follow from a distance. We're halfway home when she makes a detour toward the water. My racing heart and sweaty palms remind me that my chaos has no cure without her in my life. It causes a sad awareness I've never known.

When she rips her shirt over her head without a care in the world, I stumble.

What the hell is she going to do?

Her skirt comes off next, and she tosses it carelessly to the ground. My head is on a swivel, making sure no one is witness to her striptease.

"Rylan. What the hell are you doing?" I growl as a new wave of possession washes over me.

Reaching behind her, she unclasps her bra and drops it by her feet as she moves toward the water. I'm following behind her now, collecting her clothes.

"Rylan," I bark again. "What the fuck?"

Her panties are the last to fall, and when she glances over her shoulder at me, a small smile appears on her face.

Maybe she's lost her damn mind?

"I'm skinny-dipping, Hatty." Her voice is so melancholy, I shiver. The only other sounds are my breathing and the ocean lapping at the shore.

"You can't fucking swim, Rylan."

She turns to face me, and I blackout for a moment at the sight of her naked in the moonlight. She's so goddamn beautiful I can't breathe.

Raising an eyebrow, she shrugs one delicate shoulder and walks straight out into the surf.

Motherfucker. What the hell do I do now? It's not like I have a choice. I won't let her drown out here.

"Why are you playing games with me?" It comes out strangled. I'm trying to yell so she can hear me, but stay quiet enough I don't attract any unwanted attention.

"No games, Hatty. Not anymore," she calls over her shoulder, but she never slows her pace. The water is at her thighs now, and she's still moving forward.

Dropping her shit into a pile, I do the only thing I can. I strip and follow her into the water. It's so fucking cold I feel my balls shrivel up and die, anyway.

Screw it. Diving headfirst, I swim to catch up with her. When I finally surface, I've blocked her from going any deeper. The water hits just above her nipples, and I can't help but stare as her perfect tits float in the moonlight.

"What's going on here, Rylan? You're scaring me."

She cocks her head to the side as she stares at me. Too many emotions to count flicker in her shimmering eyes.

"I'm stripping us down. I want nothing between us. Just you and me. Honesty."

"For what?" I ask, but I'm already shaking my head no.

"You love me, yet you say it isn't enough. You're willing to let me live with a broken heart because you don't think you can have me. I deserve to know why. Why would you hurt me like this over and over again, Hatty? What could mean so much to you that you'd give up on us like this?"

181

I can't take the pain anymore. I want to kick and scream. I want to fight. However, when I raise my gaze, all I can see is the hurt I've caused.

"I never wanted to hurt you, sweetheart, but Colton loved you first. Dad said … Dad reminded me I couldn't do that to him."

Rylan blinks, but otherwise, doesn't move a muscle for a really long time.

"Sweetheart?"

Blink.

Blink.

Blink.

A rage I've never seen mars her beautiful face. Rylan's lips press together in a tight line as her face turns an unnatural shade of red that glows even in the moonlight. Her shoulders shake with a tension I can feel building, and I'm helpless to stop any of it.

"All this pain," she seethes. "All these lies and heartache were because you think Colton loved me first? So, what? He just gets me? Are you fucking kidding me, Hatty? I'm not a goddamn Lego set. No one calls dibs on me. Do you have any idea of the torment I lived through? How lonely my life was because I couldn't just cut you from my life? I also had to take a step back from my best friend because it was too painful to have that physical reminder. You hurt us all because of some childish code of ethics? Y-You didn't give me a choice." Her voice, so full of rage and anguish, cuts me to my core. "Can you see how stupid that is, Hatty? You ripped my heart out, set it on fire, and walked away because Colton called dibs." An almost maniacal laugh escapes, and her eyes are glassy and wild. "The worst part of this all? Colton never even wanted me that way. You did all this, and all he's ever wanted was to be my friend."

"But he's always loved you, and I can't do this to him." I

take a step back, putting more ocean between us, but Rylan isn't having it. She mimics my moves.

As she stares at me, I start to feel really stupid. *Do I have this all wrong? Have I made a tragic mistake all these years?*

In a fit of anger, she splashes water at my face and doesn't let up. I have to sink into the ocean to escape her constant barrage of water, and when I surface, I pin both of her wrists behind her. The movement forces us together, and her tits smash against my chest.

"How could you be so stupid, Halton?"

I flinch, but she speaks over me. This time, I deserve to be called Halton. It's better than asshole, I guess.

"Yes, of course Colton has loved me forever. I love him, too."

A strangled cry escapes my throat without warning. Rylan might as well drown me now, because I'll never survive this conversation.

"I ..." I don't know what to say, but I also can't bring myself to let her go. I fear if I do, I'll never hold her again.

"God, Hatty. I hate you so much right now." Tears cascade down her cheeks, taking her residual mascara with it.

I shift her wrists to one hand and use the thumb of my free one to erase the black marks. The small gesture feels monumental in my heart.

"How could you do this, Hatty? How could you be so dumb? You've hurt us all for so long. And for nothing."

I suck in a painful breath. "It isn't nothing, Rylan. Family has to come first. You know that."

"You ... You just don't get it, do you?" A hiccup escapes, and I've never seen her eyes so sad. "Colton loves me, yes. Just like he loves Lexi and Ari. He loves us all, Hatty. He isn't in love with us. He isn't in love with me. He never has been and never will be. How can you not see that? He calls me freaking Ryguy because he thinks I'm one of the guys. I couldn't ever belong to him because you've owned my heart since I was six years old." She breaks on a sob, and my shoulders cave. The pain in my chest feels like a gunshot wound. "You're my panacea, too. You always have been. I'm lost without you. I've been lost for years, Hatty. Please, please help me find my home."

Colton isn't in love with her? Does that matter? He will be someday ... won't he?

"How?" I force out. It sounds pained, and I struggle to form a clear sentence. "How do you know he doesn't love you?"

Slowly, Rylan wiggles an arm free and raises it toward me, placing a soft palm on the side of my face.

"Oh, Hatty." My eyes close as I soak in her touch. "How do you feel when you're with me?"

"Whole."

"That's how I know. You're the other piece of me. A love so rare no one else could fit. We're like a puzzle that only has two pieces. Colton doesn't fit with me. His other half is still out there, and if you'd ever stopped to ask him, he would have told you this. Anyone would have told you this. Why did you keep it to yourself? Why didn't you ever talk to someone? You could have saved us all so much pain."

Shame sits heavy on my soul as her words take root.

"My father died because of our fight."

Without warning, I spill the last of my secrets. The reason I lied in the first place, and the guilt I've carried ever since.

CHAPTER 24

RYLAN

*W*e stare at each other long after he finishes speaking. He blames himself for the death of his father. He truly believes that Colton is in love with me. *Hatty still loves me.*

A breeze picks up from the ocean, and it cools my over-heated skin, causing me to shiver. Hatty notices right away.

"We should head back in. You're cold." His voice is devoid of emotion. It's a skill he's honed, and if I didn't know better, I'd think he'd retreated. But his eye twitches with the pain he just set free, and I'm not willing to let this go.

Glancing around, I realize we're still standing naked off the shore of Block Island like we're the only two people on earth. My heart is heavy, and my mind is swirling with so much activity I can't think. Instead, I act. I act on every feeling, emotion, and memory I've ever had with this man because it all comes back to love at the end of the day. I love him. My heart is in love with him, and it'll never beat for anyone else. I know that with certainty now.

Pushing him like this was playing dirty. I know it was, but goddamn it, I need him. I'm demanding honesty from him. It's only fair he gets the same in return. I'm angry. So freaking angry, but love truly is a powerful thing, and it outweighs years' worth of built-up angst.

Reaching up, I wrap my arms around his neck as he watches like a stone statue. With no effort at all, I wrap my legs around his waist, the water helping me float to him.

"Rylan," he warns as his cock bobs and nestles at the crack of my ass.

"Do you love me, Hatty?" I ask again for reassurance. For him, and for myself.

"Yes, but …"

My anger ebbs to the recesses of my mind at his declaration.

"Ask me." It's a demand, and he follows orders.

"Do you love me, Rylan?"

"I always have."

Loosening my arms around his neck, I allow my body to drift a few inches lower.

"Fuck," he gasps as I find my target. Sliding my body up and down, I rub his dick slowly along my slit. "You don't know what you're asking."

"I know that I need you. I need you with me. I need you beside me. I need you in me, Hatty, like I need my last breath."

His hands finally move to my hips, and he stills my movements. His eyes are haunted, and I can tell he feels as though he's betraying his brother, but I know deep down in my soul that the fear is unfounded.

"I need you, Hatty. Please don't deny me again."

I feel the thick, round head of his cock notch at my entrance, but I don't move.

"I'm already living in hell. I might as well rot there, too," he growls.

I open my mouth to protest his sentiment. To tell him he has to trust me about his brother. To trust me. But his hands close painfully around each hip, and I know I'll have bruises there tomorrow. Before I can make a sound, he slams me down onto him with such force the air is knocked from my lungs, and I can't catch my breath.

"For eight fucking years, I had to imagine you with someone else. For eight years, I haven't been able to look at another woman without pretending she's you. And for what?" he bellows over my head.

His pace is frantic, and my body moves with him as my brain tries to catch up. And when it does, I know we're about to set the ocean on fire.

Hatty rears back, and when he pumps his hips forward this time, I meet him thrust for thrust. Surprise has him dropping his gaze, almost like my body brought him back to this moment.

"For eight years, I pretended real love, soul-crushing love, didn't exist. I made myself believe I could be okay with companionship because you pushed me away."

He growls, then lifts me higher so he can wrap his teeth around my nipple as he continues to thrust his hips in the water. Waves crash into us. Around us. Through us, but we never lose our connection.

"Do you know what it was like to get a glimpse of your life through pictures on Instagram? To see you living your life like I never existed?"

I gasp, and he uses my shocked silence to slip a hand between us. Twisting his hand, he finds my bundle of nerves ready to explode.

"I've fucked my hand hundreds of times, imagining it was you, wishing it was you, but it never compared. The memory of you in my head can't compare with the real thing. Fucking hell, Rylan, you're so perfect."

My brain stops working, and I'm no longer capable of forming coherent sentences. "More. Harder, Hatty, please. Harder."

"You're going to come, aren't you, Rylan? Right here in the middle of the ocean on my fucking cock."

He slams into me at an unnatural pace now, and I'm floating somewhere above consciousness.

"You want me to fuck you harder, baby? But I want to mark you as mine."

"Yours," I pant.

"Say it again," he demands.

"Yours. I've always been yours, Hatty."

He thrusts harder two more times, then swivels his hips so his pubic bone grinds into my clit, and I scream with abandon. I release years of pent-up frustration, pain, and love in a garbled, incoherent scream of ecstasy, and Hatty swells inside of me a moment later. A string of curses escape as he buries himself so deep inside of me, I have no doubt I will feel him in places I never knew I had.

Swirling blue lights and a siren have us both sobering to the moment much faster than our bodies can uncouple.

"Hands up. Release her now," someone yells from the shore.

Hatty immediately raises both hands.

"Oh my God. We're going to get arrested. Sh-Should we make a swim for it?"

A boyish smirk plays across his face. "Not likely, baby. Our IDs are on the beach."

I attempt to slide down his body, but my legs are like jelly, and I sink into the ocean, fully prepared to die of embarrassment.

Before my face even touches the water, Hatty has hauled me back up him and is yelling to the officers on the shore, but I can't make out the words with the ringing in my ears.

Holy shit. Hatty just fucked me stupid. I try shaking the cobwebs from my head and notice we're moving toward the shore.

"Sir, we're, ah … well, we don't have any clothes on.

Would it be possible for you to turn around so she can get out of the water?"

That wakes me from my sex-induced coma faster than a burger after a tequila night.

"Miss? I need verbal confirmation that you're okay."

Glancing up, I find an older gentleman who appears ready to die of embarrassment and a young kid who can't be more than twenty years old trying desperately not to laugh.

"Yes, sir. Sorry, we were, ah, fornicating?"

Hatty's burst of laughter rings loud in the quiet night.

"Fornicating? Seriously, sweetheart?"

"Jees-us. I'm too old to deal with this kind of shit," the older man grumbles, but turns, then yells at his understudy to do the same. "Hurry up and get your clothes on. I can't leave you here."

Hatty reaches for my hand, drags me toward the beach, and hands me my pile of clothes. We both struggle to pull them onto our soaking wet bodies, and I can sense the officer growing even more impatient.

"Are we going to get arrested?" I whisper, panic setting in now.

"I-I don't know," Hatty whispers back. "I've never been in trouble before." Turning to face me, he adjusts my top so my boob isn't hanging out.

"Was that? Did we? Was that a hate fuck?"

The kid chuckles behind us.

"No, sweetheart. How could it be? That was ..." Hatty rakes a hand through his dripping wet hair. "That was eight years of pent-up stupidity."

"Love will do that to you," the older man says. "Come on, now. I'm Officer Jacobs. This is tonight's community service officer, Jeffrey."

"What's a community service officer?" I whisper, but Jeffrey hears.

"Oh, I'm a college student. I'm studying Criminal Justice

189

at Champlain College. Block Island hires a bunch of us in the summer, kind of like interns, to help police the thousands of tourists they have in peak season."

He's way too excitable.

"This way. Follow me," Officer Jacobs repeats.

"Are we, um, are we being arrested?" I finally ask.

"Well, I have to take you in. I can't have tourists fornicating on my beaches. It's just a couple of blocks. Can you walk that far in those shoes?"

Hatty sighs, then stoops down so I can climb on his back.

"We're walking ourselves to jail?"

Jeffrey laughs. It's an awkward sound. "It's like the worst walk of shame ever, huh?"

"Jeffrey," Officer Jacobs admonishes.

"Sorry," he mumbles.

"So, what does that mean? Do we have to sleep in jail?" My voice raises uncomfortably high.

"Well, we do arraignments by Skype around here, and to be perfectly honest, it's a huge pain. We don't get much crime, and you look like a nice couple."

"It sounded like you were killing her, though," Jeffrey cuts in, and I feel my body flush from head to toe.

"Yeah. I don't remember her being so, ah, vocal," Hatty mutters, mostly to himself, but I bury my face into his back as mortification sets it.

"Hatty," I screech. "What the hell is going on? Oh my God, this is like some sitcom nightmare. We're walking ourselves to jail after fucking in the ocean. We were caught by an officer and an intern."

I feel Hatty laugh before I hear it. His shoulders shake beneath me, and his head rolls back as he adjusts his clasped hands under my ass. Somehow, his knuckles graze my sensitive flesh, and I gasp. He squeezes my thighs like he did it on purpose.

"Listen, it's not that bad. There are two rooms. I'm

supposed to separate you, but Blake got here first, so I'll let you shack up for the night. You'll need someone to come bail you out tomorrow, though."

Hatty's body goes rigid at that news.

"Ah, you mean someone has to physically bail us out?"

"Unfortunately, yes. We're about fifty years behind the times with our equipment here. We can arraign you via video, but I have to release you to someone."

That doesn't sound right to me, but it suddenly hits me as we enter what looks like an old saloon. We're stepping back in time. Hatty slides me down his body to the floor as he glances around. Before us is a giant open room with two jail cells straight ahead, like the special attraction at a show.

I gulp, and Hatty silently reaches for my hand.

"Do I have to be fingerprinted?" Why that scares me more than anything makes no sense, but it's all I can think about.

"No. I'll just run your license. We don't have the technology to run prints out here. They would sit in a pile until someone could get them over to Providence, so we only run them for violent crimes."

I nod, but have no more questions.

"So, there's a latrine in the cell, but you may want to take a moment to use the restroom before we process you," Officer Jacobs says kindly, and I waste no time escaping to the ladies' room.

When I see my reflection in the mirror, I almost laugh. Here I am being arrested on a tiny island in Rhode Island, and I've never looked happier.

I pee, wash my hands, and splash some water on my face. When I'm done, I still see the happiest version of myself staring back. That lasts right up until I enter the main room and see Hatty's face.

"What? What's the matter?"

"I called home. Colton will be here in a few hours."

CHAPTER 25

HALTON

*P*rocessing us isn't what you see in the movies. Officer Jacobs takes our license and all our belongings, then escorts us into one of the cells. In the other cell, a man about my age lays on the bed staring at the ceiling without a care in the world.

"Blake? You have some company tonight," Officer Jacobs says kindly. "This is Rylan and Halton. Jeffery will be here for the night. I'll be back in the morning."

"Sounds good," Blake replies, then rolls over to face the wall without even glancing our way.

Rylan shakes beside me, and Officer Jacobs turns his kind eyes to her.

"Blake is a regular here, though he shouldn't be. He isn't dangerous in the slightest. Just a lost man searching for redemption."

Blake grunts from the other cell but doesn't offer any words. Rylan glances between him and Jacobs before nodding silently.

"Well, that's it for me tonight. I have to make the rounds one more time. Jeffery will be here, and we'll get you settled in the morning."

The reality of our situation slaps me in the face as he walks away. I fucked Rylan in public, and we ended up in jail. And Colton is the only one free to bail us out. Given a choice between him and my mother, he was the only option.

"Well, this is going to force a conversation with Colt much sooner than I thought," I grumble.

"Hatty. I'm so sorry."

My head whips to hers. "What are you apologizing for?"

"I shouldn't have forced this," she says, motioning between us with her hands. "I-I just didn't know how else to make you see. I ..."

Sighing, I flop myself down onto the hard bunk and open my arms to her. "I'm not mad about that, sweetheart." I can't contain the smile that spreads across my face. "Though, next time, maybe wait to show the seductress side of yourself until we're in the privacy of four walls."

Rylan buries her face in her hands, but I'm not having it. Reaching up, I tug her hands free until she lands in my lap.

"I am confused, though. I can't deny that. I have to talk to Colt, too. I should have done that before any fornicating happened." I grin even through the seriousness of my words. "Without talking to Colt first, I feel as though I betrayed my brother. You know how hard that is for me to justify."

"But you didn't, Hatty. I promise you didn't."

"All this time wasted because he called dibs on you."

"Jesus, Hatty. He didn't call dibs on me. He's my best friend, that's all he's ever wanted to be, and all I've ever seen him as. My heart has been yours since you hid in the hallway with me when I was six years old."

"But my father died thinking—"

"Your father died because he had a genetic heart condition. End of story."

"H-He thought I wasn't good enough for you."

A sound of shock escapes her throat. "He said that to you?"

"No, he didn't have to. I cut him off before he could, but he was going to."

"That doesn't sound like your dad at all, Hatty. He would never say something like that to any of you."

"But I saw it on his face when he was telling me Colton loved you first."

"You stupid fuck."

I bristle at the deep baritone that comes from one cell over.

"Excuse me?" Rylan beats me to the punchline. My feisty little fireball is ready to fight for my honor, and my heart nearly explodes.

Blake rolls over and sits up to face us. He's handsome under the layers of dirt and unshaven hair. He's also familiar, and I can't figure out why.

"I expected more of a Westbrook," he growls.

Tension coils in my spine. Warning bells go off as I glance around our space, searching for a way to protect Rylan if it comes to it.

"Do I know you?" I ask, still trying to place him.

"No, but we used to run in the same circles. Who I am doesn't matter. I don't exist anymore. However, if you're sitting here telling me you pushed away the love of your life for your family, you're a fucking idiot."

Rylan jumps from my lap as she seethes, "You don't know what you're talking about."

"Kingston? Don't go picking fights with the newbies. That's not your style," Jacobs says on his way out.

Kingston. My gaze snaps to his. Blake Kingston. Suddenly it makes sense. We did run in the same circles for a while. Charity functions, country clubs, all the places you'd expect to see two of the richest families in the county.

What the fuck is he doing as a regular in Block Island lockdown?

194

"Family is what you make it, asshole. Not what you're born into. Don't you forget that."

Recollections of news stories float through my mind from a few years ago about a girl connected to Blake dying in a car accident, but I'm sure his family wiped the truth from ever reaching the media.

He glances between Rylan and me one more time, and a sadness so strong it's heartbreaking takes over his entire body. "Nothing matters more than love, Westbrook. Nothing. Without it, you're just a vessel for the emptiness to fester in. Don't let anyone dictate your forever. The consequences aren't worth it. Trust me on that one."

Blake rolls over, leaving Rylan and me gaping at him. The pain radiates off him and slaps me in the face. Memories of gossip try to take root in my brain. Stories of him eloping with someone his parents didn't approve of. Rumors she was pregnant. Rumors he told his family to go to hell. Then the news that she'd died.

I was so lost in my own hurt I didn't pay it much attention, but staring at his back now, I desperately wish I knew what happened to him. The need to help him is greater than anything I've felt in a very long time. But that makes no sense. He's almost as rich as I am. *Why the fuck would he be a regular in a jail like this?*

"I can hear your brains working from here. My story ended years ago. Don't waste your time trying to figure it out. Just fix your shit before you're left alone in hell," he growls.

Fix my shit.

Holy fuck.

I've never believed in signs. Not before GG and her damn wine. Yet, when I peer up at a slack jawed Rylan, somehow, I just know. This is exactly where I'm meant to be. Not Colt. Me.

Now I can only pray she's right about my brother, and

pray even harder that they'll forgive me for walking away from our father the day he died. If I hadn't, maybe he'd still be alive today.

Jesus Christ. I am an asshole.

~

"*I*t's pretty fucked up that the happiest I've seen you in years is asleep on a twin cot, in jail, with my best friend curled up next to you."

I bolt upright at the sound of Colton's voice and take Rylan with me. Peering down, I see that her hair is a fucking mess. Her drool covers the front of my shirt, and I feel almost happy. Scared shitless about this conversation with my brother, but the happiness outweighs the fear for the first time ever. Blake's words drift through my head, and I turn toward his cell, but it's empty.

I turn my gaze back to my brother with a heavy sigh, releasing Rylan as I do.

"Ryguy? Can you wait outside for us?" Colton asks, but I think his gaze is focused on me. It's hard to tell through the mirrored aviators he's wearing. It's a power move we got from our dad.

"Colty, I don't—"

I squeeze her hand gently, a silent reassurance that we'll be fine, and Colton raises his brow at the contact.

"Fine. But if I hear even one punch being thrown, I'm going to kick both of your asses. Where is Officer Jacobs? Am I allowed to just leave?"

Colton's chuckle has me relaxing slightly. "Yeah, I posted bail while you two were sleeping. You're all set."

I stare at my brother. His posture says he is ready for a fight, but I don't yet know what we're going to fight about, so I stand guarded across from him. Rylan gives him a hug, whispers something that has my hands clenching at my sides, then leaves us alone.

The tension ratchets up tenfold as we stand, arms crossed over our similar build, staring, waiting for someone to make the first move.

"Did you take that bet?" Colt's voice is even, but I see the muscles straining in his neck. The answer to this question will determine how we proceed, and, for once, I'm happy not to lie.

"I never would have done that, Colton."

"But you told her you did. Why?"

"Colt, I-I've loved her my entire life—"

"Why?" he interrupts.

"Dad caught us coming into the house the next morning. He called me into his office." Swallowing thickly, I sit back down on the cot, suddenly exhausted by eight years of lies. Resting my head in my hands, I tell him the truth, "Dad didn't think I was good enough for her. He said I couldn't do that to you either because you loved her first. We didn't really fight about it. I was too weak to stand there and listen to him tell me how you were the better man for the girl my soul lived for. I yelled at him. I cut him off before he could finish, and when I got back, he ... he had died."

"So, you pushed her away ... for me? Without ever talking to me about it? Allowing yourself to die a little more every day because your soul, as you call it, was halfway around the world with another man?"

Lifting my head, I find Colton tucking his sunglasses into the neck of his collared shirt.

He slowly crosses the room and sits beside me before continuing, "And you think it's your fault Dad died."

My head is swimming. For eight years, I've kept all my lies buried deep in my heart, and now within twelve hours, they're being ripped from me for a second time.

"If I'd stayed ... if I'd fought for her, I would have been

there with him when he collapsed. I could have gotten him help, and maybe he would still be alive."

"Shit. What the fuck is wrong with our family?"

Turning my head to the side, I stare at my brother in confusion.

"Halton, you weren't the last person to see Dad. You weren't even the last person to fight with him. Did you not listen to anything that night in the hospital?"

"I ..."

Did I? I don't remember much after seeing the pain I caused on Rylan's face.

"I don't remember being at the hospital at all," I admit.

"Why does everyone in this goddamn family think they have to be a martyr? For Christ's sake, Halton. Dad wasn't your fault, but we'll talk about that with everyone when we get home. These fucking secrets are killing us all. As for Rylan? I'm sorry."

I'm so shocked I choke on a breath that gets lodged in my throat.

"You're sorry? What the fuck for?"

Colton flashes a shy grin while gripping the back of his neck. "I never noticed. I wasn't a very good friend to her when we were kids, and apparently, I was an even shittier brother. I missed what everyone else in our life saw. If I hadn't been so selfish, I would have seen the love you guys had for each other, and I would have known to put an end to this bullshit before it ever happened."

"What? What are you—"

"Halton. If I had paid attention, even once, to the relationship you guys had, I would have known when you hurt her that something was wrong. I've spent all this time thinking it was some faceless asshole from school. If I'd known it was you, I would have fucking killed you, then brought you back to life and told you to fix it. So, I'm sorry

I'm so selfish. I'm sorry I wasn't there for either of you the way I should have been."

"Colt. No, this isn't your—"

"No, it's not all my fault, but I accept my piece in it. Do you love her?"

"So much it scares the shit out of me."

"That's the only kind of love worth risking heartache for, though, right?"

I stare at him for a moment. "You say that like you know from experience. Something you want to tell me?"

He forces a grin. "Nah, I'm leaving the touchy feely shit to you guys."

Something tells me Colton is holding back, but I won't push him. For now.

"Halt?"

"Yeah?"

"If you ever hurt her again, though, I will fucking kill you. You nearly destroyed her. Don't do it again."

Bile tickles the back of my throat. "Trust me, I've been punishing myself every day."

He cocks his head to the side and lays a heavy hand on my shoulder. "I know that now, Halt. I'm sorry you've been hurting so much, and none of us saw it."

A lump forms in my chest, and my eyes are as misty as his.

"I'm sorry I hurt you, Colton. I'm sorry we lied to you."

"Nah," he says, clapping me on the shoulder before standing. "If you'd told me back then, I probably would have thrown a tantrum. Worried you were taking my best friend away from me."

"And now? You're okay if we see where this goes?"

Colton stops in his tracks and turns to me, a serious expression on his face that's so foreign to him. I misstep and have to catch myself.

"What do you mean 'see where it goes'? Halt, you've been

in love with her for over twenty years. There's only one place this can go … with her becoming a Westbrook in name, too. If that's not what you see, then you need to walk the fuck away right now."

My eyes go wide as I wait for the panic to set in. Just yesterday, I thought I'd have to watch the best part of me start a relationship with my brother, and today he's asking me to commit to her for life.

Is this the GG effect? Is she that fucking powerful?

"I'm not dicking around on this, Halton. If you have to stop and think about this, then maybe—"

"No. God, Colt, no. I just have whiplash. If I have the option to make her mine forever without tearing my family apart, then I'm never letting her go again."

His goofy smile relaxes his face, and he barrels into me for a Westbrook special.

"Did you know I'm planning her bachelorette party? Jesus, now it's going to be epic." He pulls away from our embrace with a troubling chuckle.

"Colt, hold on, speedy. We haven't even had a conversation about us, ah, dating." I nearly choke on the words. How is this my fucking life? Two days ago, I thought I couldn't have her. "Don't go planning a wedding just yet." But the thought has a smile so large sneaking its way across my face that Colton laughs.

"Yeah, this is going to be good, Halt. Real fucking good."

The door bursts open, and Rylan comes flying through.

"I can't take it out there for another minute." Her hands are flapping wildly as she speaks, a sure sign she's nervous. "The door was too heavy for me to hear anything through. What's going on? Is anyone hurt?"

Colton and I both turn to her with matching grins, and her gaze ping pongs between us. He raises his eyebrow in my direction, and all feels right in my world for the first time in years.

"Yeah, sweetheart. For once, I truly believe everything is going to be just fine."

"Fuck. This is going to take some getting used to. If you're about to play tonsil hockey, can you at least wait until I drop you off?"

"Peter-freaking-Pan," Rylan giggles, and I don't hesitate to wrap her in a hug. The chains I've kept around my heart finally fall free, and it's like taking my first breath all over again. The darkness I've carried is nowhere to be found, and I smile.

Standing in a tiny, outdated jailhouse, I'm happy.

"I'd forgotten what this feels like," I admit as we walk outside into the rising sun.

"What's that?" Rylan and Colt ask at the same time.

"Being happy."

Colton stutter steps, then places a hand on his hip and stares between Rylan and me.

"Yeah, this is weird."

My chest seizes. Is he going to say he can't handle us together? After all that?

"I'd almost forgotten what your smile looked like. Happy to have you back, brother. Now come on. I'll drop you delinquents off. You still need to find Pacen. Ash is ... well, Ash is losing his damn mind."

Guilt punches me in the face, but I don't dwell on it. With Rylan by my side, we'll find Pacen. *I hope.*

"We'll never live this down, will we?" Rylan slaps a hand over her forehead, and I tuck her into my side as we follow Colt to his golf cart.

"Oh, Ryguy. Never. This is going to be fodder for years. I mean, you got arrested for ..." He laughs so hard he can't finish.

"Yeah, yeah. Fornicating in public. Can we not tell our parents, though? Geez," she groans.

"Technically, you did not get arrested. You were just

detained. No cuffs were used, and Officer Jacobs didn't even file the paperwork."

"Really?" She glances up at me with those green eyes, and my heart skips a beat.

I'm happy.

Pulling the golf cart onto the road, Colt fills in the details of our bail. "Yeah, I talked to Jacobs this morning. Apparently, Blake Kingston put in a good word for you. What the hell was he doing here, anyway?"

"Struggling, I think."

"Hmm. I'll have to call Lochlan. He was closer to Blake than any of us were. Speaking of, did you submit your portfolio to his sister, Nova?" Colt calls over his shoulder so Rylan can hear him from the back seat.

"I did. Just before we left Burke. I haven't heard anything yet, though."

Colt takes the turn into the driveway at full speed and almost flips the golf cart.

"Jesus, Colty. What the hell?"

"Just having a little fun," he laughs, but it dies on his lips as the lean-to comes into view.

Sitting on the edge with her feet dangling below her is Pacen Macomb.

CHAPTER 26

RYLAN

*a*s soon as the golf cart comes to a stop, I jump out.

"Freaking hell, Colty. You're a menace some-times, you know that?" Stomping my foot, I turn toward the lean-to and stop mid-stride. "Pacen? Geez, we've been looking for you."

"I figured. How's Ash?" She sounds sad, and the closer I get, the more I notice the void in her eyes. There's no emotion there.

"He's struggling," Hatty replies. He must notice her vacant stare, too. "Pacen? Are you okay?"

Colton steps forward and wraps her in a hug. He's either oblivious to her state or ignoring it. With him it's hard to tell. Hatty and I stand back and watch as he wraps her up with her arms hanging listlessly to her side.

"Ash has been so worried." Colton holds her by the upper arms but leans back to get a better look at her. "He wants you to come home with us. I honestly don't know what he wants, but he isn't the same, Pacen. Whatever's going on, we need you to come talk to him so we can get him back." His words are gentle, like talking to a wounded animal.

I guess he isn't as oblivious as he leads everyone to believe.

"I'm sorry." She takes a step back. "He needs this."

Hatty and I have crept closer, so when she reaches down into her bag, we all notice the barrel of a gun.

My shocked gasp has her turning to me with a sad smile, and she quickly closes the zipper, effectively shielding us from the weapon she carries.

"Everything isn't always as it seems, Rylan." Her voice is wispy, airy in a way I don't remember. Come to think of it, I don't really remember her ever saying much.

"Fuck. Pacen, what is going on? Are you in trouble? Are you hiding from your father?" Colton's words are much calmer than I feel.

"Hiding?"

Her voice reminds me of a ghost from every movie I've ever seen, and it sends a chill down my spine.

"I don't need to hide, Colton. I'm on assignment, and these two nearly blew my cover. Everything Ash needs is on this USB drive—"

"Ah, he was pretty adamant about you coming back with us," Hatty interrupts.

"I'm sure he was," she says sadly. "He and I never could agree on my assignment, but I can assure you, I won't be returning with you."

"You work for SIA, too," Colton surmises.

"SIA doesn't exist anymore, Colton. I know Ash will be unhappy, but tell him to stop searching for me. This is my decision, and I've made it. When I disappear this time, I'm gone forever."

She places the USB into Colton's palm, then reaches down to grab her bag. The three of us stare at her in shock. *Who the fuck is this woman?*

"Pacen? Please, is there anything you need? Could you at least talk to Ash on the phone?" Hatty pleads.

"No. Just tell him I never betrayed him. It's all on the USB, and I promise your father's secret is safe. I've made sure of it."

Hatty and Colton both go ashen at her words.

"Ash said you haven't touched your accounts. How are you surviving? Do you need money? Anything?" I ask.

Both men stand guard on either side of me with slack jaws.

"No. Ash knows that money is dirty. I'll be fine."

Hatty breaks free from his stupor first. "What about our father? What do you mean, secrets? What are you talking about?"

Pacen's lips thin to a straight line. It's the first real emotion I've seen from her since this exchange began.

"The secrets Ashton keeps are going to kill him one day. He doesn't agree with me, but it's true. And not because someone will find him in a dark alley, but because it's rotting his soul from the inside out."

"What the fuck does that mean?" Colton's voice carries an edge I've never heard from him before.

"That's a question for your brother. Take care of each other. You're truly the best family I've ever met, don't let secrets ruin that."

Colton takes a step forward like he's going to physically restrain her, but she quirks a brow in silent warning, and he holds up his hands.

I stand in shock, flanked by a Westbrook on either side, and watch some version of Pacen Macomb walk straight into the day and disappear.

"What in the mother fucking hell was that?" Colton asks with wide eyes.

Halton paces beside me, so I quietly slip my hand into his, and he halts to stare at our joined hands. A half smile crooks the corner of his mouth, but the worry etched on his face matches Colton's.

"How long will it take to pack up?" Colt asks. He sounds pissed off, and I know the Westbrooks are about to welcome a new kind of chaos to Burke Hollow.

"Twenty minutes tops. Can you get us on the next ferry?"

"No. I'm getting a helicopter to pick us up. Fucking Ashton has some secrets to spill."

~

*M*y insides shake like they're in the middle of an ice storm as I sit next to Hatty in GG's lodge. Glancing around, I can't believe the difference the construction crew has made in here. They must be close to opening it up to guests again. The place looks brand new.

After some asshat took advantage of GG last year, the lodge started falling apart. Literally. It was Hatty's brother, Easton, who realized someone had vandalized the property on purpose. It's why we're all here, or at least why all the Westbrooks dropped everything to be here. They're better than the army that way. The Westbrooks really leave no man, or granny, behind.

Colton had called a family meeting while we waited for the helicopter and hasn't been himself since Pacen left. The man who has never taken a single thing in his life too seriously looks murderous as he stands with crossed arms over a puffed-up chest.

"Jesus, Colty. What the hell is going on with you?" Preston asks, entering the main sitting area of the lodge.

"Language, Preston," Sylvie Westbrook, the family matriarch, chides, walking in just behind him. "Oh, Rylan, dear. I'm so happy to see you."

Rising quickly, I rush her for a hug. I saw her briefly after the Summerfest auction, but once the shit hit the fan, everything happened pretty fast.

"I'm so happy to see you, too, Sylvie."

She wraps me in a hug much tighter than her formal appearance would lead you to believe her capable of. "Happy to have you home, Rylan." Her words are whispered but full of emotion, and I feel myself tearing up. Clasping my hands, she stares into my eyes. "We'll catch up soon, okay? Let's find out what the emergency is that has Colton calling a family meeting."

Sylvie winks like this is all fun and games. I don't think she has any idea of the ambush about to happen.

The back door swings open with so much force it bounces against the wall. Ashton comes barreling through on the next breath. His gaze searches wildly around the room.

"Where is she? Did you find her?" he rasps. He searches my face, then moves to Halton. "Did you find her?"

"More like she found us," Colton says calmly from across the room. However, when I turn to him, his body language is anything but relaxed, and every person in the room notices.

Glancing around, I note Sylvie has taken a seat next to Loki on the couch across from us, while Preston and East are perched on bar stools behind them. To my left, I'm surprised to find Easton's childhood friend, Dillon, sitting quietly. He and I make eye contact, and I know he's thinking the same thing.

Shit is about to get real. Should we even be here?

As if sensing my unasked question, Hatty reaches over and takes my hand in his lap. The gesture doesn't go unnoticed by the peanut gallery across from us, and my cheeks go up in flames.

"Well, where is she?"

Ashton's raw words draw my attention back to him. I have no doubt he just attempted to yell. His white knuckles on the chair he's holding prove I'm right.

"She said she's on assignment. She refused to come, and I wasn't about to kidnap her," Colton announces coolly.

"Fuck." Ash pulls at his hair with both hands.

"She gave us this, though. She said everything you need is on here."

All eyes move to the little rectangle in Colton's hand.

"But it's the other thing she said that was really curious." Colton's voice has turned deadly, and Preston stands to cross the room, sensing something's off.

Hatty releases my hand and stands, too. The testosterone in this room is suffocating.

"Time out," Sylvie says calmly. "I don't know what this pissing match is about yet, but you all need to take a step back. Family first."

Colton's bark of laughter sounds anything but happy.

"Family trusts each other, Mom. All we know how to do is keep secrets."

"Watch your tone, Colty."

His face softens as he turns to his mother.

"Now, why don't you tell us, calmly, what's going on."

Colton widens his stance and narrows his eyes at Ash, who returns the same position. Hatty twists his fingers together as he paces in front of me. Reaching out, I place a hand on his leg as he passes, and he stills.

My heart beats rapidly in my ears, and I realize I'm holding my breath as Colty and Ash face off. It comes out in a whoosh when Hatty speaks first.

"Pacen found us, and gave us the drive," he repeats. "But then she said Dad's secret was safe, too."

"Fuck," Ash quietly curses.

"Dad's secret? What secret?" Preston and East ask at the same time.

"That's what I'd like to know. Apparently, Ashton has been keeping secrets from us for a long time. Just like Preston. Just like Easton. Just like Halton. And don't get me started on Loki." Colton's angry words barely mask the hurt I hear just below the surface.

"What the fuck is he talking about?" Preston directs his

question to Ash, but I realize everyone is searching for answers as I glance around the room.

When my gaze lands on Sylvie, she's staring straight ahead at Ash with tears in her eyes.

"How long have you known?" she asks him gently.

CHAPTER 27

*E*very muscle in my body tenses as I turn toward my mother.

"You have got to be shitting me," Preston grumbles as he brushes past me to sit on the couch next to Loki.

Ashton shakes his head, then pinches the bridge of his nose with his eyes closed as if he can make us all vanish if he only tries hard enough.

"Listen, I don't know what the hell is going on, but I've almost lost too many brothers in the last six months. First Preston, then Loki, and then you, Ash. I can't take this shit anymore." Colton's voice is calmer now, but his body is still wound up, looking for a fight.

"Sit down, Colton." Turning back to Ash, Sylvie waits for him to speak.

"I was with Dad when he died."

All heads in the room turn to Ashton.

"I thought you found him?" *That's what he told me. Didn't he?*

Ash shakes his head no, then sits in the empty seat next to Preston. We all shift his way, waiting for an explanation as Dillon slips from the room.

Silently, I sink into the couch next to Rylan, and she immediately takes my hand.

"I was in the butler's pantry when you were fighting with him, Halt. You stormed off before I could catch you. I told Dad he was wrong. I told him you had always loved Rylan. But he knew it before I said anything."

Dillon reappears and hands Ash a water. I'm suddenly grateful the guy has been working so closely with him recently. None of us thought to do that.

"But I had been in the pantry for a long time. There was a specialized router in there that I probably wasn't supposed to know about. I was …" He turns to Sylvie and shrugs. "I was doing some stuff I shouldn't have, but I heard Dad talking to Ryan on the phone."

Confusion sets in as we glance at one another until we all come to the same conclusion. We only know one Ryan, and we've known him our entire lives.

"Ryan? Nichols? The owner of Envision Securities?" Preston asks in disbelief.

Ash nods, and we wait for him to swallow another sip of water. "Except he wasn't the owner back then."

"Who was?" Loki asks, his bouncing knee giving away his deceivingly calm tone.

"Daddy was. Clinton, I mean."

Rylan tenses beside me, and she may not have been the only one, but I can't be sure because my ears are ringing as my heart races uncomfortably fast. No one in the room says a thing, so my mother continues.

"It all started years ago with Macomb," she explains. "He came to Daddy with a business proposition that didn't sit right with him. Daddy had heard rumblings of his under-handed dealings, so he did a little digging before he turned him down. He found out he was putting employees at risk, and he refused to have our name tied to that. We later found out that Macomb was already indebted to someone who only wanted Daddy's business for a cover as payment. Macomb became desperate, and it arose all kinds of suspicions. The next thing we knew, we had SIA on our doorstep. Preston was just a baby at the time, but the more we heard, the more we knew we couldn't say no to helping them catch these people. But we never had any idea it would turn into what it did."

Holy shit. Before we were even born, my father was working to take down the Blacks, a Boston area mob family.

Her misty eyes land on Loki. "That's how we met you. Saving your mother was his first assignment, but there was a leak on the inside. Clinton was so angry that he couldn't get her out from under Black's web quickly enough. He hired an elite force and removed her on his own. That's when we met Ryan and then your stepdad. Shortly after you and your mom relocated to Waverley-Cay, he started Envision."

My mother takes a deep breath and places her hands in her lap as if she didn't just drop a bomb on us all.

"You let us play with their children," Preston accuses. "Easton dated one of them."

"For a long time after Daddy started Envision, Macomb steered clear of Black. His girls were innocents. They didn't deserve to be punished. And, it allowed Daddy to keep tabs on them. That's why they always played at our house where I could watch them."

It's like I'm seeing my mother for the first time.

"What happened?" Colt turns to Ash.

"I didn't have all the information. I only heard part of their conversation, but it was enough for me to confront Dad before I yelled at him about Halton. He had just grounded me for hacking, and he was doing things that were far more illegal. Or so I thought."

Ash drops his head into his hands, making it more difficult to hear him, and I find myself moving closer.

"I'd never seen him so angry." When Ash lifts his head, his

eyes are unfocused, and his fist clenches above his heart. He's lost in a memory. "He grabbed his chest. It's like he knew what was happening. He was rushing around the room. Then he handed me a key, a password, and a disk drive, and told me to get it to Ryan. I-I didn't know what was happening. He was trying to write you a note, Halton. You see? It isn't your fault Dad died. It's mine."

My mouth is so dry my tongue sticks to the roof of my mouth. Rylan wiggles her fingers in my grasp, and I realize I'm probably hurting her with the death grip I have on her hand.

"You've been working with Envision ever since." Loki's voice cuts through the silence. "That's why there was never any pushback from SIA when you started helping me."

Ashton nods his head, and I don't know what to do with any of this information. I wasn't the last to see my father. Ash has been pulling strings since he was a teenager. It's all too much. Too much information. Too intense. Too many lies. And it's suddenly too much for me to handle. Jumping to my feet, I hear Rylan whisper beside me, but my vision is tunneling with the first signs of panic. Rushing past her, I ignore the shouts coming from my brothers.

I need to get out of here. I-I ... holy fuck. I don't know what I need other than to not be here right now.

"You see? It isn't your fault Dad died. It's mine."

Ashton's confession, however misguided, plays on a loop in my head. My fists flex and tighten as I jog down the stairs. I have no location in mind. I just know my body needs to move.

It's not Ash's fault, I know that. However, if it's true, why have I been blaming myself all this time?

I enter the unfinished game room but see nothing in my anxiety haze. Scrubbing a hand over my face, I turn and barrel through the double doors that lead to the basement, only to backtrack as my breathing becomes erratic.

The swinging door to GG's industrial kitchen flies open with a deafening snap that startles me. I'm not surprised I ended up here, but I'm unable to streamline my thoughts even as I pull ingredients from the pantry. My hands shake, and the full body tremors take over as I attempt to measure the flour.

Dad knew I loved Rylan, and he was okay with it? That can't be true. I saw his face. I know he was about to tell me I wasn't good enough. *Wasn't he?* Did my father seriously start Envision to take down Loki's biological father? Ashton. Holy fuck. *Ash, you were just a kid. What the fuck have you been doing?*

My fist slams into the stainless-steel counter, and my mixing bowl goes flying, sending flour and baking soda all over the room. My knuckles throb against the cold surface, and I sink to the floor. I want to scream as I rest my forehead on the hard steel. My fingers tingle, searching anywhere to find an outlet for these emotions I don't know what to do with.

"Hatty?" My name is a breathy whisper on Rylan's lips before she rushes around the counter and sinks to the floor with me. "Talk to me. What can I do? What do you need?"

It's a struggle to focus, but when I do, her eyes tell the story of her soul. She's the air that I breathe, the warmth I feel.

"Ry," my voice cracks, and I cough to clear it. "I forgot I had you."

She nods as tears fall down her face. "It's kinda new. I'm not surprised." She tries to smile, but her face reflects my pain.

When I hurt, she hurts. How could I have ever pushed her away? Her delicate fingers cradle my face, and I sink into her touch.

"What do you need, Hatty? Are you okay?"

Am I okay? No. No, I'm not. Every darkness that has held me in its grasp was just upended. I found out everything I believed to be true was wrong. That I hurt us all for nothing. My life just spun out of control, so no, I'm not okay, but I don't tell her that. I can't. I just got her back, and I'm going to hang onto her with both hands.

"Please, Hatty. You're scaring me. What do you need?" Her gaze is pleading, and though I don't deserve her, I need her.

"I need you. I just need you."

An almost unhealthy need to dominate her takes over, and I swear she can read my mind. A heavy second passes between us, and as her tears dry, they're replaced with pools of pure sin. She lunges forward, and our lips crash in a frantic clash of teeth and tongues.

Slipping a hand between us, she cups my cock through the denim. With nowhere for it to grow, it fights against the confines of the zipper. When she squeezes, it's almost too much for me to take.

I rise to my knees, taking Rylan with me. She claws at the button of my pants, and I growl, realizing she's as needy as I am. She wastes no time ripping open the button or lowering the zipper before her hand slips below to find me commando.

"Fuck the pants," I grind out, then release her to toe off my shoes and remove my jeans. My gaze never leaves hers, and it somehow turns me on even more. I'm a hairsbreadth away from beast mode, but I don't want to hurt her. I've never felt so out of control before, and I tell her so.

"Are you sure, Rylan? This is what you want? I don't think I can be gentle right now."

Her chest rises and falls as if she was sprinting. I can feel her arousal from here, but she'll have to say it.

"There are a lot of ways you could break me, Hatty, but sex isn't one of them. I'm not the timid, little girl you knew back then."

Rage roils in my gut at the thought of her living her life

with other men … a fury so hot I scare myself, and take a step back.

"Tell me what you're thinking." Her words are a demand as she confidently steps out of her own tiny shorts.

My jaw clicks as I try to gain control. She steps into my space and runs one long nail down the center of my chest, stopping at the top of my pubic bone.

"You won't break me. Not this way, Hatty. I'm yours. Show me what you need."

Something in me snaps. I'm no longer the distinguished CFO of The Westbrook Group. I'm not the wannabe artist. I'm not the black sheep or the panic-riddled man afraid of the spotlight. No. When that last tether breaks, I'm set free, and every obsessive, dominating caveman instinct I have rears its ugly heads.

There's no stopping me, and there's no turning back. Rylan just set me free, and I won't be able to stop until I own every goddamn inch of her.

CHAPTER 28

*M*y breath hitches as I watch Hatty transform before my eyes, and I take a tentative step back. My false bravado of a second ago vanishes as he glares at me with wolfish intent.

"H-Hatty?"

"Are you nervous?" His voice is low, dangerous, and sets my sex on fire.

I gulp past my nerves and steel my resolve. This is Hatty, after all. He won't hurt me. Not physically, anyway. Emotionally is still up in the air.

I nod, unable to form words.

His eyes flash with warmth for the briefest of seconds. "I won't hurt you," he whispers. When he blinks, the warmth is replaced with an inferno. "But this is going to be fast. Hard. I'm going to fuck you, Rylan. I don't care who enters this room. I won't stop until you're screaming my name, and it's echoing through every inch of this mountain. I'm going to fuck that twatwaddler right out of your memory. I'm going to fuck you so hard that the only thought you'll ever have again is me. Between your legs. With my tongue. My fingers. My dick so deep inside you'll have to beg for breath. When you move, it will be me you feel. It will be me you think of. Me. Do you understand?"

Nodding, I try not to swallow my tongue. I've never seen Hatty like this, or been more aroused than I am at this very moment. Jesus. He hasn't even touched me, and my pussy is so wet I flush crimson.

I don't ever remember him being this worked up. This intense. A part of me feels the need to flee, or remind him that he pushed me into someone else's arms, not the other way around. But staring into those haunted, glacier-blue eyes, now is not the time for those words. Now is the time to show him I've always belonged to him, even when he didn't deserve me.

"Words, princess. I need your words."

His voice pierces the silence, startling me into action. "I-I understand."

He steps forward, his cock bobbing angrily between us until it pokes me in the stomach. I'm not short, but he seems to have grown to behemoth size as he towers over me. Every muscle in his body ripples with awareness. From his broad shoulders to his pronounced pecs, down to his toned abs, and into that insane V I've never found sexy until this very moment.

He's going to wreck me.

"Mine," he growls. His hand slides through the hair on my scalp until he has a fistful, then he tugs my face to his. "I will never let you go again."

My eyes go wide while unshed tears threaten. "Promise?"

His body ripples with tension. "Oh, Rylan. Like I ever had a goddamn choice? I've been hanging on to you in here," he rasps, shoving an angry finger against his temple. "If I can have you here?" He points to his heart. "They'll have to pry you from my cold, dead hands."

Leaning in, his teeth graze my earlobe. "Tell me, sweetheart. Did you let him fuck your mouth?"

Holy shit. Hatty is angry at the world, and right now, his focus, his anger, is on erasing every sexual encounter that didn't include him.

I shake my head no, as I shift my weight from one foot to the other, causing a blissful pleasure between my legs. He presses his body firmly into mine, but his hands stay clenched in tight fists at his sides.

"Words," he snaps.

I narrow my eyes, not sure if I like his tone but unable to deny the insane arousal it causes.

"No, Hatty. He didn't fuck my mouth. Sex …" *Shit.* I've never talked openly about sex with anyone. His eyes narrow, and his nostrils flare as he waits for me to continue. "Sex was never emotional. It was never all-consuming. It was a connection that ended the second we pulled apart." I chance a peek up at him through my lashes. His face is an unreadable mask. "Sex was never like it is with you."

His chest puffs out on a quick inhale of breath.

I know what he wants before he speaks. He's already putting pressure on my head to guide me to my knees, and I lick my lips. I've given blow jobs before, but I have never once been turned on by doing it. I knew before I even touched him that was about to change.

"Get on your knees, princess."

I bristle at the nickname, but with one glance into the stormy depths of his eyes, I forget all about it.

I sink to the floor. The cold tiles press unforgivingly into my knees. Hatty stares down at me, and his cock jerks against his stomach. I don't need to be told what to do. With my hands on my thighs, I lean forward. Then I keep leaning until my face is close to the weeping head of his shaft.

He holds my gaze as he widens his stance and bends his knees to give me better access. His cock stands at full attention, and I tilt my head, so my nose grazes the side of it, then

219

stick my tongue out and run it along the underside from root to tip.

"Fuck," he hisses before a growl erupts when I take him into my mouth fully.

I take him in as far as I can, pulling back when my eyes begin to water. Then, he threads his hands into my hair, and I whimper at the contact.

He wants to fuck my mouth. I nod and mumble my consent through a mouth full of him. Hatty takes full advantage as I relax my jaw and watch in awe as he pistons in and out between my lips. I gag when he reaches my limit, but he doesn't pull back right away. He holds himself there, concentrating on my eyes as something I'm too afraid to name passes between us.

"Mine," he roars before he rips himself from my mouth.

Gasping for air, I sit back on my knees, but he's already reaching for me. He hauls me to my feet with no effort on his part. I blink away the tears his cock caused, but I don't have time to recover from one sensation before another assaults me. Hatty rips my clothes from my body and lifts me, so my bare ass sits on the stainless-steel counter.

It's cold, and I gasp as he places a hand on my sternum and guides me to lie back. Flour covers the cool surface, adding to the strange sensations buzzing through my body.

"Open your legs, Rylan."

Lifting my head, I find him standing in front of me, his gaze watching, waiting for me to open to him, and I do without hesitation. There isn't much I wouldn't do for this man. With my inhibitions gone, I lift my legs so my heels are on the edge of the counter and let my knees fall open.

"Fucking perfect."

Seeing the rapture on his face is too much, and my head falls back. Turning to the side, I have a moment of panic that we're in GG's kitchen. A working kitchen with no locks and a lodge full of Westbrooks. *Anyone could walk in at any—*

I lose all thought as Hatty's tongue takes one aggressive swipe at my slit.

"Gah!" I'm panting, and it was one lick. "Hatty," I beg.

His mouth closes over my pussy, and he sucks, flicks, tugs, and teases until I'm writhing in a mess of flour and sweat.

"You're going to come on my tongue first, princess. Then again on my fingers, and then on my cock."

I'm blinking and panting, trying to catch my bearings, but he doesn't let up. With my clit between his teeth, he flicks and tugs and flicks again just before he enters me with one long finger. He flattens his tongue and laves at me like a man dying of thirst in a rainstorm, and my body convulses around him.

"One."

"Wh-What?"

He doesn't give me a chance to finish that thought. My insides are still quivering when two long fingers explore my sex and enter me with no warning.

"I-I..."

"You're going to come again, princess. This time on my fingers."

My head is shaking no, but my body bends to his will. His fingers twist and turn, opening me to his every whim, and I feel the pull start deep in my belly before the first one has even fully subsided.

I have no words. I have no thoughts. All I can do is feel. Feel and watch as his gaze is laser focused on my every reaction. My body is hot, electric. I'm buzzing from head to toe. His touch is almost too much.

"Hatty..."

"Fuck, Rylan. Scream my name."

"Halton."

He pinches my clit so hard I see stars and doesn't let up.

It's bordering on the verge of pain, and tears prickle the backs of my eyes.

"*My* name, Verity. My. Fucking. Name."

"H-Hatty," I wail, and he releases my clit. Sensations flood my body, and the stars I was seeing before are replaced by full-on fireworks in vibrant shades of pink and blue. My back arches off the counter, and sweat slides down my body, the exertion of orgasms tiring me to the point I think I might blackout for a minute.

"Hatty. I'll always be your Hatty," he's murmuring over me. Kissing my neck, my collarbone, my tits. His tongue leaves a damp path along my skin as he whispers words of praise. Just as I think my breathing is evening out, he sinks his teeth into the crook of my neck, and I scream out.

I'm like a live wire. Each new sensation sends sparks coursing through my over-sensitized body. I feel his cock notching at my entrance, and my hips lift on their own accord, trying to suck him in, but his hand on my hip holds me still.

Slowly. Painfully fucking slowly, Hatty guides his erection through my dripping sex. He repeats the motion, hitting my clit each time. Making me gasp. And starting the process all over again.

Leaning over me, he lowers his lips to mine. His gentle kiss is a stark contrast to the unbridled demands of his body. Strong hands glide up my torso, circle down my arms, and back in an erotic path that keeps my body keyed up.

He reaches above my head, and it forces him closer. I use the moment to arch into him and lick a line down his neck before sinking my teeth into his shoulder.

"Christ, yes," he bellows.

We should be concerned about the noise. We should be aware of our surroundings. We should be doing a lot of things. However, at the moment, I don't have it in me to worry about anything but getting this man inside of me.

Hatty leans back and shows me his fingers. A frown forms as I attempt to comprehend what I'm seeing. A thick, white cloud of something seems to be melting into his fingers. I crane my neck, trying to figure out where it came from. With my attention behind me, I don't notice his hands moving lower until they're on me.

My body automatically lurches forward as Hatty smooths something up and down the crack of my ass.

"Wh-What is that?"

"Coconut oil."

The devilish smirk kicks up a notch, but he doesn't lift his gaze to mine. His eyes stay locked on his fingers and what they're doing. I gasp as one finger presses at the puckered hole, and I again try to scoot away. His hand clamps down on my thigh, holding me in place.

I'm terrified by how turned on I am. His finger continues to massage and prod, but never enters me. When he does finally lift his gaze, it's filled with a hunger I've only ever read about. Lowering his lips to mine, he takes them in a possessive kiss, slanting my face with a hand on my jaw so he can devour my mouth. His tongue commands mine to submit, and it does because my mind is focused solely on Hatty's finger circling my ass.

"Has anyone had you here?" he growls.

I cry out as his finger slips past the ring of muscle. I cry out a second time as he twists his hand and slides in deeper.

He's stolen the air from my lungs as he moves closer, folding me up by bringing my legs to rest on his shoulders. His finger rims the tight muscle, and the slight pang of discomfort morphs into a new kind of pleasure.

"Has anyone had you here?" he repeats, but I'm gasping for breath, so all I can do is shake my head. That's not what he wants, though, and I know it as soon as he tries to slip a second finger into my ass. "No, no one," I choke out.

As soon as the words leave my mouth, Hatty rears

forward, sliding his dick into my pussy in one hard thrust. He doesn't remove his fingers, though. The scissoring motion mixed with the feeling of his cock so deep inside of me is too much to take.

My orgasm rips through my body like a tsunami as wave after wave of pleasure wrecks my body. I'm crying out Hatty's name when he finally removes his hands, but his cock is just warming up.

Grabbing my legs around the knees, he slides me through the flour and slams into me again and again. I can't see. I can't hear. I can't speak.

Hatty's lips move, and I think he's saying mine, mine, mine, each time he bottoms out, but my body is careening down a slippery slope of orgasmic torment.

"Look at me," he roars.

My hazy gaze snaps to his. There's a hungry gleam in his blue eyes, his thick hair matted to his forehead as his body glistens from exertion.

"You're mine. Promise me."

With one final thrust, his body tenses, and I feel him twitch and expand within my walls.

"Rylan." It's a groan and a moan. A wail, a promise, a need that escapes his lips as he empties himself inside of me.

And just as I predicted, he's ruined me for life.

CHAPTER 29

HALTON

*M*y body trembles as I hover over Rylan's spent form. With my face pressed tightly into the crook of her neck, I can feel her heartbeat racing against my lips.

What the fuck did I just do? What was that? Shame hits my gut like a lead weight, and I pull back to see if I've hurt her.

Rylan's eyes flutter open when our bodies, both covered in a sheen of perspiration, separate with a loud slurping noise. I scan her face for any signs that I've been too rough, but a smile eases across an otherwise tired expression.

"Sweetheart, I-I'm so sorry."

Her smile fades quickly. "If you're about to push me away again, you have another thing coming, Hatty."

She's pissed. I'm confused.

"What? No! No, that's not it at all." That ugly ball of shame festers in my gut, growing by the minute. I'm hovering over her delicious body, still semi erect inside of her warm, wet pussy, and I don't know what to say to her.

"Then what is it?" She gentles her voice and ghosts her hands up and down my back.

I rest on my forearms over her, unable to pull out of her

just yet. "I've never done that before, Rylan. Not like that. I've never lost control so completely. I've never been so …"

Hello, shame, my old friend.

"Aggressive? Dominant? Rough?"

My face snaps back to hers. "Did I hurt you?"

She stretches like a cat, and my erection grows to its full length inside of her. She glances left, then right, before wrapping her arms around my neck again.

"Nothing feels hurt. A little sore from lack of use, maybe. But not hurt. I liked this, Hatty. I like the way you make me feel. I like the way you took control, as if your life depended on the outcome of our lovemaking."

She winces at her choice of words, but my heart expands so much I'm afraid it won't fit inside of my chest for much longer.

"I've never," I glance away, unable to shake the shame, "made love like that, Rylan. What if I'd hurt you?"

Soft, delicate hands land on either side of my face. When she turns me to face her, I see a sad understanding in those deep green irises.

"Hatty? You've always needed control. That's why you're the CFO. Numbers and equations have rules. It's why you always felt so out of control when you'd draw. There were no rules to that. You had to run purely on instinct. They are very different sides of the same man, and that's okay. That's what makes you, you. And I …" She trails off, and I find myself desperately needing to hear her words.

"You what?" I whisper as I finally ease my erection out of her.

She bites her bottom lip so hard I know there will be an indentation left when she removes it. Rylan searches my face, and I wonder what she needs from me.

"I've always loved both sides of you, Hatty. Someday, you will, too."

That ball of shame speed rockets up into my throat and rattles around there as emotion overwhelms me.

Lowering my face to the crook of her neck, I inhale deeply as I slide my hands beneath her body and raise her up. She's sticky, and when I pull my hand back, I find that the flour has mixed with our sweat and made a paste of sorts that's all over her.

I yank her naked body into mine, hugging her so tightly my arms shake. "Say it again?"

Turning her face so she can see me, she does as I ask. "I've always loved both sides of you. My entire life, I've been in love with Hatty Westbrook."

Some people would say it's too soon for those words, but to me, they're twenty years in the making, and my eyes glisten with emotion.

"That's not going to happen, Beast. No chance in hell am I—"

The kitchen door snaps open, and I twist my body to shield Rylan.

"Holy shit," Easton's voice calls out.

Rylan tries to shift us. "What are you doing?" I scold. "Easton is not going to see you naked. Hold still."

Glancing over my shoulder, I see East is doing the same dance with Lexi in an attempt to block her from my ass. Rylan spins us, and so does Lexi. Four sets of eyes are wide open in shock as we go around and around, trying to block the other from view.

"Stop. Just stop," East yells.

Turning my head again, I see he has one hand over his eyes and another firmly over Lexi's. She's grinning like a lunatic and attempting to pry his hand away from her face.

"Beast, cut it out. Let me go." A hint of mischief is evident in her tone. If ever there was someone to push every single one of Easton's buttons, Lexi Heart is that girl. Easton closes his eyes tight and uses his free hand to wrap around Lexi's middle, slowly dragging her backward.

"I'm not going to let you get a look at my brother's dick, Locket. No matter how nicely you ask," he growls.

"Aren't you seeing Rylan's tatas? What's the difference?"

"No, I'm not," Easton chides, and I feel the need to weigh in, too.

"No, he's not fucking seeing anything," I bark.

"I don't even know what to say right now, other than get yourselves cleaned the fuck up." Easton's voice is like acid, bursting the bubble we'd found ourselves in. "If the two of you are into some kind of kinky voyeur shit, do it somewhere else. Not GG's goddamn kitchen." He backs up, dragging a laughing Lexi with him.

"Way to go, Rylan!" she calls through the door. "Disinfect everything."

"Oh my God."

Laughter erupts from deep in my chest. It feels foreign, but the harder I try to hold it in, the more it wants to come out until finally I'm doubled over with tears streaming down my face.

"Hatty," Rylan hisses, "this is not funny. This is the second time we've had sex, and the second time we've been caught."

Straightening, I'm suddenly serious. "Third, princess. This is the third time we had sex. Just because I fucked up afterwards doesn't discount the act. It's something that has lived in my head for years. A memory I could never give up, even when it hurt."

She opens her mouth to speak, but I grab a hand towel and tell her to turn around. We can't keep standing here naked. Who knows who will walk through that door next.

Emotions swirl in my chest as I attempt to wipe away the flour that's turned to sludge on her body. I've marked her. On her delicate neck, there is a nip mark, and as I wipe her down, I see more marks.

What the fuck got into me?

Rylan's breathing hitches when I stand in front of her. I like that. I like the reaction I cause every time I'm near. She responds to me in a way that just feels right.

"I don't think you're going to be able to get your shirt on with all that shit on your back."

She glances behind her and winces. I reach for my T-shirt and slip it over her head.

"This should cover you enough," I explain as I pull it down over her body, hating that it covers her and grateful that it does, too. "Why don't you go shower? I'll clean up here, and then we can …"

Can what? Talk? After this, I know I can't give her up. She stopped the panic attack. She truly is my panacea.

"Hatty?"

I glance up to realize I drifted into my own head mid-sentence.

"Are you okay?" Green eyes bore into my blue ones, and I know she can see all my fears. For once, I don't try to hide them.

"Yeah. I'm good. I'll meet you upstairs when I'm done here, okay?"

She nods, seeming uncertain, so I lean in for a tender kiss.

"Are you sure you're okay?" My words turn husky. "I-I didn't hurt you?"

"I may break from time to time, Hatty, but I'm not made of glass."

"The most beautiful stained glass comes from something broken," I whisper. "I'm so sorry if I broke any piece of you, Rylan. I thought I was doing the right thing for you. For Colton. For my family. I thought it was what I had to do."

"Hatty," she lowers her gaze as if she's disappointed, and my gut clenches, "putting everyone else first all the time will ruin you. Sometimes, you have to be a little selfish and go after what you want."

"And if what I want is you?"

She smiles, and the glacier sitting on my heart melts away. "Then all you have to do is stay."

Stay? There isn't anywhere I'd rather be. A goofy smile lights up my whole world, and I set about righting GG's kitchen. Jesus, I hope she never finds out about this. We'll never hear the end of it.

CHAPTER 30

RYLAN

*R*acing up the back stairs, I pray I don't run into anyone. The last thing I need is to explain why I'm wearing Hatty's shirt and covered in flour and sex.

Holy shit. Not just sex. Galaxies could collide and not burn as hot. I have never in my life experienced sex or intimacy like that.

Is that what I've been missing all this time? It's not like I really have a lot of experience to compare it to. I was ruined in college trying to get over the man who shattered my world for the second time in my life. Then I met Matthew, and things just happened.

After unlocking my door, I rush through and immediately turn on the shower. I'm starting to feel like I'm in some sort of plaster cast as the flour gunk hardens. Removing Hatty's T-shirt, I fold it as neatly as I can, then drop it on the bed to return to him later.

I glance around the room like I'm seeing it for the first time, but really, I think I'm living for the first time in years. Hatty does that to me.

Will it last, though?

Negative thoughts enter my head unbidden. I have to

focus on the here and now. Nothing can be done about our past. It's time to look to the future.

Is that what he wants? Are we together? Holy shit, we haven't had any kind of meaningful conversation that wasn't during postcoital bliss. Taking a deep breath, I enter the bathroom. I need to slow this ship down before I'm swept away and lost at sea because I wasn't kidding earlier … I won't survive him leaving me a second time.

I lift my gaze to the mirror and am shocked by what I see. Hatty marked me. My neck, my chest, and my hip bones bear his mark. Warmth spreads through my body, making me realize just how intensely he fucked me.

Stepping into the spray, I let the water cascade over my body, soothing my nerves and bringing me a sense of calm. I do my best thinking in the shower, I always have, and it's here that I decide not to push him. We'll take this day by day, minute by minute, if we have to.

There is no doubt in my mind I'm meant to spend my life with Hatty, but something tells me he still has demons to slay, and I can't do it for him.

When the water runs cold, I shut it off and wrap a towel around my body. I can't help the grin when I see the lightest red mark on my neck.

"You're mine."

Gah, Hatty. I hope you meant it.

I've just stepped into some sleep shorts when there's a knock at my door. *Hatty.* Rushing to open it, I'm greeted by the Westbrook smirk, just not the Westbrook I was expecting.

Colton stands leaning against the door with his arms crossed over his broad chest.

"Hey, jailbait." He slides into the room, and I roll my eyes.

"Very funny, Colty. What's up?"

Colton, my best friend, the eternal Peter Pan, belly flops onto my bed just as another knock comes.

Shit.

Hatty doesn't wait for me to answer. He just waltzes in and heads straight for my mouth. I try to protest, tell him Colton is here, but his mouth descends on mine before I get a chance.

"For fuck's sake, Ryguy. Why does your bed smell like a bakery and ..."

Hatty pulls back and rests his forehead on mine. Annoyance is written across his body, but he says nothing.

There's a loud crash as Colton bolts from the bed. He knocks over a lamp while swiping at his body like a swarm of bees are after him.

"Oh my God. Did I just lay in my brother's jiz?" *Bleh.* He dry heaves dramatically. "I-I ..." *Bleh.* "Did you two just have sex? Jesus, Halton. Look at her neck! Are you out of your mind? Mom is going to kill you."

Colton has lost his mind.

"It's not like we're fifteen anymore, Colt," Hatty growls in response, but smirks at seeing his mark.

Bleh. "Did I or did I not just lay in his jiz?"

I roll my eyes so hard I see stars, and I get no satisfaction from it this time.

"We haven't even had sex on that bed, Colty."

"Yet," Hatty adds in warning.

Colton's entire body shivers like it's the most disgusting thing he's ever heard.

"I don't think I can do this. It's like hearing about your parents having sex. I can't do it. Ryguy, I'll be your man of honor, but I cannot be the one to listen to you gab about sex. With my brother."

Colton is on a roll, and sometimes it's just easier to let him get it out.

"So, you're together. For real now?" he asks pointedly, gaping between my perplexed expression and Halton's exasperated one.

"We haven't had *the talk* if that's what you're asking."

"I mean, is it really necessary? I know I was late to the game, but you've obviously been pining after her for years. So, it's official. Yes?"

Hatty turns to stare at me, the first signs of panic forming behind those sexy, blue eyes, so I reach down and squeeze his hand.

"We've got this," I whisper.

"Okay, so let me think about this for a minute. Ry, you're going to have to meet with the designer and tell them how you want your house."

My head spins to him so fast my ponytail flits across Hatty's chest.

"What are you talking about?"

"On the mountain? You might as well decorate it. Halton has no style, and since it'll be yours, too, you might as well get in on the décor. These houses are going to go up quickly."

"We just fucked, Colt. You have us moving in together already? I haven't even asked her out!"

My eyes close painfully, Hatty's words slicing like barbed wire.

"Fuck. That's … That's not what I meant. Rylan, that's—"

I hold up a hand to keep him from spiraling. "It's fine."

"The hell it is," Colton barks. "Halton, we talked about this. You need to get your shit sorted. If you're doing this," he gestures between Hatty and me, "then you're all in. I won't let you hurt her again."

"I don't plan to," Hatty grinds out.

"Yeah, well, I didn't plan to break my arm in fifth grade either, but I did. You're not going to break her again."

Placing my fingers between my lips, I let out a loud, ear-piercing whistle.

My two favorite Westbrooks slowly turn their stormy gazes my way.

"I'm right here. You're talking about me as if I'm not, and

234

I don't appreciate it. Hatty, Colton's right. We do need to talk about what's going on before anyone gets hurt. Colton, I know you're trying to protect me, but this isn't your fight. You have to let us go at our own pace. Marrying us off tomorrow isn't the path we're on, so you need to back up at least twenty steps."

Both men bow their heads but nod in silent agreement.

"This is going to suck." Colton pouts. "I'm going to be the third wheel now. Will you still let me snuggle during movie nights?"

"You snuggle him during movie nights?" Hatty growls, and I know Colty is going to have a field day riling him up.

"No, I don't snuggle him."

"Will I have to sit on the opposite booth by myself, or can I squeeze in with you guys?"

Hatty raises his head, finally realizing Colton is fucking with him, and they both laugh.

"Listen, Halt. You seriously need to figure this out, okay? Don't ruin a good thing. I'm sorry about how everything went down."

Hatty grabs the back of his neck with a rough squeeze.

"Have you talked to Ash?"

Colton shakes his head. "Dillon said Ash sent him home today. Wouldn't even let him into the trailer to get his laptop. But …"

Hatty and I both raise our gaze in concern at Colton's tone.

"What?" Hatty barks.

"Dillon said he thinks Ash isn't in a good place."

"No shit."

"No, you don't understand. Dillon said as he was leaving, things started crashing. Like, smashing and breaking. He couldn't see anything, but he could hear it. He thinks Ash went ape shit about an hour ago."

"Well, did anyone go check on him?" Hatty sounds

panicked, and I don't blame him. That doesn't sound like Ashton at all.

"I tried. He wouldn't let me in. He told me to go away."

Hatty glances at his watch. "It's late. What was going on when you went up there?"

Colton sighs heavily, and I can tell he's worried. "He had a broom in his hand. Whatever he did, he seems to be cleaning it up now."

"Should you guys go check on him again?" I ask, my eyebrows pinched in worry.

"No," Hatty says without hesitation. "Let's give him the night to get his shit together. We'll all go first thing in the morning."

"What do you think set him off?"

Colton and Hatty share a look. I can't begin to imagine what's been going on with Ash since I haven't been here, but the look they give tells a story that's full of pain.

"For whatever reason, he feels like he has to be the keeper of all our secrets. I think having Dad's secret come out the way it did, and whatever Pacen put on that drive, pushed him over his carefully constructed walls."

"Sounds familiar," I grumble. "You guys love each other like I've never seen with your family first, and welcome to the chaos, but you can't communicate for shit."

And that's what it all boils down to, isn't it? Communication. And it's the one thing we can't seem to master.

ASHTON

CHAPTER 31

I see red. Everywhere I turn. There's no escaping this, and the rage that's been building for months finally explodes. I couldn't get out of the lodge fast enough. Fucking Pacen. Who the hell does she think she is?

This was not her story to tell. How dare she? How fucking dare she? And now she's gone? Just poof, into thin air, and all I have is this goddamn USB.

I stormed out of the lodge with nothing but the USB drive in my hand, and now I sit staring at Pacen on the screen, telling me the secrets I keep will kill me.

I hit pause. I've already watched this video at least five times. She's made her decision. She's going in deep, on her own, and it's my fault. She never would have even gotten involved with SIA if it hadn't been for me.

Naïvely, I thought by bringing her into Envision when I did, I'd be able to save her. But in some ways, I think she was lost before I ever brought her in. Now she's willingly putting her life on the line to save others, and there's nothing I can do about it.

She won't come to work for me. SIA is no more, and because of her, I now have to bring Loki and Seth into this world. They're partners at Envision. They deserve to know the truth. However, once they know, there will be no turning back. I wanted to shield them from this. They have families. Lives to live. And fucking Pacen made the choice for me.

I make the decisions. I keep this family together. Me. Standing, I flip the table and relish the loud crash as the computers hit the floor. Turning in place, I find the next monitor and send it hurtling through the air to crash against the far wall.

The sound of breaking glass and crunching metal is the soundtrack of my life. Damaged.

Screen to screen, room to room, I tear this house down. Tomorrow, I'll rebuild. Tomorrow, we'll be stronger. Tomorrow, I'll get my shit together. But tonight? Tonight, I set the monster I've become free.

CHAPTER 32

"Are you sure you don't want me to check on him first?" I ask my mother, but my nervous gaze finds Sadie tucked into her car seat in the back. "Colton said it was pretty, ah, loud at Ash's when he was there last night."

Sadie squeals in delight, clapping her hands and wiggling as much as her harness will allow. Seth's little girl is truly a ray of sunshine and seems to be the only one Ashton is incapable of pushing away.

"Yes, I'm sure. We've made a lot of mistakes in this family, Halt. I'm not too proud to admit that. Your father ..." She sighs and stares out the window. "He always meant well, Halton, but he could be a stubborn mule when he got something stuck in his head."

"There's something Ash isn't telling us about Dad and SIA, isn't there?"

"I'm beginning to think so. I knew the basics. After Easton was born, your dad and I decided it was best if I only knew of Envision, not the details. I'm worried whatever your father started, Ash has carried that burden since he was a child. That means I failed him." Her voice wavers, and for the first time in years, Sylvie Westbrook isn't in control.

"Mom," I say gently, "that's not true. You have to know that. Whatever he took on, he should have told us. All of us. You couldn't have known. Whatever secret he's keeping, he's doing it because he thinks he has to protect us. We should have always been a team, and he didn't give us that option."

"Sounds very familiar, doesn't it? Keeping secrets to protect this family? You've all done it. You're all so much like your father in different ways. I swear it's like he's still here," she says sadly.

A humorless laugh escapes, even though I try to rein it in. "I'm nothing like Dad. I've never fit in, you know that. Preston and Colt have his outgoing, sometimes outlandish personality. Easton has his temper and his drive, and Ash? God, Mom. Ash is so much like Dad it's scary. Or, at least he used to be …" I break off from my train of thought. I shouldn't be dumping all my worries on her right now.

We pull up to the construction site where Ashton's home is being built. He's the farthest up the mountain, so his was the first to break ground, hoping to get it done before the first frost. With the number of crews we have working, though, they'll finish all the homes before winter falls.

"Halton Westbrook." I can tell by her voice I'm about to be reprimanded. "How could you say that? You are all your father's sons. You may not like the same things your brothers do, but that's what makes you, you. No one ever expected you all to be carbon copies of each other. I would be sad if you hadn't all found your own way."

I'm about to argue when the door to the trailer Ash is staying in swings open, and he drags out a thirty-gallon barrel.

What the hell is he doing?

I put the SUV into park just as Sadie spies Ashton on the steps.

"Uncle Ash! Uncle Ash! Oh, he's goin' be so 'cited, Nanna Sylvie. So 'cited to see me," she squeals.

Jesus, I hope she's right.

I take one last peek at her in the mirror. If ever there was a ray of sunshine in human form, it would be Sadie Foster. Stepping out of the car, I head toward Ash while Sylvie goes to the back to unbuckle Sadie Sunshine.

"What the hell happened here?"

Ash ignores me and walks to the side of the trailer, where my jaw drops. He has the door of a dumpster open, and he walks the barrel inside and dumps it. Glancing around in shock, I realize he's dumping computer screens, a TV, and a chair that's been shredded.

"Is this all the shit from inside of your trailer?"

"I had some stuff to work out," he grumbles just as Sadie Sunshine comes barreling around the corner.

As if he's expecting her, he lowers himself to catch her just as she propels her little body into his arms.

He stands with her on his hip, and she places two tiny hands on either side of his face and squeezes his cheeks together, so his lips pucker out. I see a hint of pain flash in his eyes, but he doesn't tell her to stop. Instead, he stands and allows her to scrutinize his face up close and personal.

"Hi, Uncle Ash. Miss me?"

Ash nods his head, and she grins, twisting in his arms to call over her shoulder. "See, Nanna Sylvie? I told ya. He's so 'cited to see me."

Her pudgy, little face turns back around, blonde curls bouncing with the movement. "Your booboos is looking so much better, Uncle Ash."

He flinches as she leans in and places a big, messy kid kiss on his cheek. Right over his scar. "Feels better?"

"Yeah, Sadie Sunshine. Feels better," he whispers as my mom comes up beside me with tears in her eyes.

I'm suddenly very understanding of her insistence on bringing the beautiful, little girl. All Ash can see through his pain is darkness and evil. Sadie is the antithesis of both.

She clears her throat, and I know Sylvie Westbrook is about to lay down the law. I can feel it in my bones. I feel like I'm twelve years old again, and we're about to have our asses handed to us.

"Ashton, Sadie is your new Friday night date. Indefinitely."

Ashton raises his head and blinks a few times, like he is unsure of what he just heard. I cross my arms and try not to smirk. My mother has never gone for subtle.

"Seth and Ari are in a good place, but they need some alone time as well to explore their relationship further. So, as long as you're planning to stay in Vermont, I volunteered you to pick up Miss Sadie Sunshine every Friday at six p.m. and drop her off back at home at ten a.m. on Saturday mornings."

She brushes her hands together like that's final and turns on her heel.

I can see Ashton's mouth moving, but no words come out.

"Isn't that so fun, Uncle Ash? I loves sleepovers. Do you have a bed for me here? I have a sleepin' bag with all my favorite princesses on it if you don't."

Ash's eyes go wide as he realizes our mother is about to enter the trailer. After what I just saw, I have a feeling there is nothing left inside. With a pointed stare at Ash, I jog to catch up with my mom.

"You know, it might be better if Ash stays at the lodge with Sadie for now. His trailer isn't really set up for kids."

He's caught up to us now, still carrying Sadie. That kid is like a koala bear. I don't think he could put her down if he tried.

"I-I don't know how to b-babysit," he stutters.

"I isn't a baby, Uncle Ash. I'll help ya." Happiness radiates off Sadie like lightning.

He glances back and forth between Sadie and our mom. He knows he can't say no, so he sets his jaw. But I see the

242

subtle nod of his head. A silent thank you for not allowing our mother to witness his meltdown.

"Good. Now that that's settled ... Sadie, dear, why don't you hop down and start collecting the rocks you need for your pets?"

Ash and I watch on, thoroughly confused.

"We're gonna make a pet garden, Uncle Ash. I gots paints and everything." She wiggles out of his arms, and he lowers her to the ground.

"Don't go near the dumpster, and stay on this side of the trailer. There might be nails and stuff over by the construction site," he says softly.

I raise my brow. "And you don't know how to babysit?"

"I don't want her to get hurt," he grumbles softly. His voice is still weak but not quite as raspy today. I hope that's a good sign.

Sadie grabs a basket I hadn't noticed my mother holding and runs to the dirt pile to start digging. It's funny to see all the pink tulle of her dress bouncing around in the dirt.

"Now," my mother says in a tone that has my hackles rising, "we need to talk."

Ash and I exchange a glance that says 'oh shit.'

"Ashton. What have you done?" she asks without preamble.

"What I needed to."

I bite my tongue, but I know that answer isn't going to fly.

"You're not your father, Ash. This doesn't have to be your fight. It should never have been your fight. Envision was supposed to go to Ryan, and everything else dismantled if anything ever happened to your father. I may not have known the details of his day-to-day, but I do know there was a plan in place should anything ever happen to him."

"There was."

Staring at my baby brother, I realize it's like I don't even know him. How many secrets can he possibly keep? My mother must realize Ash has no intention of expanding on his answer because she tries another tactic.

"What could Pacen have given you that sent you into such a tailspin?" She nods toward the dumpster. I should have known better. Nothing gets past my mother.

"Everything I need to bring her father down. Proof of all his crimes, corruption, everything from when he first contacted Dad to when he tried to steal GG's mountain. She found proof of it all and gave it to me."

"No shit," I grumble. "So, you can stop him?"

Ashton's jaw tightens. "Eventually. I can cut off his attempts at the mountain by bringing in Fontaine, the town accountant, but I need to follow Macomb for a while. I need more information on …" He breaks off on a cough. "I will take him down. Just not yet."

Our mother stands between us, and I don't dare say a word.

"Ashton, you know Daddy's death was not your fault," she says with an air of authority he doesn't question. "You also need to know that you are not responsible for keeping this family safe. You are not our protector. Whatever secrets you're keeping from us, and I have a feeling there are many, they aren't yours to carry."

She turns to me, and my neck gets hot.

"Honestly, how could you have both blamed yourselves for Daddy's death for all these years, and I never knew? Am I that blind to your needs?" A single tear falls from her left eye. Ash and I both step forward on instinct.

"No. That's not it at all," we both promise.

"He was just like you both. You know that, right? He never kept a secret in our marriage. I wouldn't have allowed it. But his work was another story. If he thought he had to protect us, he would do whatever he needed to. Even if it hurt him in the process. Please don't hurt yourselves on our behalf. Let us in. Let us help."

My throat is uncomfortably tight, and I have to work multiple times to swallow.

"Your dad thought he was Bruce Wayne sometimes, but he was never Batman. Remember that, Ash."

Ash and I stare at her like she has three heads, but where I'm thoroughly confused, Ash seems taken aback. When he nods, I realize there is so much more to Envision than he's letting on. I also realize until he's ready to talk, he'll be a brick fucking wall.

"Now, Halton."

My spine stiffens as she turns her motherly glare my way.

"You have been in love with Rylan Maroney since she was six years old. Are you telling me that you hurt that girl on purpose because of something Daddy said?"

I narrow my eyes at Ash, but he shrugs. One of my brothers ratted me out.

"I don't know what the two of you talked about that day, but let me tell you what he and I would talk about late at night. It started when you were around eleven. The two of you spent so much time together, and you thought no one noticed, but we did. We whispered to each other about how cute you were and dreamed about what you'd be like as you got older.

"As you grew, so did your relationship. It was a love we recognized. Your father worried about Colton's feelings, but he knew it was a different kind of love for you. Our only concern back then was that the flame that burned between you and Rylan would grow so hot that you'd fizzle out before you grew into the adults you needed to be to appreciate what you had. But never once did he think you weren't good enough for her. Never once did we doubt that she was your soul mate.

"So, the dark hole you've dug yourself over the last few

years needs to be buried again. Find yourself, Halton. Find the amazing, talented, caring man I know you to be. Then fix this shit and get your girl."

Ashton and I both sputter, and I swear he chuckles. Sylvie Westbrook does not say the word shit. Ever.

But it's another person I love telling me to fix my shit. They make it sound so easy, and yet not a single one has mentioned how I should go about doing it.

"Now that I've said my piece, let's get you guys back to the lodge. Sadie Sunshine has a big night planned for you, Ashton, and it begins at The Marinated Mushroom for pizza."

He freezes, and his hands ball into fists.

"I know this is hard for you, Ash. But if you think I'm going to just sit by and watch you become a bitter, old hermit, you haven't been paying attention. One night a week, Ash. For me. I know you want to climb into that dark hole Halton is trying to get out of, but I'll be damned if I don't pour some sunshine on the both of you every chance I get. I failed as your mother where Daddy was concerned. I won't do it again."

Ash and I try to dispute her claim, but she's not having any of it. She's made up her mind, and now she's made it her mission to bring us both back from the dark.

As Sadie Sunshine comes barreling into Ashton's open arms, I can see her plan working its way into the recesses of his heart. But I'm still floundering out at sea, unsure of how to bring my ship home.

CHAPTER 33

*H*ome.

Such a strange word to think of the second you wake up, but that's what I feel as my body gains consciousness.

I'm calm, is the second thing I notice before I even open my eyes, and when I do, eyes the color of rolling hills in Ireland stare up at me. A smile breaks, and I don't try to tame it.

Rylan lays with her hands clasped under her chin on my chest. Staring at me.

"Are you watching me sleep?"

"We can't have you being the only stalker in this rela … in our friendship."

"We've been sleeping in the same bed for over three weeks now. I think it's okay to call this a relationship," I tell her, even as warning bells go off behind my eyes.

We haven't had *the talk*. It either hasn't come up, or we're both avoiding it, but as she stares at me like this, I have to wonder why I'm so hesitant to put a name to it.

She nods slowly while biting her lip. She focuses her attention on a spot next to me, so I take a minute to watch her closely. Worrying her lip is new. I've always known when something was bothering her, but as she chews on her bottom lip that I want so badly to kiss, I glance away.

Maybe she isn't ready to put a name to us either? I'm still fearful I'll hurt her again, even unintentionally. Could she have the same concerns?

Deciding to gloss over this conversation for now, I go back to her original statement. "I never stalked you, sweetheart."

"You lied when you told me you didn't have Instagram." Her voice is quiet and shaky. I've told so many lies at this point I can't keep track, but even the asshole I am, I know if I want anything with her, I can't do it anymore. I can't lie to her face knowing the pain I've already caused.

"It wasn't necessarily a lie," I begin, and she furrows her brow, then attempts to pull away.

Grasping her upper arms, I pull her closer and hold her to me. "Halton doesn't have Instagram, or Facebook, TikTok, Twitter, Discord, or any of the other ones either."

"But you said, in the ocean. On Block Island, you said—"

"I don't have social media, but Hatty's Heart does." My voice cracks with shame.

A loud sigh escapes her, and her brow creases in concentration. That damn lip is between her teeth. I'm fucking this all up. Again.

"It isn't like I checked it all the time. Only when I was weak. The times late at night when I would miss you so much, I couldn't breathe. Then, and only then, would I allow myself a glimpse into your life. Well, at least until the car thing," I admit. "I was a fucking wreck worried you would get kidnapped, or worse, taking those godforsaken buses through the worst parts of London. I was a goddamn maniac checking every twenty minutes, praying you'd give some mundane update so at least I'd know you were alive."

I tilt my head toward the ceiling. I hadn't intended on spilling all that.

"We haven't really … I mean, I don't know what you—"

We're interrupted by something that sounds like a cross between a bullhorn and a fisher cat, and we both sit up quickly. The sheet falls to her lap, and I'm momentarily distracted by the pebbling of her perfectly pink nipples.

"Do they have tornado warnings here?" she asks, while scrambling to her feet.

"Shit." Do they? I have no idea. "That is what it sounded like ri—"

"This is your warning call." Colton's distorted voice rings loudly through the door. "I'm coming in. I don't want to see any nips, bits, wrappers, or any other freaky thing you've got going on in there."

"I'm going to kill him," I growl.

"Hurry up and get dressed. You know what he's like. He isn't kidding. He's coming in …"

"Countdown begins now. Twenty. Nineteen …"

"He's insane."

"He's taking advantage of the fact that there are no paying guests at the lodge right now."

I'm slipping a shirt over my head when Rylan starts bouncing into her denim shorts to pull them over her perfectly round ass. Commando.

"Fucking hell, sweetheart. There are maybe two inches from your pussy to the bottom of those shorts. I'm going to be trying to get my fingers in there all day if you don't put on some panties."

"Five. Four …"

"There's no time," she screeches. Diving into the bathroom, she slams the door just as Colton starts banging on the outside one.

I've only managed a T-shirt and boxer briefs. He'll have to deal.

249

Yanking the door open, I cross my arms over my chest. Then my scowl deepens when Colt, East, Preston, Seth, and Dillon all brush past me as they walk through the door.

"What the hell are you doing in here?" I try to control my temper, really, I do, but being interrupted by my brothers when a girl … no, not just a girl, *the* girl is naked on top of me, pisses me off.

The bathroom door swings open, and Rylan squeaks as she takes in the overcrowded room.

"Ryguy!" Colton quips happily.

I can't contain the growl low in my throat when he wraps her in a hug that lifts her off her feet.

"Easy there, killer. She is his BFF, remember?" East whispers beside me.

Shaking my head at the ground, I rake a hand through my hair until I can tug at the bunched muscles in my neck.

"What are you guys doing here?" I ask again. This time with more self control.

"We needed to talk to you," Preston discloses.

I narrow my eyes as I glance around. "You all look guilty."

Everyone's gaze moves anywhere but on me. Except for Colton. That asshole just stands there and smiles.

"You have a girls' day, Ryguy. Lexi is waiting for you downstairs. She said she didn't need to be part of the ambush."

"We said that, too. You wouldn't listen," East mumbles.

"Out you go."

I scan the room, and notice Colton is the only one moving. He's ushering Rylan out of the room like her ass is on fire. She's pushed out the door a second later. Colton kisses her on the cheek, which causes a low rumble in my throat, but not a full-on growl, then he slams the door. In her confused face.

"What the hell, Colty?" she yelps through the door.

As soon as it's shut, every eye in the place turns its gaze on me.

"Wh-What's going on?" I'm suddenly fucking nervous. It feels like I'm about to be initiated into some secret society, and I'm not sure I want to be a member.

"Well, we could have done without Colton's theatrics." Preston pauses to gape at our younger brother, who just cannonballed into my bed.

"I had sex in that spot not ten minutes ago," I say to be a dick.

Colton's face turns green as he jumps out of the bed, shivering and brushing himself off.

"That's worse than planting your naked ass on my pillow when we were kids." Loki laughs.

Smirking, I shrug. I'd forgotten about that. We'd had a massive sleepover, all of us boys, plus the adopted brothers—Loki, Dillon, Trevor, and Dexter, too. One of us had read that if you farted on someone's pillow, it gave you pink eye, so we all snuck around sticking our asses on pillows all night long. It's really fucking gross to think about it now.

"What do you expect when you have a full basketball team of boys in one room?"

"I hope I have girls," Preston grumbles, and we all turn to stare at him.

"Are you? Is Emory?"

He shakes his head. "It's complicated."

After everything he's been through, I never stopped to think about the implications of what his situation could mean for him and his family long term.

Jesus. I'm an asshole. I've been wallowing in self pity, and my brothers have real world shit going on.

"Preston, I'm—"

He holds up a hand to stop me. "It's okay. We're just, we're not ready to talk about options yet. Or maybe at all." He shakes his head like he's clearing a memory, then continues, "Anyway, we're here about you."

"Me?" My eyebrows shoot to my hairline. "Did I miss a board meeting or something?"

"No," Easton interrupts. "But we're afraid if you don't get your head out of your ass, you're going to fuck this all up. Again."

"Dexter wanted to be here, but he's knee deep in diapers, and Lanie isn't feeling well, so we'll do the best we can," Preston announces.

My heart rate is accelerating with each passing word. Dexter is known as our real-life Prince Charming. He's really big into grand gestures to get the girl, and he's helped more than one of these guys succeed in a happily ever after. But for me? I'm not even sure if I can keep Rylan through next week. Forget about forever.

Instead of telling them the truth and voicing my concerns, I reach into the mini fridge and pull out a bottle of water. "It's too damn early for an intervention."

"Halt. You've been back here with Rylan for what? Almost three weeks?"

"Twenty-three days," I blurt like an asshole.

I've been spending my days holed up in an office downstairs, putting out fires as the CFO and spending my nights igniting them in this room with Rylan. Of course I know exactly how many fucking days she's been mine.

Every Westbrook in the room, both by blood and by choice, turns the same exact smirk on me.

Shit.

"You've got it bad," Seth announces. "I cannot believe GG is going to be right again."

I stare down to where my heart is. I was sure everyone in here could see it attempting its escape out of my chest, but all I see is the rapid rise and fall of each shallow breath.

At some point in the last few weeks, I'd taken to singing,

"Hello, panic, my old friend," in my head to the tune of Simon & Garfunkel's song, "The Sound of Silence," anytime my heart began to race. But when everyone gapes at me, I realize I mumbled it out loud.

"Listen, I know that was fucking weird, okay? Rylan has been doing all this meditation crap around me, so when my —" I clamp my mouth closed with an audible snap.

"When your what?" Colton asks with more sympathy than I'm used to from him.

"Nothing. It's nothing, okay? I just woke up and haven't had any coffee yet. Leave it alone. Please."

I don't have the courage to make eye contact with anyone, so instead I stare at my bare feet and count to ten. In my peripheral vision, I can see heads shaking and nodding. All my brothers attempt to have a silent conversation over my head while I pout like a little boy.

Grow up, Halton.

Lifting my gaze, I find Easton across the room, studying my face. He's wearing an expression of understanding, and I'm thankful when he speaks up.

"Listen, aren't we here to talk about him getting the girl?" Easton's voice is gruff, but he's softened since being here in Vermont.

I hadn't noticed before, but his shoulders aren't hunched around his ears anymore. The thick, bulging veins in his neck have receded, and he's no longer in permanent Hulk territory.

I've been here for weeks. How am I just now noticing this? Suddenly, I'm frantic to see what else I've missed, and I go face to face, scrutinizing every line, every smile. Have I been so wrapped up in my woe-is-me bullshit that I didn't notice these major life changes in my brothers?

Easton crosses the room and lays a heavy hand on my shoulder. While everyone else discusses my dating habits, Easton speaks low, so only I can hear.

"It just hits you sometimes, right?"

"What?" I could barely get the word out.

"Everything you've missed while buried in a cloud of grief."

My gaze snaps to his, and again, understanding passes between us. We've always been the grumpy assholes of the family. Well, at least for the last few years, anyway. Regarding him now, I see all the subtle changes in him. His relaxed posture. His softened tone. Even the way he looks at someone has softened.

"Happiness looks good on you, East."

He nods sagely before piercing me with honesty. "It would look really good on you, too, you know. You just have to want it badly enough." He allows a few seconds to pass, then glances around the room as the rest of our brothers bicker about the best first date options.

"Are they talking about me?" I ask, horrified.

"Yup. It's probably best just to let them work it out. It makes them feel like they're helping, even if you and I both know the only one who can make a change is you. Come on, I want to show you something."

He nods toward the door, and I almost laugh. When I peek back at the group, I realize they're so deep into planning, they'll have no idea I'm gone until it's too late.

"What are you waiting for?" I whisper yell. "Get me out of here."

CHAPTER 34

HALTON

"You know, I've spent years hiding my pain because I thought it was better than dumping my shit on all of you. Losing Dad, and trying to navigate life, I'd like to think I was protecting you all, but after everything exploded with Lexi, I'm starting to realize that I was protecting myself more than anything."

Easton went through the wringer with an ex-girlfriend and a giant misunderstanding between him and his best friend. We both had reasons to be assholes, but he hasn't spent years blaming himself for our father's death.

I grunt in response as he pulls back the bay doors of GG's old barn. Stepping inside, I'm surprised to see its condition.

"Who works in here?" I ask, taking in the craftsmanship of projects in various stages of completion.

"I do."

My gaze shifts to East as he rounds a workbench covered in scraps of paper, rulers, pencils, and wood samples in every shade and texture.

He glances down at something, and then back at me. "How long have you had the panic attacks?"

I would have felt it less if he'd punched me in the chest.

His words hit me like a thousand-pound dumbbell, and I can't control my feet as they stagger back.

Shame washes over me, and I glance away. We're mother-fucking Westbrooks. Alpha in all that we do. Win at everything we attempt. We don't have these weaknesses.

"It's not like that," I lie.

Easton pulls out a stool and sits at his workstation, but I can feel his penetrating gaze on me.

"You can't bullshit a bull shitter, Halt. I may not have recognized the signs at the time because I was distracted, but at the Billionaire Auction, you were seconds away from blacking out."

My feet propel me toward the back wall where he has two sawhorses set up and an old beam lying across the top. I run my hand along the rough wood and notice the splinters, cracks, and fractures that show its age. It looks like I feel most of the time.

"You know, we haven't really talked about what happened with Dad. Or the fact that you've felt responsible this whole time. I can't imagine how it was to live like that. Or, to suddenly find out it wasn't actually your fault."

"I knew after he died, and we had the genetic testing done, that it wasn't my fault."

"And yet, you still blamed yourself."

"I fought with him, East. Yelled, actually. I got in his face. If I'd stayed to listen …" I shrug my shoulders and turn to him.

"If you'd stayed to listen, you probably would have heard him tell you what we all know to be true. Rylan is your missing piece, and Colton's best friend. It's a relationship you need to navigate delicately because of how tightly she's already woven into our lives."

I grunt, feeling the collar of my shirt becoming smaller.

"Mom said something the other day about you never feeling like you fit in. Is that true?"

"Jesus, Easton. I'm fine. I'm not a ten year old that needs to play with the cool kids."

I move around the room, stopping short when I see a sketch attached to a long piece of wood. Stepping closer, I take in the details. I can't tear my eyes away as I follow the intricate lines. Scanning the piece of wood, I can see it take shape. A heavy, wooden chair with delicate detailing along the arms and backrest. I'm mesmerized by how clearly I can see his vision, and I have to shake my head when I realize Easton is speaking again.

"Is that how you see the rest of us? The cool kids?"

"For fuck's sake, East. When did you turn into Dear Abby?"

"I'm just trying to understand why you don't feel like you fit in. If you were an ugly fucker, maybe I'd get it."

He's so ridiculous, I have to turn to face him. His shit-eating grin covers his entire face.

"But, since you look like the rest of us, I know that's not it. I've spent all morning thinking about you."

"Seems like a waste of time now, doesn't it?"

"No, actually. And when I mentioned it to Lexi, she told me something I couldn't believe. Something about an art show you never made it to."

"Fucking gossips," I grumble.

"Rylan told her how your friendship grew and evolved through art. Your charcoals and her photographs. Lexi said the sample Rylan showed her was so detailed, it took her a few minutes to realize she wasn't looking at a black and white photograph. How come we never knew, Halt? Why didn't you ever show us? You have to know we would have supported you?"

"You're not going to let this go, are you?"

"Not a chance. The numbskulls up there want to make sure you don't ruin your relationship with Rylan because of your inability to open up. I want to make sure you don't ruin yourself first. You can't love Rylan completely until you love yourself."

"Did you get a subscription for self-help books or something?" I mean it as a joke, but he only gives a small smirk.

"No. But I have been going to therapy with Lexi. It helps. When I heard your little song about panic being an old friend, I recognized something the therapist had said to me. Singing that song, either in your head or out loud, you're taking control of it. Did you know that? Does it help you calm down?"

Does it? Thinking back, I realize repeating it does slow my heart rate.

Pinching the back of my neck, I peer up at him. "Yeah. I guess it does."

"Panic makes you feel out of control. Your heart rate, your breathing, your physical awareness all become something you fight for. By acknowledging it, with that song or by counting, or whatever the fuck works, you're taking the power back. It's a coping mechanism, Halt. And a good one if it works."

Easton slides his phone over, and I see a family photo taken at a fundraiser gala last Christmas. I'm in the back, slightly behind Ash.

"Scroll through them," he orders.

Picking up his phone, I do as he asks. Each photo a similar version of the first.

"It's like you're hiding in plain sight in each one?" It isn't an accusation. It's more of a question. He's trying to understand something I've been attempting to figure out my entire life. "Social situations like this cause your attacks."

I nod but keep my eyes on the screen. To the outside world, we're the picture of perfection, from our straight, white teeth to crystal clear blue eyes and hulking forms. We have more money than we could ever spend, and here I am, incapable of enjoying it.

"So, I would imagine having brothers like Preston and Colton that thrive in the spotlight makes you feel like an outsider. But what about Ash and me? Why wouldn't you have come to us? I've been a grumpy asshat, sure, but I would have understood. And Ashton? Jesus, he has always been awkward. The most gentle for sure, but awkward just the same."

He smirks, but we both know we have work to do with Ash.

Leaning forward, I rest my elbows on the table in front of me. My head falls into my hands, and I involuntarily tug on the strands.

"I have nothing to complain about, East. We were born with more privilege than most will experience in a lifetime."

"What does that have to do with how you feel?"

"I have no right to be like this. I have every opportunity. I …" I break off because I don't know what I want to say.

"Halt, you know that panic and anxiety are medical conditions. It isn't something you choose."

"No shit. Do you think I'd choose to feel like a loser? Do you think I'd choose to feel like an outsider with my own family because I like different things? I know it doesn't make any sense. I know it's not rational. I-I just can't control it." My voice rises with each word until I finish and I realize I'm full-blown yelling.

"You aren't different, Halton. At least no different from the rest of us. Yes, Preston and Colt are a different breed for sure, but they have issues they have to deal with, too."

Guilt racks my body, thinking about everything Preston put himself through in the name of protecting us.

"I also guarantee that you're more alike to all of us than you give yourself credit for. Why do you think you're so different? Because you like art and math? Because you hate social situations? Because you'd rather be anywhere than put on display? What? Tell me?"

I hate that he has summarized my existence and can make it sound like no big deal.

"Halt. If we had known, we could have protected you. Preston and Colt? They love the spotlight. There was never any need for you to be in it. We would have helped you. We would have supported any dream you had, no matter where that put you within The Westbrook Group. You understand that, right?"

"It makes me sound weak, Easton." My tone is biting, but he sits patiently, waiting for me to continue. "After Dad died, we couldn't afford a weak link. Not when the entire world was waiting to see The Westbrook Group fail. Everyone expects us to be like … to be like you and Preston. In control. Aggressive when necessary. Larger than life. If people knew I was trembling every single time I had to open my mouth, what would that have done to our reputation? What would you guys have said? Do you really think you could have understood this when you were twenty years old?"

"Yes," he bellows. "Yes, I would have understood even back then, Halt. Maybe even more so because of what I was feeling at the time. As for what the world expects, fuck you. Since when have we, as a family, ever cared what the world thought of us? But I'll tell you what we would have thought. We would have thought, we do think, you're human. You're not a robot. You're not a clone of any of us. You're our brother who is struggling to grasp the concept that we love you for who you are, not what you do. If you were weak, you wouldn't have made it through all those events," he says, nodding toward the phone still in my hand. "If you were weak, you wouldn't have been able to stay away from Rylan. You're not weak, Halton. You're probably stronger than any of us, but you don't give yourself the same grace you give us."

Easton stands, dragging large sheets of paper across the table, and turns them to face me.

"You draw people. I draw furniture. You keep journals

like Preston and Dad. You love with your whole heart, like Colton, and you have a stubborn streak like us all. A gentle soul and need to protect as big as Ashton's. You fit in this family just the way you are, Halton. You always have. Your problems are hard to fix because you're always fighting yourself."

We sit in silence. My heavy, erratic breathing is the only sound.

"I know you love Rylan, even if you haven't admitted it to yourself yet. But I'm telling you, if you don't get a handle on yourself, you're going to lose her. It's okay to have missing links in your armor, Halton. You just have to know how to let us in, so we can hold those links together. That's what family does. We're stronger together than we'll ever be on our own. Stop pushing those that love you away. You have to get a handle on this shit before it ruins you."

"Fix your shit," I mumble the words everyone seems to be saying to me lately.

"Yeah, fix your shit ... before you're buried in it."

Easton stands and claps me on the back. "I have to go find GG. She's talking about getting some cocks for the lodge. I need to make sure she's talking about the rooster variety because you never fucking know with her."

Laughter rings out in the heavy moment.

"You can always count on GG to lighten the mood," I acknowledge.

"That's for sure. Think about what I said. It also might not be a bad idea to talk to someone about this. Someone with experience that can teach you other coping skills. Seeking help for a hurt that no one else can see isn't weak, Halt. It takes strength and bravery that some men will never have. Remember that the next time you feel ashamed of something you didn't ask for. There are ways of handling this, but you have to take the first step. It takes more courage to fight for your mental health than it does to fight for a broken bone. People are quick to brush aside a disease when they can't see it, but we won't ever be those people. We're your people, Halt, and we'll always have your back. Remember that."

He leaves before I can say anything else, and I sit in the empty barn surrounded by Easton's art, his words swirling around my head until I feel dizzy.

I have to be the change, to make a change. And that's my scariest fucking thought yet.

CHAPTER 35

*R*ylan: Is everything all set?

Ari: Yup. You're good to go! I set it up myself. You should have everything you need.

Lexi: Should I warn the sheriff there may be some kink to watch out for tonight? Our jail isn't as nice as on Block Island, but ...

She's so freaking ridiculous. Neither she nor Colton will let us live down the sexcapades, as Colton now refers to them.

Rylan: We are keeping the sexcapades confined to four walls with a locking door these days.

Rylan: No need to warn the sheriff.

Lexi: Too bad. Good luck.

Ari: I can't wait to see what he does!

Me too, Ari. Me too.

In the weeks since we returned from Block Island, we've settled into a routine of sorts. It feels strange because we're all in limbo helping GG here in Vermont. Hatty spends his days doing whatever the CFO of The Westbrook Group does, taking breaks to run numbers for Easton when he needs help with something they're doing to rejuvenate the area.

I'm proud of this family in an unexpected way. They've dropped everything to be in this tiny town for someone they love, and in the process, they fell in love with the town and are doing everything in their power to give it some much needed Westbrook TLC.

Things have been relatively normal after the initial freak out about Pacen, Mr. Westbrook, and all the secrets we may never know about. Well, except that Ash won't leave his trailer. Everyone is worried sick about him, but he insists he just needs time to work through some things. The only exception is Friday nights when he picks up little Sadie for whatever date she has planned for him.

It is quite possibly the cutest thing I've ever seen.

Hatty and I spend every night together, but we still haven't put a label to us, and I can't decide if I'm upset by that or not. Everyone just assumes we're together. Hell, I think that most days, too. But the longer we're here, in this bubble without having the talk, the more a thread of doubt tries to creep in.

"You ready?" Hatty asks, exiting the bathroom freshly showered. He hasn't stayed in his room since we got back, and as worried as I am about our future, it just feels right.

"Yup." I can't contain my grin if I tried.

"Should I be nervous? You look like you're up to something." He leans against the door and crosses his arms over his broad chest. A chest I was trapped under not too long ago.

My cheeks flush at the memory.

"I'd love to know what just ran through that dirty little head of yours," he teases.

"No way. We will never get out of here, and I have a special date planned for us."

His body language stiffens, and he opens his mouth, but

no words come out, so he clamps it shut again. Eventually, he puffs out the breath he was holding and shakes his head.

"I suck. I'm sorry, sweetheart. I … they told me I need to plan an epic first date, but everything they came up with just felt … wrong."

"They?"

"The merry fucking happily ever after crew. Formally known as my brothers." He grumbles the words, but I sense a smile behind them.

"They told you to plan an epic first date, huh?"

He nods, and I love the light shade of pink that covers his cheeks.

"Do they know we're kind of past first date territory? I mean, you've been inside of me like, a lot."

A rumble happens in his chest, and when I glance up, fire has replaced his earlier embarrassment.

"Oh, no. No way, big guy. Come on. If we don't get out of this room now, we'll miss our chance."

He pounces, and I'm up against the wall before I can blink.

"We may not have an epic first date, but I can think of a lot of firsts we can still do." His hands find purchase on my ass, and I'm lifted against his body a second later.

I'm breathless, and he hasn't even kissed me yet. My phone buzzes in my hand, reminding me we have some place to be.

"Raincheck on the sexy firsts, okay? We have to get going."

Hatty growls but slides me down his body. There is no missing his erection straining against his zipper.

"Oh, geez."

A devilish grin quirks one side of his mouth.

"Later. Save that for later," I whisper as I wiggle out of his grasp.

"Trust me. It isn't going anywhere if you're within reach."

His words are low and sullen. My insides do the cha-cha, just listening to him.

"Come on. I'll make it up to you later."

"I'll hold you to it," he promises as he follows me out the door.

～

*H*atty stands in front of the canvas with his hands on his hips and a scowl on his face.

Maybe this wasn't such a good idea after all.

"So, you know, as part of Easton's revitalization plan, he's helping Ari turn this place into a rec center for the town. Mainly, it focuses on the arts because they cut most of the programs around here due to lack of funding. She painted the mural in here." He doesn't even peek at the walls, so I continue, "She's really talented, actually. Anyway, she started getting all her supplies in, and since it isn't open to the public yet, she said we could use it tonight. I-I brought a picnic and my camera, and she said she was going to buy the charcoal anyway, so I had her get the kind you used to use. I wasn't sure if you kept the tin I gave you on Block Island. You've just, I just, I see the way you look at things, Hatty. I know you miss this part of your life, and I don't know why you won't allow yourself to have it. After everything we've learned and are getting past, I-I want you to be happy. I think this will make you happy."

"I am happy, sweetheart," he says softly. "I'm happy with you. You're all I need."

His hands ball into fists, then he shakes them out, and it starts all over again. It's like his hands literally itch to touch the canvas, but he's restraining himself, and I have no idea why.

"I'm happy, too, Hatty. But I don't feel like you're whole.

266

It's like you're holding back from life and from me. I thought maybe this would help."

My shoulders slump, and now what I thought was a great idea suddenly makes me extremely uncomfortable. Perhaps I read him all wrong. Maybe I don't know him as well as I thought I did.

"I'm not trying to hold anything back from you, Rylan. I don't want to ruin us again."

"Are we? An us, I mean?" The insecurity in my voice makes me cringe.

His gaze that hasn't left the canvas flies to mine, and he's on me a second later.

"Yes, Rylan. We're an us. Maybe we haven't put a name to it, but make no mistake, you're mine."

He shakes his head like his possessive words startled him.

"I like when you get like this," I admit.

He rests his forehead on mine and cradles my cheeks in his hands. "Like what, sweetheart?"

"When you talk as if you own me," I admit, and hate the heat that creeps down my neck.

"Some people would probably say it's unhealthy how strongly I feel for you. It's not that I own you, but I can't look at you without a baser instinct screaming *she's mine.*"

"I feel it, too, you know. That primal need? That urgency to be with you? It scares me sometimes."

He pulls back but doesn't let go of my face. "What scares you?"

It's now or never, Rylan. Is it too soon? *Yes.* Am I going to scare him away? *Probably.* Can I stop the words from leaving my mouth? *Not a chance.*

"How much I love you."

His lips parting is the only sign that he heard me. As his eyes dance back and forth between mine, my nerves amp up, and I'm afraid I'll pass out if he doesn't say something soon.

"Are you sure?"

My eyebrows shoot up to the sky. "Am I sure that I love you?"

He nods, and his Adam's apple works hard to swallow.

"Hatty, my heart and my body have loved you for as long as I can remember. And even when I was trying to convince my mind that we hated you, it knew better. There isn't a time I can remember not loving you."

His lips crash over mine in a brutal kiss. Hatty's hand slides to the back of my head, and he angles me the way he prefers. There's no mistaking who is in charge of this kiss, of my body, my heart, and my future.

As his lips move over mine, I know without a doubt I wouldn't survive him pushing me away again. It's that thought that has me pressing lightly on his chest.

After a moment, he pulls back. The sincerity in his gaze has my heart fluttering an uneven pattern.

Gathering my thoughts, I know I have to tell him the truth.

"Hatty, I've loved you my whole life. I love you with my whole heart, but I won't survive you pushing me away again. I barely made it through last time, so I'm giving you my heart to hold. You have to promise to take care of it because it only beats for you, anyway."

"Christ, Rylan. I'm never going to forgive myself for hurting you."

"You have to, though. That's how we'll move on. I'm just begging you not to do it again."

"Never. I will never hurt you again. I promise to take care of your heart, just don't ever leave me. Now that I have you, really have you, I know what happiness feels like. I need you more than air, sweetheart. That will never change."

"Does this mean you're my boyfriend?" As silly as it is, I need a label. Something tangible to hold on to.

"If that's what you want to call it," he says cryptically. "But I'm going to call you my forever."

"I love you," I say again, desperately hoping he'll say it back this time.

"I'll love you forever, Rylan."

Five words. That's all it takes for the waterworks to start. I've always known words were powerful, but I wasn't expecting five words to knock me off my feet.

"Hey? Hey, did I say something wrong?" he coos.

I'm a blubbering mess and can only shake my head.

"Are you upset?"

I shake my head again, trying desperately to get myself under control. I'm not usually an emotional basket case, so this is new for the both of us.

Emotions overwhelm me, and I need to change the subject, but with his face pressed so close to mine, he's all I can think about.

Then I remember why we're here.

"Give me a word, Hatty?"

My words are a whisper in the night. A plea to let go. A promise to take care of him.

"Forever."

His lips descend onto mine, but this time he's gentle. Slow. Methodical in the way he kisses me. His hand still maneuvers me how it pleases him, and there's no doubting who is in control, but he's tender in a way I haven't experienced yet.

Where all his other types of kisses turn me on, this one wraps a vise around my soul and squeezes just tight enough to let me know it belongs to him. Forever.

His tongue glides down the column of my neck as he whispers words. Words like mine, and forever, and need. Words that tie me even closer to this man. Words that have my belly quivering before he's even really touched me.

"I love you, Rylan. Forever."

His hands slip beneath my shirt and ghost up my sides

until he's palming both breasts. With his thumb flicking back and forth, my nipples peak instantly.

"I love you so much," I reply with a gasp.

His fingers trail down my stomach and have just breached the band of my shorts when someone coughs. Hatty growls while I squeak and try to pull away, but his finger gets twisted in the belt loop of my shorts, and I tumble into him.

He catches me while glaring over his shoulder.

"So, ah … just wanted to mention that we installed security cameras in here yesterday. They're monitored by an Envision team. I can ask Ash to turn them off, but then—"

"No," Hatty barks, but Seth just laughs.

"Yeah, I figured as much. You two are going to need to set aside a lot of bail money if this is how your relationship is going to go."

I can hear his chuckle all the way down the stairs.

"What the hell is wrong with us? I've never had sex in public before. Not once, until you," I accuse.

Hatty finally untwists his hand from my shorts but hauls me close to him again.

"New rule, Rylan. I don't want to hear about any other nut monkeys you've been with. Got it? From now on, it's only me."

"Well, it was only you and Matthew anyway, so—" He cuts off my words by bending down and biting my lower lip. Hard.

"I don't want to hear about anyone else. If there's something you like, tell me. If there's something you want to try, show me. In terms of sex and love, and everything in between, I only want to hear about us."

"Okay," I reply breathlessly. Then my mind goes into overdrive. "How many people have you been with?"

Hurt flashes across his face before he schools his features. "Too many," he finally admits. "And only ever once."

"You've only had one-night stands. This whole time? So, you've never had a relationship besides me?"

"It didn't seem fair. I couldn't give someone else my heart when it's always belonged to you."

"But you ... you know, with a lot of women?"

"I wouldn't say a lot, but I wasn't celibate if that's what you're asking."

Jealousy unfurls in my gut like an angry mob, and I suddenly understand his new rule.

"I don't want to hear about them either," I say quickly.

"Okay. There hasn't been anyone in a long while, though. And I was tested at my last checkup."

"Probably something we should have discussed long before now, huh?"

He chuckles. "Yeah, probably."

Hatty smiles down at me, and my world feels right. Here in his arms, I feel like I can conquer the world, and that makes me the luckiest girl on earth.

Pulling away from him, I keep the contented smile on my face as I reach down for my camera.

"Forever, huh?"

A grin hits me first. He's the most beautiful man I've ever seen, and he's my forever.

Removing the lens cap, I set the camera up on a portable tripod, push a button, and run back to stand with Hatty. He immediately wraps an arm around my waist and hauls me up in a bridal hold. He smiles into the camera while I smile at him.

The flash goes off, and I know this will be my new favorite picture.

Lowering his mouth, he kisses me gently, and when he pulls back, I notice his haunted eyes.

"Forever, huh?" he repeats my words as he sets me on my feet.

With long strides, he crosses the room to stand in front of the easel again.

"Forever." It becomes a whispered chant as he lifts and inspects the charcoal.

I'm frozen to my spot. Afraid if I move, he'll lose the nerve.

"You want me to draw our forever?"

Silently, I move closer. I won't push him if this is too much, but I need to see his face. That's how I'll know if this was the right decision or not. Slowly, I inch closer until I'm standing at his side.

His focus is on the large, blank slate in front of him, and it gives me the opportunity to scan his face. His brow is furrowed in concentration, not fear. His breathing is regular, and his body posture is loose.

"I haven't done this in a very long time, Rylan. Our forever might end up looking like a pile of dog shit."

"Not a chance," I say confidently. "I can see our future clearly enough for the both of us. Whatever you put on that paper will be just the beginning."

"You're pretty sure I can do this."

"Hatty, I have no doubt you can do anything you put your mind to. I believe in you, but if our forever is too daunting, you can always draw me like a French girl."

I wiggle my eyebrows at him, and he pounces. With his lips to my ear, he admits to a fantasy.

"I've dreamed of drawing you naked for years, Rylan. But when I do that, it will be just for me and not where a room full of assholes can watch from a computer screen."

"Wh-When?"

He pulls away, and I stumble forward. His self-satisfied smirk is back as he glances around the room.

"Yes, when." Grabbing my hand, he drags me through the space and out into the hallway.

"What are we doing?"

Hatty glances left, then right. His hand squeezes mine in the rhythm of a heartbeat.

"I don't own you, Rylan. But I am going to own this moment."

I see the second he's formed a plan, and we're on the move again. At the end of the hallway, he opens a closet door and shoves me inside.

"There will be no cameras in here," he whispers dangerously.

Craning my neck to peer around him as he closes the door behind us, I see art supplies in various shades and mediums. Chairs are stacked to the ceiling in one corner, while folding tables lean against each other in another. Staring at our surroundings, I realize it's more of a tiny room than a closet, and my breaths pick up in anticipation.

"This moment?" I whisper.

Hatty grins, but steps away from me. Turning his back, he reaches for the chairs and lowers one to the ground. When he faces me again, naughtiness covers his features as he positions the single chair directly under the hanging light bulb. When his gaze hits mine again, I forget to breathe.

He stalks me in three short strides, and when his mouth descends on mine, I know we're about to have the hottest sex this closet has ever seen.

His movements are anything but smooth. Frantic hands rip my shirt over my head and his lips fall to my collarbone. Hatty wastes no time removing my shorts next. The telltale sound of fabric ripping hits my ears as he drags them down my legs.

"Hatty?"

Before I can form a question, I'm naked before him and he's guiding me to the chair. The plastic is cold against my ass, but when Hatty drops to his knees between my legs my body goes up in flames.

There's no preamble. No warmup. Hatty dives into my

pussy like a starving man. With a hand snaking around my lower back, he pulls me forward on the seat, directly into his waiting mouth.

"Gah, I, Hatty,"

He growls against my clit, and my back arches in response. Moving my hands to my breasts, I pinch both nipples between my thumbs and forefingers, rocketing my sensations into overdrive.

"There is nothing sexier than watching you touch yourself, princess."

I'm vaguely aware of his shuffling body, but his tongue speeds up its assault on my clit and my eyes clamp shut. When he sucks my clit into his mouth and clamps down lightly with his teeth, I see stars. My body quivers around his magical tongue as he draws out every last tremor.

With hooded eyes, I stare at the man before me, on his knees, offering a forever the only way he knows how.

"I want you to ride me, hard," he growls.

My head nods with wide eyes as he stands, bringing his cock in line with my face, and I lick my lips.

"Not today, sweetheart. Ride me," he demands. Hauling me from the chair, he turns and sits while hanging on tightly to my hands.

Once he's seated, he tugs my arm roughly, and I fall into his legs. Staring into his eyes, I step around one leg, then the other, until I'm straddling his lap.

Hatty swallows audibly as I reach between us and wrap my hand around the base of his shaft. A low groan escapes his lips as I pump him once, twice, then lower my pussy to his tip.

His hands fly to hips, and the second I sink down, he grinds into me.

"Holy hell, you're deep like this, Hatty."

A dangerous grin transforms his face. With one movement, Hatty turns into a sexual beast. His hands cup my ass, forcing my hips to roll with his dick rooted deep inside of me. My legs can't quite reach the floor in this position, so I can't get any leverage to ride him.

Hatty makes up for it. Wrapping both arms around my back, he holds me tightly against his chest, suspended a few inches above him, and thrusts up and into me with unmeasurable force. The sounds of our naked bodies slamming into each other echo in the tight space. But when I cry out, he makes no effort to silence me. Instead, he removes one arm from my back and threads it through my hair, tilting my head back.

"Let me hear you, princess. Let me hear every sound, every moan, every slurp of your aroused body, then let me fuck you harder. Come screaming my name. Come feeling me so deep inside, you're branded by my cock forever. Let me mark you as mine."

His filthy words are my undoing, and as he jackhammers into my core, I spiral around him. My body spasms and I'm unable to breathe. When he doesn't slow his pace, I feel the quivers pick up as if my body hadn't just shattered and I know I'm racing toward another orgasm.

"Hatty. Hatty, I don't think—"

"You can, sweetheart. I feel your walls milking me. I feel your body tensing and squeezing around my dick."

He's panting now, and his shoulder muscles bunch beneath my fingers. He's close.

Leaning in, I graze his earlobe with my teeth, and whisper my own dirty words, "Paint me with your seed, Hatty. Mark me as yours forever. Come for me, now."

He roars a violent sound as he locks my hips against his with strong hands, holding me to him until I feel his dick twitch and warm jets of his love paint my insides. He pushes my pubic bone into his, and my second orgasm causes my world to go dark.

Seconds or maybe minutes later, I slump forward on

Hatty's chest. He's running gentle fingers up and down my spine while whispering words of love beside my temple.

He may not have drawn our forever, but he showed me with his body, and I'll settle for that. For now, anyway. Our future will take work, but sitting here, joined together as one, I know it will be worth the fight.

CHAPTER 36

"*A*nd I'm telling you, I ran those numbers myself. There's no fucking way we were outbid without help. Whoever is selling out The WB, is on your staff."

"Mason? What are your thoughts?" Easton looks sick as he defers to the man who has taken over his position at our head office. "Everyone on our team that would have access to this information I've hired personally. We've always had a loyal team. Is something happening that I've missed?"

Preston flew back to North Carolina a few days ago, but the rest of us have been lingering in Vermont, tying up loose ends. East has decided not to return at all, for now.

"I really don't know," Mason announces via speakerphone. "It doesn't make any sense. Everyone in this office has been here for years. We know their families. We treat them like family."

"Listen, I know this is hard, but Ashton had me put out those numbers to see who bites. It is coming from your office, and it's only a matter of time before we figure out who. All I want you to do is keep an eye on everyone. If they get spooked, they'll run. Keep moving forward with the numbers I sent you. Ashton will find the mole; we just have to be patient."

"And what do I say to anyone wondering if we've lost our damn minds? Bidding this much on a rundown block in the suburbs is professional suicide." Mason isn't wrong, but it's our only chance at catching this guy.

"You smile and tell them they'll see in time. If other companies think we know something they don't, so will the mole. It's not ideal, but it's what we have to work with. Can you do that?" Easton asks through the screen.

"Yeah, I can do that," Mason grumbles. "Anything else? I have a staff meeting in five."

I glance up at Easton, who shakes his head.

"No, that's it, Mas. Thanks."

"Talk to you soon."

I end the call and scan Easton's face. "What are you thinking?"

"It's not him, Halt. I know it's not. He loves this company, and he loved Dad. He wouldn't do this to us."

I blow out a harsh breath. "Yeah, I didn't think it was him either, but it's definitely coming from someone close to him. I'm going to have to head back soon. We can't run this company with all of us holed up on this mountain."

Easton grimaces. "Are you sure that's what you want? I can't help but notice your hands. You're sketching again?"

My gaze automatically shifts to stained fingers. It's funny how quickly that happens.

"Yeah, it's … it's not very good yet. I can't get the faces right," I admit.

Rylan tasked me with our forever. In my head, that looks like the picture Ash texted me. The one with all my brothers smiling at the camera, but me smiling at Rylan. I've sketched it a dozen times, but we're always faceless.

"I saw something in the rec center. I knew it had to be

yours. It's fucking amazing, Halt. It looks like the photograph of us all as kids."

"Yeah, it's all of us without faces."

"It'll come. Just give it time. You can't force it. How are things with Rylan? Have you taken her on your epic date yet?"

Now it's my turn to cringe.

"You haven't taken her on a date? Jesus Christ, Halton. What the hell? Summer's almost over."

"We've gone on dates. She always has a plan." It sounds lame even as I say it.

"You have to put in the effort, Halt."

"I know," I sigh. "I just … what if I can't do this? What if I can't keep her?"

"If you don't try, you won't have to worry about keeping her. If you don't put in the effort, you will lose her."

"It's been weird being here. We're all in this limbo of real-life responsibilities and vacation. I don't know how to have her in my life when we're not here. What if we don't want the same things?"

"That's what conversations are for, Halt. As scary as it is, you are leaving the mountain soon. Do you want her to go with you?"

"Of course I do."

"Then you need to talk to her. Work it out. Make a plan. Grab ahold of your future before it's too late."

"I'm afraid of holding her back," I admit, and immediately hate the catch in my voice. "What if Dad was right, and I can't hold her up in the spotlight she deserves?"

Easton sits back in his chair and observes me for so long it becomes uncomfortable. He rubs his chin between his thumb and forefinger before speaking.

"You want to know something else we have in common?"

My eyebrows lift in confusion. Is he just going to ignore my concern? *Nice, East. Way to be there for me.*

279

"We're not quitters, and we don't let fear control us. I was fucking terrified of spilling my guts to Lexi, but I did it because I knew I wanted her. Whether you want to acknowledge it or not, you've been doing scary shit your entire life. You've never backed away from an event, even when you would struggle to stay standing through it. You showed up. Show up for her, too, Halt. Show up for yourself. Don't allow fear to ruin your future."

His words are rattling around in my head when the front door opens, and Colton bursts through.

"She got it! She got the job. Can you believe it? She's going to kill it in NYC! Models, and parties … hey," he stops mid-stride and calls to someone behind him, "will I get to meet the models?"

"What the hell are you talking about?" Easton asks when Colt pauses for a breath.

That's when I notice Rylan standing quietly in the doorway with a flush to her cheeks.

"Rylan. She got the photography job with Lochlan's sister. Ryguy! Holy shit, this is going to skyrocket you to the next level. Red carpets, parties, interviews, after parties. This is it for you. This is everything you've been waiting for. Everyone will know your name by October, and you'll be able to cherry pick your jobs after this. You'll be the next Annie Leibovitz."

Colton is speaking so fast I can't keep up. My gaze hasn't left Rylan's. She seems happy but nervous. My brain is still unraveling everything Colton is saying.

Hello, panic, my old friend.

It pops into my head before I even realize my heart is racing.

"This is good news?" I know it is, but I need to hear her say it. I need to hear that this is what she wants.

Biting her lip, she nods. "I think it is good news. It's not really the direction I thought I would go, but Colty's right. If I nail this show, I could do everything I've always wanted."

Parties. Red carpets. After parties. Interviews.

I'm going to end up holding her back from her dreams.

Her phone rings, and a pretty smile graces her face. Holding it up, she seeks me out. "It's ... I've got to take this. I'll see you tonight?"

I smile even though my heart is cracking.

I can pretend to be strong. I can pretend to fit in, but for how long? I won't survive in that life of parties and models, and I can't very well ask her to give up her dreams.

What the fuck am I supposed to do now?

"Hello, panic, my old friend," I mumble the words, and I don't care who hears. Silent words aren't cutting it right now as I clench my jaw and force air in and out through my nose.

"Breathe, Halton. Just—"

"I'm going to run and call Loch. See if he has any more details for our girl!" Colton bolts from the room without a care in the world. He has no idea I'm seconds away from blacking out. He has no idea that my world is silently crashing in on top of me. He's happy for *our girl* in a way that I should be, but I can't even get my ass out of this chair. He's always going to be the one to raise her up while I drag her down.

The next thing I know, Easton is in my face and shaking my shoulders.

"Fucking breathe, Halt. Jesus Christ," he grinds out. "You really can't control this, can you?"

I shake my head no and begin to count. Every time I get distracted by a thought of Rylan, I start over. It takes eleven tries before I'm able to count to ten without interruption.

"Tell me what you're thinking," Easton demands when I appear to have a semblance of control.

"This is big for her. This is her career, what's she's worked

281

so hard for. Colton is giving her an opportunity of a lifetime."

"He gave her a connection. She got the job on her own," he clarifies, obviously aware of the direction of my thoughts.

"It's a career that will involve parties and red carpets. Interviews and travel."

"All the things your nightmares are made of. So, what are you going to do? Are you going to let her go? Push her away again?" He scowls, then shakes his head. "Can you walk away?"

"Jesus, East. Do you think I can handle this shit?" My voice echoes off the lodge's high ceiling, and I jump out of my chair to pace the room. "Rylan's life will include literally everything I hate. Everything that kills a little piece of me every time I have to participate in it. She deserves someone who can walk the red carpet, proud to have her on their arm. She needs someone that can handle the spotlight. Someone that won't fucking pass out if he has to give a speech. She deserves the world, man, and I'm broken inside. I don't know how to do any of that shit without physically hurting. Just thinking about taking her to that show has my stomach turning in so many knots I think I'm going to vomit. What kind of man ..."

Glancing up, I find Easton watching me. His fingers steepled under his chin, waiting for something.

"What?" I bark.

"Those are all problems. But you're a fixer, Halt. So, what are you going to do?"

"She deserves better than me." Dropping into my chair, I run both hands through my hair and shake my head, secretly hoping I'll dislodge the piece of me that's broken.

"I agree." He smirks. "Most women deserve better than us. That's not what I asked, though. I asked, what are you going to do? Can you live through losing her again?"

"No."

Raising my gaze, Easton's eyes find mine with an expectant expression.

"Fuck. No, I can't live without her."

"So?" he prods.

"So, I'm going to fix my shit, okay? I don't know how I'm going to do it, but I'm going to try. She's worth more than my effort. She's worth more than my pain or my pride. I'll fight through my weakness if it means I won't ever have to let her go again. Sh-She brings the magic into my life. GG was right. I live in black and white, but Rylan busts through my dark cloud, bringing all the colors of the rainbow with her. And I don't want to live in the dark again. Not now that I've felt what it's like to live in her sunshine. I need her, East. I need her so fucking much it terrifies me. Is one human supposed to depend on another so much?"

"Yeah, little brother. It's called love. But the first step to fixing your shit is understanding it's not your weakness that makes you this way. It's your strength. Your compassion. Your need to protect and love. If you didn't care so much, you wouldn't have so much anxiety festering around inside, winding you up tight. You're not weak, Halton. You're strong in all the ways that matter. You just have to learn how to harness it."

"It's not that easy," I grumble.

"Nothing worth it ever is, right? Welcome to the chaos, Halton. The world is your oyster and all that, you just have to …"

"Stay." The stinking Taylor Swift song muddles my brain. All I have to do is stay.

"Well, yeah. If you're strong enough to stick it out, you can work through anything," he affirms, not understanding I've tuned him out in favor of a pop song.

CHAPTER 37

RYLAN

"*T*hanks, Mom. I'm not sure what's going to happen. I just got the call, but I'm so excited."

"And what does that mean for Halton?"

"I'm not sure," I admit.

There's a long sigh before she speaks again. "Rylan, honey, you know I love Halton. I love all those boys, but he's hurt you once already, and you almost missed out on a life that makes you happy. Halton will be miserable in New York City, but he'll try, for you, I'm sure of it. He's too stubborn not to. This is a once in a lifetime opportunity for you, though. Think long and hard about what you want. It might be time to focus on you for once in your life. If Halton is the one, a few months apart will only make that love grow stronger. I think you know this is something you need to accomplish on your own."

"I know." My voice is uncharacteristically quiet.

"Honey, I understand the draw to him. Really, I do, but I don't want to see you hurt again. He destroyed you. He snuffed out your light, and it took him years to come clean. I don't want to see you place all your hopes and dreams in his hands again. Sometimes, it's okay to be selfish. If he can't give you this time to flourish, maybe he isn't the man you think him to be."

"We haven't really had a chance to talk about any of it, Mom. It literally happened a few minutes ago."

"I know, sweetie. Just take care of yourself this time around, okay?"

I know she loves Halton. Even after everything that happened, she found it in her heart to forgive him, but I'm her little girl. I'll always come first, and she isn't saying anything I haven't already worried about privately.

Hatty would destroy himself to be with me, but I'll find a way to make sure that doesn't happen.

I'm still holding the phone to my ear long after we've hung up. That was not the phone call I was expecting. *Holy shit.*

"Rylan? Are you okay?" GG's voice calls out.

Turning, I see her on the side of the lodge digging in a flower bed. I can't handle her right now.

"Yeah, GG. I'm good. I, ah, I have to talk to Hatty. I mean, Halton. I mean, yeah. I'm good," I blurt as I run up the steps toward the lodge.

My hand is on the doorknob when Hatty's raised voice stops me in my tracks.

"Jesus, East. Do you think I can handle this shit? Rylan's life will include literally everything I hate. Everything that kills a little piece of me every time I have to participate in it. She deserves someone who can walk the red carpet, proud to have her on their arm. She needs someone that can handle the spotlight."

I stumble back. His words hit me like a two-handed shove. *He's going to push me away again.* Or leave. He isn't even going to give me a choice. I can feel it.

"She deserves the world, man, and I'm broken inside. I don't know how to do any of that shit without physically hurting," he yells.

285

Oh, God. Oh, God. My insides shake and my outside trembles. He can't be with me without hurting himself, and he isn't even giving me the option to choose him.

"Rylan?" GG's voice barely registers.

"Ah, I forgot. Something. I forgot something," I mumble as I backtrack down the steps.

Walking in a daze, I make it to the back door and run into Colton.

"Ryguy! Loch has a place for you to stay whenever you arrive in New York. He said ... Rylan?" Colton holds me at arm's length, searching my face. "What's the matter with you?"

I bite my tongue to keep the tears at bay. "Nothing, Colty," I say with fake cheer. "I'm just so excited. I've got to pack."

His shocked expression tells me he wasn't expecting that.

"When are you leaving? Loch said you have a couple of weeks before Nova needs you." He crosses his arms as he scrutinizes my face. Colton isn't known for being very perceptive, but he chooses this moment to learn the skill.

"Oh, I know," I trill. "But I have so much I need to prepare for. I need to get the lay of the land. Check Nova's portfolio and the surroundings to make sure we're on the same page. Creatively, you know? It's just best if I get there as soon as I can."

"How soon is that, Rylan?"

Hatty's voice makes me jump. I don't dare turn his way.

"I'm going to catch a bus tonight." *Shit. Do they have buses here?* "Or maybe a train?" I giggle, and it sounds borderline psychotic. "I guess I have a lot to work out still."

"Ry, what's going on? Halt, you're going with her, right?" Colton asks over my head.

"Yes," he growls.

"No," I squeal at the same time. "No, I mean, Hatty needs to get back to Waverley-Cay. The WB. All that stuff. I'll be fine."

Turning to Hatty, I finally dare a glimpse. "I'll be fine," I say again.

"What the fuck is going on, Halton?"

I keep my gaze down. "Nothing, Colty. I-We just have stuff to do."

"I'm going to kill you, Halton."

"I didn't fucking do anything, Colt. Give us a minute, would you? I don't know what the hell is going on."

My throat closes, and I squeeze my eyes tight, count to ten, then pull myself together. The only way this works is if he hurts me, or himself, and I won't allow him to do either. I have to take control of this situation, or he'll never forgive himself.

"Fine," Colton eventually agrees. "Rylan, I'll be back here in twenty minutes for you to tell me what in the actual fuck is going on."

I force a smile. "You're worrying too much, Colty. Everything's fine."

"Fine my ass," he grumbles, pulling me in for a quick hug, then stomping off toward the lodge.

"What's going on, Rylan?"

Hatty's voice is quiet, subdued, but his expression is full of angry emotions, searching for a fight.

It's now or never. *Hurt or be hurt? Hurt him and let him hate me, or allow him to push himself so hard he hates me in the end, anyway?*

Shaking my head to erase those thoughts, I know there's only one thing to do.

"Hatty, I know you have to go back to Waverley-Cay. The WB needs you, and I need to go to New York. This is big for me. An opportunity of a lifetime."

He steps forward, but I sidestep him to keep some distance between us.

"I know it is, sweetheart. I'll figure out the WB. I want to be there for you. I want to support you, so I'll go with you."

287

"No."

He rears back as if I struck him. "No? What do you mean?"

"I have to do this on my own, Hatty. I've always depended on someone. This is something I have to do myself. You hate the city, and the crowds. You hate the spotlight, and that's going to be my life for at least the next few months. I don't know what will happen after this show, but if you come with me, you'll end up resenting me."

"That's not true, Rylan. Yes, I hate all that shit, but I'll do it. For you, I'll do anything." His tone is pleading. His eyes beseech me to listen to him, but as his fists curl and unfurl in an unconscious nervous habit, I know dragging him to New York would be the end of us. He practically admitted it earlier.

"I know you would, Hatty. That's why I'm asking you to let me go."

"Let you go? Are you out of your fucking mind? I can't live without you, Rylan. If I have to go through hell every day to have you, then that's what I'll do. Don't ask me to let you go. I already promised to stay. So did you. Don't forget you made promises, too."

His accusatory tone gets my hackles up.

"I think you know better than anyone how easily promises can be broken, Halton. I've given, and given, and given. I've put in the effort. I've made this a relationship while you've skated along, never fully invested or putting your heart on the line. Why was that, huh? So, it's easier for you to walk away if you decide I'm not worth the effort anymore?"

"It's not like that," he growls.

"No? That's what it feels like. I feel like a convenience. What did you think would happen when everyone left Vermont? You've had one foot out the door this entire time, just waiting for your escape."

"I may not be putting in an effort in a way you can see, Rylan, but make no mistake, I am invested. I'm all in. If I'm holding back, it's because I don't want to be responsible for keeping you from the life you deserve. I'm trying to protect you, even if that means protecting you from me. You deserve the best. Everything good in this world, and half the time, I'm in the dark. How can I give you everything when I'm still trying to figure out how I fit in this world without the panic that grips me daily? I don't want that for you, sweetheart. I have to protect you from that."

Tears fall down my face and soak my shirt.

"But don't you see, Hatty? That's no better than when you pushed me away before. You made the choice to do that without ever talking to me about it. You made the decision to protect me, but it isn't your decision to make. A relationship is fifty-fifty. We compromise. We make decisions together, but you keeping me at arm's length is the same as pushing me away again. You keep choosing to exclude me from the narrative of our story, and that's not how love works."

"What about you?" he bellows. "Aren't you doing the same fucking thing by going to New York and deciding for me I shouldn't be there? How is that any different?"

He moves swiftly, and I'm in his arms a second later.

"I know I'm fucking this up, Rylan, but I'm not done with you. Please don't be done with me. I have so much shit to figure out. I-I'm broken, but I want to do better for you. I want to be better so I can support you in the things that matter in your life. Please don't push me away."

"You're not broken, Hatty. But we both have things we need to work on and figure out. New York isn't the place for you to do that."

Stepping away from him is shredding my heart into a million pieces. I know I'm the world's biggest hypocrite. I'm lecturing him on equality and fairness in a relationship when in reality, I'm doing the same thing he did. I'm going to push him away to protect him, even if it's from himself.

"I'll do it wherever you are, sweetheart."

I can't swallow past the lump in my throat, and I choke on an inhale.

"No, Hatty. I-I think we need to take a break."

"You're breaking up with me?" It's a hoarse whisper that has me shutting my eyes tightly.

"My life is the things your nightmares are made of, Hatty. Our timing is off."

"You're leaving me," he says again. "That's it? You're just going to decide that I don't get a chance to make this work? My world doesn't spin without you in it, Rylan. Do you understand that? I don't know how to live without you in my life anymore."

Pain lances through my chest. "Is that all I am to you, Hatty?"

"What do you mean is that all? It's everything, Rylan. You mean everything because you're my entire world."

"As much as I want that to be true, I can't, Hatty. I can't be your happiness. You have to be happy with yourself first. You have to love yourself before you can love anyone else."

"Bull shit. I've loved you my whole life, Rylan."

"For how long, though?" My head tilts as I stare at him.

"How long what?" He exhales a frustrated breath.

"How long can you be happy putting all your joy on me? That's a lot of pressure, Hatty. What if I change? What if we get old, and I'm not the same person I am right now? What happens to your happiness then?"

"It'll change with you. I-I don't understand what we're even fighting about right now," he admits.

"I don't think I did until just now. But, I know you can't expect me to carry your happiness for you. Everything I'm going to accomplish in New York is the same things that fuel your nightmares, right?"

He stares at me for a long while but says nothing.

"This is something I've worked for, Hatty. For years. This one event could make all my years of work worth it."

"I know," he rasps.

"If you come with me, you'd destroy yourself before you'd walk away. I don't want that for you, or for us, because regardless of what you think right now, you would grow to resent me for dragging you there."

"So, you're going to leave me. Just like that?"

No. Not just like that. Nothing about this is easy. I want to scream. But no words come.

"I'm not agreeing to a break, Rylan. We're either together or we're not."

My gaze flashes pain as I stare at him. My mouth hangs open, but all I can manage is a strangled cry.

His eyes dart back and forth between mine, then his head drops, and he takes a step back.

"I love you with everything I am, Rylan. I'm sorry that's not enough." He turns on his heel and is gone while I drag in a haggard breath.

This is what I wanted, right? A break so we can both work on ourselves? Our careers? This was my idea. So why does it feel so final? Why do I feel like Hatty just walked away from me for the last time?

CHAPTER 38

HALTON

*B*uzz. Buzz. Buzz.

The alarm goes off at 5:45 a.m., but I'm already wide awake. Sleep is an elusive bitch when your heart is shattered beyond repair. Tossing back the covers, I swing my legs over the edge of the bed and come face-to-face with one of the many easels now filling my apartment.

I can't get her face right. The charcoal doesn't want to bend to my will these days, so I have at least a dozen half-started portraits throughout my home. I rise to my feet, and wadded-up sketches crunch under them. Glancing down, I find my floor littered with paper. Hundreds of attempted drawings tossed aside in various states of progress.

I ignore them all and head to the kitchen for coffee instead. Entering the galley-style room, shame tries to peek through at the state of it. Beer bottles, pizza boxes, and left-over Chinese take-out containers litter the island and counter space.

And I can't bring myself to care. Work is the only solace I have these days, so abandoning the idea of coffee, I shower, dress, and head to work. The stubble along my jaw is unkempt, an outward sign of the state my emotions are in.

I fucking miss Rylan. I'm suffocating without her, and there doesn't seem to be a damn thing I can do about it.

~

*M*y office door slams open, and Mason Dennery strides through it like a man on a mission. We've known each other for more than half our lives. He's been a great friend to Easton, and he started working here with our father at the same time we did. But never in all that time have I seen him look so … wrecked.

"East, Mason's here," I say into the webcam. "And he isn't looking so hot. Hold on a minute?"

"What? Why? What's wrong, Mas?"

I notice his shaking hand as he slams a stack of papers down onto my desk. When he leans over, Easton gets a glimpse of him over the video call.

"Jesus, Mason. What the hell happened?"

His entire body shakes, and as I adjust my focus to the papers he placed in front of me, I realize why.

"Fuck," I curse, then wipe a hand over my face.

"Fill me in here, Halt." Easton is a grumpy asshole, most of the time anyway, but he loves hard, and Mason is one of us.

"Mason just handed me Jonathon's bank statements," I tell East. Jonathon has been Mason's live-in boyfriend for over a year.

"Why would he …"

"If I check, I'm guessing the dates of these large deposits will correspond with major deals we've lost recently?"

Mason nods his head and drops into the chair opposite my desk.

"I'm so sorry. I had no idea," he begins. Leaning forward, he places his forearms on his thighs. "I trusted him."

The pain in Mason's voice is reflective of my own feelings right now. It's almost too much to take.

"Mason, this isn't your fault," Easton assures.

He nods his head but doesn't glance up.

"Mas? How did you get these?" They aren't regular bank statements, they're for offshore accounts, and I need to know what we're getting into here.

"I started going through everything a couple of days ago. Once you set the false numbers and they started circulating, I knew it was coming from someone close. I just never suspected he could do this to me. I gave him everything. I loved him."

"Jesus. This is going to get ugly, you know that, right?"

"Do what you have to do, Halton. He didn't have any concern for me. I'll need to get over my feelings. I ... He doesn't know that I've found them. Just let me know what you need me to do."

He stands to leave, but the devastation is evident in his expression.

"Mason, I'm really sorry about this. What do you need from us? How can we help?"

He barks a humorless laugh. "I just told you my boyfriend caused you to lose nearly a billion dollars in revenue over the last year, and you're still concerned about me?"

"Don't do that, Mason. You're one of us, and we take care of our own. You know that. This isn't on you." Easton leaves no room for debate, and I silently nod in agreement.

"Thanks, East. I ... shit. I'm going to stay at a hotel tonight. I'll tell Jonathon I have a last-minute work trip. I just can't face him in person without exploding, so the sooner you can make a plan, I'd appreciate it."

"I'll fill Ash and the legal team in now. Let us know if we can do anything for you, okay? This isn't your fault, Mason. We trust you completely."

"Thanks. After this, I really appreciate that."

He leaves my office, but my gut twists painfully at his dejected state. He looks like I feel.

I don't realize I'm staring after him long after he's gone, until Easton interrupts my thoughts.

"I've forwarded a message to legal and to Ash. We'll need to move quickly on this."

"Yeah," I mumble, trying desperately to get back to the stone-faced, emotionless statue I was a half hour ago.

"Have you heard from her?"

My gaze cuts to the computer screen. Eyes so similar to my own stare back at me, and I shake my head. "We texted a little yesterday, but I-I think it's over."

"She's been in New York for two weeks, Halt. You need to do more than text if you want to get her back."

"I don't think that's what she wants, East. She left me, remember? I wanted to go with her, and she said no, but she'll let Colton stay there this whole time?" It feels like a betrayal that he's there, and at the same time, I'm fucking glad she has him. It's a double edge sword that stabs me in the heart with every breath.

"I don't fit into that world, and she realized it the second she got that job. She didn't even give me a chance to try. She assumed because her life was my nightmare, we needed to take a break like we're fucking Ross and Rachel. Taking a break never works out for anyone."

"She said her life was your nightmare?"

I glare at him through the screen. "Yes," I growl, but he just reclines in his seat and clasps his hands behind his head.

"That doesn't seem odd to you? Where were you when she said this?"

"Odd? No, I said the same fucking thing. To you."

"I know. That's why I said it's odd that she used the same exact verbiage you did to spew that nonsense. When did she say it?"

"Are you out of your tits? What are you getting at?" A

295

niggling feeling attempts to scratch the surface of hope, but I tamp it down.

"Well, according to Colton, everything went to shit immediately after our conversation. I think we've proved that our family has a communication problem, so is it possible that she overheard you screaming about not fitting into her life?"

I flop back into my seat and take the same stance as East. Folding my hands behind my head, I stare into the screen.

"If she did, she would have heard me say that she was worth it. That I would do whatever it took."

"Not if she heard you freak out. She probably would have tried to get out of there as fast as possible. Which brings me back to Colton, who was pissed off at you. He thought you'd hurt her again, so she must have been out of sorts, right?"

My clasped hands pinch the back of my neck. "She would have said something," I mumble.

Easton quirks his eyebrow. "If she thought her lifelong dream was going to hurt you? Do you really think she would ask you about it? Or do you think she would have drawn from your history and assumed the worst?"

"Which is what?" My teeth grind together, afraid of his answer.

"That you would push her away again, or that you'd force yourself to live in a nightmare. Neither option seems all that great for someone you love, now does it?"

My fist comes down on my desk so hard the monitor wobbles for a full minute before evening out again.

"She left," I growl.

"She did, but is she worth fighting for?"

My gaze is stern as I find his on the screen.

"You know she is." I glance out the window, feeling the familiar sensations of panic rising. "But what if she doesn't want me to fight for her? What if this is karma coming to collect for my stupidity?"

"I don't believe in that shit, Halton. You just have to decide which is worse. Fighting for her and risk being rejected, or living in this hell you've been in for the last two weeks? I gotta tell you, though. I liked you a lot better when you were with Rylan. You're kind of a miserable bastard on your own."

He's not wrong. Even my assistant threatened to quit today if I didn't ease up.

"There's not much of a choice, is there?" I grumble.

"Not if you want to be happy."

"I have some shit to do. Can you get Ash up to speed and check in with legal for me?"

"If you promise me something first."

I don't respond because his tone makes the hairs on my arm stand on end.

"Just promise me you'll do what it takes to get the girl, and if you need help, you'll call Dex. He's itching to put his Prince Charming hat on again."

His smirk tells me he isn't joking about Dex, but the other part? I'm going to do everything I can.

"I don't like to lose, East. You know that."

"That'a boy, Halton! Go get your girl. I'll talk to you soon. By the way, Colton will be back in Waverley-Cay tonight. I hear he's on the warpath, so be prepared to defend yourself."

He hangs up before I can ask any questions.

I chuck my pen across the desk. Just great. What the hell do I do now?

Removing my suit coat, I lay it over the back of my chair, then cross the room to the small easel I set up this morning. I pick up the charcoal, rolling it between my fingers to heat the oils within, but I can't bring myself to touch the paper.

I've attempted this draft at least a hundred times, and I yield the same results every time. The bodies of my family are all there. The details of their clothing, their hair, their posture, all exactly how they appear in the photograph, but they're all faceless. The few expressions I've attempted seem haunted when I'm finished, and I end up tossing the entire project in the trash.

"But my cards are showin' that you're the only one needing help."

GG's words from weeks ago rattle around in my head. Staring at the unfinished sketch, I have to wonder if my inability to finish it has more to do with my pain than I'm willing to acknowledge.

Why can't I show happiness on the page? It's haunting my dreams now, too. Faceless people all waiting for me to draw their forever.

"I can't be your happiness, Hatty."

Rylan's words cut through my chest, and I step back. How the hell am I supposed to find my happiness if I can't even draw it on my family?

CHAPTER 39

RYLAN

"*Y*ou know I love you, right?"

I stare at Colty over my coffee cup. I never know where he's going, but when he just stares back, I put down my cup and nod.

"Yeah, Colty. I know."

"Good. Then you know what I'm about to say comes from a place of love. But what in the actual fuck is going on with you and Halton? I thought you were depressed after prom-hole, but that is nothing compared to you now. Ry, you don't look like you've slept in two weeks, and according to office gossip, Halton has been such a prick we're on the verge of losing some key employees. You're obviously both miserable, so what am I missing here?"

"It's complicated. Can we just leave it at that?"

"No, we can't because I cannot take seeing your puffy, swollen eyes for one more minute. Plus, if Halton pisses off my staff and they quit, I'm going to lose my shit."

"He's not that bad."

"Oh yeah? How do you know? Did you finally call him? Return his phone calls?"

Guilt washes over me, and I stare into my coffee cup again.

"Rylan, please. Please explain to me why, in God's name, you're both punishing yourselves?"

The alarm on my phone goes off, and I'm literally saved by the bell.

"Ready? I don't want to be late to meet Nova."

Colton sighs but wraps his enormous arms around my back. The Westbrook special.

"Yeah, we can go, but you do realize you're making my case for never falling in love, right? If love makes you this miserable, count me out."

"It's complicated," I repeat.

"Yeah, yeah, so you've said. But from where I stand? The only thing making it complicated is the both of you being too stubborn to actually communicate."

My shoulders droop because, unfortunately, Colton is one hundred percent correct. And there is nothing I can do about it.

~

"*T*hat is your sister?" Colton asks with his jaw on the floor.

"Stepsister, but yes. And don't go getting any ideas, Colton. She's too fucking good for you, and she's focused on making a name for herself. She's not interested in dabbling in Neverland with you, Peter."

"Jesus, does everyone call me Peter Pan?"

"If the shoe fits." Lochlan chuckles.

I take a moment to observe him. He's relaxed with an air of confidence that comes from having money. As the heir to the Bryer Hotel empire, he's on par with the Westbrooks financially. He also has a straight nose, white teeth, perfect smile, and cocky stance that gives off an 'I'm sexy but don't fuck with me' vibe.

"Nova? Your creative genius is needed over here, love."

I tilt my head as I watch him. He has an almost British lilt to some of his words, but his affection for his sister is evident. Lochlan catches me staring and flashes me a wink.

"She's worked her ass off for this and refuses to let me help, so I'm not about to let this bloody asshole distract her."

Gaping at him, I can't help but smile. He has that effect on people I've noticed. And not just me, but everyone running around the ballroom of his Gramercy Hotel seems to be smitten with him.

I'm still staring at him when Nova flits over to us. She's about my height, with light brown hair with golden highlights that frame her delicate face. She's beautiful in a youthful, innocent way. But observing how her eyes dart from one thing to the next, I can tell she's also brilliant.

"Rylan?" she finally asks, drawing her attention away from the activity in the room.

"Yes. Hi, it's so nice to meet you." Holding out my hand, I'm caught off guard when she swats it aside and hugs me tight. She's strong for such a delicate thing. "Oh, okay."

"I am so glad Colton suggested you to Loch. I can just tell by your portfolio you're the one to get my vision for this show. I want the clothes to be the star, obviously, but nature has to play as big a part, too. That's really important to me. It's going to be so romantic," she says dreamily. "Picture the most epic love story known to man played out before your very eyes. That's what I want you to capture."

"No pressure or anything though." Lochlan chuckles. Affection for his sister is evident on his face, and I wonder what their story is. "She's been obsessed with happily ever afters since she was in middle school."

Nova rolls her eyes. "How would you know? You were in college when I was in middle school."

Lochlan shrugs his shoulders. "Someone had to keep an eye on you." A frown crosses his face, but she ignores him.

"So," she turns to me and grasps both of my hands in hers, "I have it all planned out. Well, except for the grand gesture at the end. Nothing seems to be quite right. But, I'll get it. We have a week. It'll come to me. I hope. Anyway, let's show you around. We've got so much ground to cover."

She drags me deeper into the ballroom, and I hear Colton chuckling at my wary expression.

'Chance of a lifetime,' he mouths.

Yeah, I just hope I can deliver.

~

"You're sure you'll be okay?" Colton asks for the tenth time in the last hour. He's heading back to Waverley-Cay, and I'll be alone in New York City for the first time.

"Yes, Colty. I'll be fine."

His expression is skeptical, and I can't say I blame him. It didn't even sound convincing to my own ears.

"Loch lives upstairs in the penthouse. If you need anything, anything at all, he'll take care of it. You just have to ask."

"Thanks, Colt." I bury my face into his chest, and he gives me a squeeze.

"Call Halton, Ryguy. Please? I hate to see you like this."

"I will ... eventually."

Colton shakes his head in sadness. "I just don't fucking get it, Rylan. How can two people love each other as much as you guys do, and you still can't figure out how to find your happy?"

"Sometimes, love isn't enough," I whisper. Even as the words leave my lips, I know they're a lie.

Colton kisses my head and promises to call when he

lands. I head deeper into the hotel suite Lochlan has put me up in. The room has every luxury you could ever want or need, but to me, everything feels dreary.

Deciding to skip dinner again, I climb into the king-sized sleigh bed with Egyptian cotton sheets and burrow deep beneath the soft fabric just as a text message chimes on my phone.

Halton: I miss you.

Halton: I know I'm probably supposed to give you space on this break, but I fucking hate it.

Halton: I know you can't carry my happiness for me, but what if the only thing I need to make me happy is you?

Halton: I love you with all that I am, Rylan. That will never change. Please tell me how to fix us?

Instead of answering, I turn off my phone and cry, full bodied, heart wrenching tears that wreck my soul. I'm doing this to protect him. That's what I tell myself in moments like this, but as I protect him, my heart dies a little more.

Love shouldn't hurt this much. Love shouldn't make me want to give up on all my hopes and dreams, but as I lay here, night after night, I have to wonder if any of it is worth it. I've been in a cloud of pain and sadness since I walked away from Hatty, and for what? A career that may or may not take off?

Tears flow harder as fear grabs hold of my thoughts. Have I been lying to myself this entire time? I said I was pushing him away to protect him, but how is that any better than what he did to me years ago? Deep down, I worry we'll never be able to have love without the pain that keeps separating us.

Maybe, sometimes love just isn't enough. And it's that thought that shreds my heart in a million different ways.

CHAPTER 40

HALTON

*H*itting refresh, I scroll through Rylan's Instagram feed again. She hasn't posted anything today, and it's driving me fucking nuts.

I really have turned into a stalker. I tried to call her yesterday, but it went straight to voicemail, the same as the day before.

Slamming the lid of my laptop down, I stand and stretch my arms over my head. I've been sitting at my desk for hours, not at all interested in going home to an empty house. I miss Rylan. I miss having her in my bed, and I really miss her goddamn voice.

I was miserable when I pushed her away in high school, but nothing compares to the near constant ache of loss I feel now. It's overwhelming and all consuming. There's no greater pain than knowing what it feels like to live in her light but be forced to stay in the dark. It's like a knife to the chest that twists painfully each passing day.

Falling back into my chair, I open my laptop again to the video app. It only takes a second to pull up the home movies because I've been watching them on a loop for the last week.

"Give me a word, Hatty?"

"Ebullience."

Rylan turns toward the camera and rolls her forest green eyes that seem to glow on screen.

Fast forwarding the video, I find the next clip.

"Give me a word, Hatty?"

The camera follows her around the gardens of my childhood home. I remember telling her I was capturing nature, but we both knew it was a lie. I zoom in on her face, and it brings her freckles into view, but it's her smile that takes my breath away. I fucking miss her smile. I miss her.

"For fuck's sake. You're as bad off as she is."

Colton's words startle me, and I nearly fall out of my chair. It's after ten p.m. I thought the office was empty. The lid of my laptop slams closed. Again. I'm going to break the damn thing at this rate.

"What do you need, Colt?"

I don't have the energy to fight with him.

"You look pathetic."

"Thanks for the observation, *brother*. Do you need something, or are you just here to give me shit?"

He waltzes into my office and takes a seat across from me.

"I didn't think it was possible, but you might look even worse than she does."

My spine stiffens, and I hate that he's spoken to her while I'm getting the silent treatment. "Is she okay?"

"No."

I'm out of my chair before I know what I want to do. "What do you mean? Is she hurt? Sick? Is that why she isn't answering my calls? Where is she? Why are you here? What do I need to do?"

His laughter pisses me off, and I'm close to punching the asshole. I have to take a step away so he can use his fucking words. Then I'll punch him.

"I guess that answers my question."

"What question?" If I grind my teeth anymore, they're going to whittle down to nubs.

"If you love her."

"Of course I love her. I told you I did."

"And yet, she's in New York, as miserable as I've ever seen her. Then there's you."

"What about me? I'm not in the mood for games, Colton. Just tell me what you have to say."

"You're here, angry at the world and taking it out on our employees. Why aren't you in New York fighting for her?"

I've been asking myself the same question all damn day.

"Listen, I don't know what happened between the two of you that had her jetting out of Vermont like her ass was on fire, but she's miserable. You're miserable. Get your head out of your ass and fix it."

"Fix your shit," I grumble. "Fuck, Colt. I don't even know what I'm supposed to fix at this point."

"Good thing I brought back up then."

Lifting my head, I close my eyes and shake my head as Dexter saunters into my office, dragging a large whiteboard on wheels. As Preston's best friend, he's the OG of my adoptive brothers. He's also slightly obsessive about happily ever after.

"Jesus."

As he rubs his hands together like a kid on Christmas morning, I really start to question his sanity.

"We've got some planning to do, huh?" His grin matches Colton's, and I know I'm in trouble. "Let's start with figuring out what the hell you did to fuck this up. Then we'll make a plan to get the girl."

CHAPTER 41

HALTON

"*A*re you sure you can handle this?"

"It's a little fucking late for that question, isn't it?" I bark.

Easton backs up with his hands raised in the air.

The truth is, I don't know if I can handle this, but I'm going to try.

"Did you take the medicine the doctor gave you?" Lexi asks, her tone lacking any of her usual sarcasm.

I must look like I'm going to pass out.

"Yeah, I took the pill about twenty minutes ago."

I finally broke down and called Lexi's therapist last week. Luckily, she does e-visits, so I'm able to meet with her online once a week. Somehow, that makes talking about shit easier.

"That's good, Halt. It will help, but this is still like some form of psycho emersion therapy. Are you sure this is what you want to do?"

"I need something big, Lex. I need to prove to her I can handle her world. That I want to try, anyway."

Lexi stares at me in confusion, then shakes her head. "Did she ask you to accept this world? Did you ever ask if this," she says, gesturing around the backstage setup of Nova's fashion show, "is what she wants?"

Now it's my turn to stare at her, dumbfounded.

Shaking her head, she laughs, and I know it's at my expense.

"When will the all-powerful Westbrooks learn? Talk, Halton. Having a conversation can save you a hell of a lot of heartache, and yet you all seem hell-bent on making things harder for yourselves."

"Could you maybe, I don't know, lecture me another time, Lexi? I'm doing my best not to pass out here."

Not overly demonstrative, I'm shocked when she drags me in for a giant hug.

"I'm proud of you, Halt. It takes a lot of courage to face your fears like this, and it takes a lot of strength to seek help for things you can't control."

Emotion clogs my throat, then Lexi punches me in the shoulder. Hard.

"Next time, don't listen to your idiot brothers, though, okay? You have a family full of sisters now. Dexter should hang up his cape. Not everyone needs a grand gesture. Sometimes, a few words and a hug are all it takes."

"Thanks, Lexi. I'll keep that in mind. I'm sure I'm going to fuck this up a few more times before I make Rylan mine for good."

She smiles then. Part evil genius, part loving sister-in-law.

"I'm sure you will, Halt. But what matters is that you keep trying."

"Move outta my way. Let me see my Fibby before he blacks out up on that stage."

Turning, I find GG pushing her way through models and tsk-ing at some of their outfits.

"What the hell is she doing here?" I hiss.

"Oh, Halton. It's cute you think we can control her. The second she found out you were making your move, she sat

308

her ass in the truck and waited for someone to drive her to the airport."

This crazy old bat. I smile as she approaches.

"There he is. My Fibby. I'm proud of ya. But just in case you pass out before you get your girl, I made you these."

She hands me a plate piled high with Rylan's favorite coconut cookies.

"You've got this, Fibby. I believe in you. Deep breaths. Trust your love to get you through this, and you'll be just fine."

"HEA. Five-minute warning to the HEA."

My eyes go wide, and I feel the sweat trickle down my spine. That's my five-minute warning to showtime.

$\sim$

Rylan

$\mathcal{T}$he air is electric. I'm running from one side of the stage to the other, then back again to capture each shot. Nova's show has been spectacular. From the clothing to the models to every choreographed detail of the art presentation I'm photographing. It's nothing short of amazing.

The constant gasps and oohs that fill the air is a testament to the work she's put in. I have no doubt Nova is about to become a household name. And, by proxy, my work will be displayed literally everywhere.

My chest aches when I realize the one person I want to share this moment with isn't here. I don't regret pushing him away. He would have ruined himself to be here for me, but I never would have been able to forgive myself if he had. Instead, I focus my attention back on the project at hand.

Nova has me freaked out a little about her surprise ending. It's not common for it to be so secretive. I just hope I have the right angles to capture the essence of whatever she has up her sleeve.

The room fades to black, and I haul ass to the top of the catwalk. Whatever she has planned, she wants me ready to shoot from the top when the lights come back up. I'm out of breath and rushing to get set up for the shot by the time I'm in position.

"Give me a word, Hatty?"

What the fuck? That's my voice on the speaker.

"All you had to do was stay," Taylor Swift sings.

My head is on a swivel in the pitch black. *What the hell is going on?*

Lights flicker, and I lift my gaze to the jumbo screens on either side of the stage. It's a video of me when I was thirteen.

"Give me a word, Hatty?"

"All you had to do was stay."

My voice alternates with the Taylor Swift song, then I hear him.

"Halcyon."

The screen flashes, and a picture I took as a teenager appears.

"All you had to do was stay."

"Give me a word, Hatty?"

The other screen flickers to life, and it's Hatty's charcoal version of my photo. I'm lightheaded as the words keep coming, paired with photographs and drawings.

"Dulcet."

"Lilt."

"Mellifluous."

"Talisman."

"Panacea."

Tears stream down my face, and I gasp as a live video of my tear-stained face shows up on the jumbo screen. And then, a spotlight shines on the center of the stage, and Hatty steps into view.

"Our life is made up of moments in time. Some moments we capture. Some moments we royally screw up, and some moments bring you right where you were always meant to be."

My mouth hangs open, and any hope I had of stopping the tears goes out the window as Hatty stands up on the stage in front of a thousand people, speaking into a microphone.

"When I was seven years old, I found my best friend hiding behind a bunch of rain gear."

The screen behind him shows a stick figure drawing of us, and I gasp when I realize it's something he drew when we were kids.

"Everything changed for me that day."

My gaze drifts back to Hatty.

"I didn't know it at the time, but that was the day my heart found its rhythm. I fell in love with a little girl who spoke with a lisp and had the saddest green eyes I'd ever seen."

The image behind him cuts to a closeup of an eyeball. As the camera zooms, it comes into focus. It's a recent charcoal, and there's no mistaking my face. He did it. He drew my face.

"Our story took a wrong turn a few years ago."

The montage changes between photographs and drawings in rapid succession. It makes it difficult to tell where the drawings end and the pictures begin.

I'm vaguely aware of models walking the outskirts of the stage around Hatty, but my focus is solely on him.

"I made a lot of mistakes. I told a lot of lies. I thought I was doing the right thing, and it nearly cost me the only person that has ever mattered. The only one who has ever made me feel whole. The love of my life. I'm not very good at planning dates or expressing my feelings. But I'm trying."

The music changes to another Taylor song; "this is me trying" plays on a loop.

"I will keep trying. I will make mistakes, but I promise to own up to them. I promise to talk to you and ask for help. I promise to put myself out there because I want to be with you. I want to be wherever you are at all times. I just want you, Rylan."

I can't take it anymore. I clamber to the stage, shocked by how high up it is. I recognize a deep chuckle at my side a second later, and Colt and Easton lift me up onto the platform.

"This is me trying, Rylan. This is me staying. Please let me love you. Let me show you all the ways you matter. J-Just let me love you forever, please."

I don't know if it was intentional or not, but the music has faded, and the lights are slowly coming up. I realize every person in the room is waiting for my answer.

"It's only ever been you, Hatty. I love you. I've always loved you."

"Thank fuck."

There is a loud roar from the crowd, and we're drawn from the bubble we'd been in. Hatty's eyes go wide as he takes in the audience all around us, and a second later, he crumbles to the ground like a sack of bricks.

"Oh my God." There are gasps from everyone, and the next thing I know, Preston's wife is being lifted to the stage.

She cracks something in her hands and waves it under Hatty's nose. Lifting her gaze, she smiles at me. "I carry smelling salts with me everywhere this family goes now."

Hatty's eyes flicker open, and he's adorably confused. Chaos erupts around us as Nova takes the stage, followed by wave after wave of models. When she gets to us, she winks.

"Best ending ever," she shouts.

EPILOGUE

HALTON

lanked by my brothers, their wives, and friends, I fade into the background of the after-party. My skin is crawling with the first signs of anxiety, but there's a smile on my face as I watch Rylan work the room like the angel she is.

"You know, I'm sure she'll be fine if you want to meet her in her room? I don't think she expects you to go through all this just because she's here."

I'm grateful for Colton's words and worried that perhaps I'm not holding it together as well as I thought I was.

"We have a lot to talk about. We kind of suck at communicating, and I don't want to leave her side until I know for sure that we're on the same page."

"What page is that?" he asks with a smirk. The asshole.

"The forever kind," I declare without hesitation.

Colton barrels into me, and I'm embarrassed to admit that his embrace eases the panic building inside of me.

"I'm happy for you, Halt. Just remember, she was mine first. You can have your forever, but she's always going to be my best friend."

His words are playful, but there's a hint of sadness behind them, too.

"Colt? Do you really think I'd keep Rylan from you? You're the one that was there for her when I couldn't be. I'll always be grateful for that."

He smiles and claps me on the back just as our girl burrows into my side.

"I'm going to grab a drink. I'll check in with you two later." Colton leans in to kiss Rylan on the cheek, and his whispered words punch me in the feels. "Take care of him, Ryguy. He's the best man I know, and no one deserves to be happier than the two of you."

When he steps back, I know he sees the moisture in my eyes but doesn't acknowledge it. Instead, he tips his empty glass and walks away.

Rylan's head rests on my chest as she smiles up at me. "How are you doing, Hatty?"

"I'm okay. I love watching you shine out there." I sweep my hand across the ballroom. "I'm so proud of you, princess."

"You didn't have to stay, you know?"

I shake my head. "I wanted to. I won't always be able to do it, but I'm … I'm seeing Lexi's therapist, and she prescribed some medicine that takes the edge off. I want to support you any time I can. Tonight, I could. But …"

I don't want to cut the night short for her, but I know I can't handle this crowd much longer.

"But you've had your fill," she offers with a brilliant smile.

"Yeah." Leaning down, I kiss her gently on the forehead. "I don't want to leave us like this. There are things we need to discuss. Things I need to say, so there's no confusion. Our communication has sucked so far, and I don't want to make any more mistakes with you. So, when you're done here, can we meet up? I'll come to you if that works."

"Hatty," she smiles sadly, and my heart pinches in panic, "I only want to be where you are. This isn't the life I want." She indicates the room with her hands. "It was a means to an end for me. If you're ready to leave, let's go."

Staring into her eyes, I see my forever, and happiness overwhelms me. I grab her hand and drag her from the ballroom. We pass Lexi on the way, and she grumbles about the Westbrooks and their caveman tendencies, causing me to pause. Glancing behind me, I see Rylan practically running to keep up with my long strides, and I slow my pace.

I'm ready to start our forever, but I can wait a few more minutes.

～

"This is your room?" Rylan gasps, twirling in a circle and taking in the suite.

I shrug sheepishly because I know it's excessive, but I was hoping she'd stay here with me for a few days, so I splurged.

"It's amazing, Hatty." She's standing at the floor-to-ceiling windows, and my heart thunders in my chest. Moving quickly, I stand behind her.

"You're amazing, Rylan." She turns her head, but I step into her space and wrap her in an embrace from behind so she can't turn around.

"I'm so sorry for hurting you." The words fight through the emotion, but there's no mistaking my sincerity.

Rylan leans into me, resting her head on my chest. "Me too, Hatty."

"I want to be very clear about my intentions, princess. I'm all in. I will make mistakes, but I swear to you, I'll fight for us until my dying breath. I'll never push you away again, but I'm going to need help. I'm never going to fit in certain situations, no matter how much I want to. Be my talisman. Ground me with your sunbeams, Rylan. I need you to help me fit when I want to run and love me, even if I do. You're all the best parts of me. I only fit when you're beside me, and I never want to live without you again."

"H-Hatty." She sucks in a ragged breath before turning in my arms. Placing her palms on either side of my face, she draws me closer. "I've always been yours, Hatty. And, I promise you, I'll force communication if we need it. I can't live without you either. You're my missing piece. I'm whole when you're with me. I love you so much."

Unable to control myself, I drag her into my body and hold her tight.

"Sempiternal," I whisper, and I can feel her smile against my chest.

"Sempiternal," she repeats.

Standing here, with Rylan in my arms, a weight lifts from my chest, and I feel ethereal happiness for the first time in my life. It's here that I realize I'm going to be okay. Life isn't going to suffocate me. Today is the start of my happily ever after, and my body vibrates with a joy I've never known.

~

One Year Later
Halton

"*I*s it all set?" I ask Ash for the tenth time.

"Yes, Uncle Hatty. Geez. We got it all set up just like you wanted. Promise."

Glancing down, I'm greeted by Sadie Sunshine and her smiling eyes.

"Thanks, chipmunk."

She scrunches up her nose, obviously still unhappy with my nickname for her.

"I don't like that name, Uncle Hatty." She places her tiny fists on both hips and scowls.

"Well, you shouldn't fill your cheeks with my cookies then," I tease.

I almost laugh when she crosses her arms over her chest in a huff. Her mannerisms have taken on a hint of Ashton, and it makes me smile.

I dare a peek in Ash's direction, and he's fighting a smile, too.

"So, what do you two have planned now?"

Ash groans at the same time Sadie squeals. She's clapping her hands and bouncing from foot to foot.

"Uncle Ash is taking me to get my recital dress. Isn't that so 'citing?"

My eyebrow shoots up in surprise, but a smirk breaks free, anyway. "That is very, ah, exciting, Sadie Sunshine. You're very lucky. I've heard Ash is a great dress shopper."

Ashton coughs, and it sounds suspiciously like "fuck you," but he recovers quickly.

"We should get going, Sadie Sunshine. The store is only open until four." Ash turns to me, and though his voice will never be the same, relief at the strength in his words weighs on me. "We set everything up from your entryway to the great room, just as you requested. Good luck. You have the ring?"

My hand flies to my pocket out of habit. It's silly, really, since I can feel it like the elephant in the room.

"Yup. I'm actually doing this."

A rare smile crosses Ash's face, and he nods happily. "You are. I'm happy for you, Halt. Truly."

Emotions clog my throat, cutting off any chance of a reply. My baby brother has fallen even deeper into his own personal hell over the last year or so. The only glimpse of the man we once knew comes out in Sadie's presence. It's a blessing and a curse, but it gives me hope that we'll find our sweet brother again one day.

"Have fun shopping." I meant it honestly, but a chuckle escapes, too.

"Fuck off," Ash grumbles. "How the hell do you say no to this girl?"

I smirk because I know it's impossible, and that's precisely why our mother insisted on his Friday nights with her.

Ash pats me on the shoulder and points behind me. Turning, I find Rylan exiting the yoga studio with Lexi and Ari, and I smile.

"Good luck," Ash whispers, taking Sadie by the hand and leading her to his car.

I'm so mesmerized by Rylan I'm not even sure if I said good-bye, but the closer she gets, the broader my smile becomes.

"Hey, you. What are you doing here?" she asks, flinging her lithe body into mine.

I catch her on instinct and drag her into me. "I was running an errand with Ash, so I thought I'd see if I can give you a ride home?"

Ari and Lexi mumble their good-byes and quietly fade away. We're in Vermont for Sadie's dance recital, and as soon as I decided I wanted to ask Rylan to marry me here, I knew I'd need some help. These two women jumped at the chance, and now we're about to find out if our planning worked.

"That's great!" She turns to tell the girls and frowns when she realizes they're already gone. "That's weird."

"Nah, they probably just knew I couldn't wait to get you alone."

"Is that so?"

"Yup." Holding out my hand, I drag her toward the car and closer to our forever.

The road up the backside of GG's mountain was paved recently, but it's still a mountain road that requires slow speeds, and right now, that's freaking brutal.

When we finally pull into the tongue and groove log cabin we've been slowly making our own, a thrill goes up my spine. Ash and Sadie have the lights dimmed just the way I asked for, and my palms sweat as Rylan climbs the front steps.

"I can't believe we left all these lights on," she sighs. "That's unusual."

"Mmhmm." I don't trust myself to speak as I push open the front door.

Rylan glides past me and comes to an abrupt stop as my first sketch comes into view.

"Oh my God, Hatty. What did you do? Look at this," she whispers through tears.

Her delicate finger traces the charcoal lines of two sad faces partially hidden by raincoats.

"Hatty?" Her voice breaks off as she notices the second one down the hall. It's of us at her birthday party sitting on the stairs.

Tears fall freely down her face as she enters the great room and makes her way from easel to easel. Us in the hammock. Us on the street at my failed art show. Us on prom night. Camping. Her fashion show. Us on the couch of our home in Waverley-Cay. Sitting on the porch of this log cabin.

Her shocked gasp tells me it's go time. Dropping to my knee behind her, I wait as she takes in the drawing of this exact moment. It seems to go on forever, and just as I'm about to lose my nerve, she turns.

Trembling hands cover her mouth as a sob escapes.

"Words have never been my thing, sweetheart. I'm trying to get better because I refuse to lose you again. But I realized something the other day. Even if I can't find the words, I can express what I'm feeling through these." I wave my hand around the room. "Sometimes, they might even be better since my communications skills are obviously lacking.

"I won't promise to be perfect, but I will promise to try. I'll try to be the best version of myself for you every day. I'll try to be a friend when you need one, even if I have to kick Colton's ass to be that friend. I'll try to be the partner you deserve in life and love. The only thing I'll never have to attempt, though, is loving you. That's as natural as breathing to me. Sometimes loving you is actually easier. I promise to love you with all that I am. I promise to find the words when the need arises, and I promise to make you happy for all of our days. You're my sunbeam in a dark sky. You make me a better man every day, and I want to prove to you for the rest of your life that I'm worthy of you. Please let me do that, Rylan. Marry me, and let me show you all the ways I'll love you, sempiternal."

Rylan drops to her knees beside me. A second later, her lips are on mine. It's a possessive kiss. One that bonds us together for all time, but I need words. I need to hear her say yes.

Pulling away, I cradle her face in my hands. "Is that a yes, princess? Will you marry me?"

Through sobs, Rylan nods her head, and a broken yes comes out on a cry. "Yes, Hatty. A million lifetimes of yes."

She stares into my eyes as an ugly cry takes over her beautiful face. I can't help but laugh through my own tears.

"Can I make one request?"

Rylan nods frantically.

"Please don't ever make me listen to you shit again. I think a little mystery in a marriage is okay."

A strangled laugh erupts through slobber, tears, and snot. My girl can ugly cry with the best of them, and she's never looked more beautiful.

Leaning in, I kiss her in thanks, in love, in happiness, and in hope.

"Thank you for saving me, my sweet Verity."

"Thank you for loving me so much you never let me go."

We've been through hell and back. I still have demons to fight, but I know I can face anything with Rylan at my side. We are truly stronger together, and I vow, at this moment, to never take our love for granted because my dad was right. A love like ours only comes around once in a lifetime.

I say a silent prayer of thanks to my dad. Wherever he is, I know he's looking down on us and smiling. It's that knowledge that lets me put to bed my fears over what he thought of Rylan and me. He loved us all, and I know he would be proud of the man I've become, even if it took a few wrong turns to get here.

Holding Rylan, I breathe her in in contentment. I know, soon enough, the chaos will surround us, wishing us well. It's how my family operates. But it's in these quiet moments that I find the strength to face it all.

My panacea for a happy life is the little girl my heart has longed for since I was seven years old. And now she's mine forever.

"Welcome to the chaos," Colton bellows as the front door snaps open. "Now you get to be my BFF and my sister-in-law. This bachelorette party is going to be ah-maaazing!"

Before I can complain, the dickhead has Rylan out of my arms and is flinging her around the room. I haven't even put the damn ring on her finger, and yet, I can't seem to find any anger as I watch my family filter in one after another. Happiness and love radiating from them all and directed at Rylan and me.

I really am the luckiest grumpy asshole in the world.

Want to see what happens when Ash takes Sadie Sunshine dress shopping?

Download the extended epilogue here!

Or visit my website:
www.averymaxwellbooks.com

If you loved this book please consider leaving a review.
Reviews are how Indie Authors like myself succeed.
Thank you!
<u>Please leave a review here!</u>

Turn the page for a sneak peek at the next Westbrook
brother to fall in love in One Little Kiss, coming soon!

ONE LITTLE KISS

COLTON

"Wha-wha, wha-wha-wha-wha."

It's never a good sign to be woken up by your oldest brother sounding like Charlie Brown's teacher.

I turn my head toward the sound, only mildly alarmed that I'm unable to open my eyes. Lifting my hands feels like a herculean effort, but I do it and stab numb fingers at my face until my fingertips land on my eyelids. Prying them open with both index fingers, I wince.

"Who blew saw dust into my eyeballs?" my voice croaks, and it's followed by a groan.

What the fuck is wrong with me?

Something hard sails past my face, landing less than an inch away from my head. Rolling my neck to the left, I find an iPad.

"Why the hell are you throwing shit at me, Pres?"

He yells again, but it sounds like we're underwater, so I don't answer him. Before I know what's happening, he rips the covers from my body. Cool air glides over my skin, and I shiver. My dick takes notice, and I realize I must be nude.

Halton sits on the edge of my bed. I hadn't even realized he was here. Someone definitely pissed in their Cheerios, though, because as he hands me a cup of coffee, anger radiates off him.

"Get the fuck up, Colton." Preston's words are finally taking shape.

"What is your problem? Why are you breaking and entering this morning?"

"You don't remember? Jesus, Colton. Our family doesn't get press like this. We work our asses off to stay out of the tabloids, and you ruin that in one fucking night you can't remember?"

My head throbs as I scoot up in bed.

"What are you talking about?"

Preston jabs an angry finger into the iPad, and the screen comes to life.

"How could you do this to us, Colton? You've always been a little selfish, but never destructive. Any chance we had at splitting The Westbrook Group into separate entities is gone after this little stunt. There's no way our board will vote in favor of us diversifying. You've essentially fucked every one of your brothers over. I hope a little pussy was worth it, you asshole."

"Do you have any idea what this is going to do to Mom?" Halt asks quietly.

"What the hell are you talking about?" I try to yell, but my throat feels like the Sahara, and it comes out gravely and weaker than I intend.

Preston practically throws the iPad in my face.

"Preston, calm down. Beating the shit out of him won't help matters."

I stare between Halton and Pres. Whatever they think I've done must be big. Preston has never once threatened me.

Peering down at the tablet, I see TMZ is open, and my naked ass sits slumped over in between two girls I've never seen before in my life.

"This isn't real. I've never seen these girls before."

. "Oh, yeah? Then why did we just escort them out of your living room with threats of a lawsuit?" Preston snarls.

My head snaps to his. "No way. I didn't even ... I didn't even drink last night."

Preston gives an undignified huff, and Halton shakes his head.

"You party every night, Colton. You have no responsibility to anyone."

I know that's how it appears, but I rarely drink, and last night, I ordered a fucking root beer.

"This is bullshit, Pres. You can check my tab from The Loft; that's where I was last night. I was drinking fucking root beer, watching the Braves game."

"And you woke up hungover, naked, with two girls rifling through your kitchen." Preston sneers.

"I'm not hungover, you dipshit. I didn't fucking drink."

Memories of last night try to pierce my consciousness, but everything is fuzzy.

"Was one of the girls a redhead?"

"So you do remember?"

"No ... I mean, sort of? She sat down and asked me to buy her a drink." Scratching my head, I try to remember if I actually did. "I think I bought her one but told her I wasn't looking for company. I just wanted to catch the end of the game."

"You should have watched it at home," Halton mumbles.

Anger and sadness fill my chest. "I don't like watching the games by myself, and you two assholes were too busy."

"We have responsibilities, Colton. Families that depend on us. We can't just drop everything to have a fucking beer with you when you're feeling lonely." Preston turns to Halt. "I'm so done with the Peter Pan bull shit."

"What's that supposed to mean?" I growl.

"It means you need to grow the fuck up. You may have just ruined this opportunity that would allow Halton and

325

East to run a branch of The WB the way they want to. That fucks up their plans, Colt. Do you even give a shit about anyone but yourself these days?"

I admit, I've been a little more carefree lately, but what does he expect? Every person I know and love is in a committed relationship that doesn't always include me.

"You know I do, Preston. None of this makes sense. I swear to you I wasn't drinking last night."

"So what? You're telling me they drugged you?"

I hadn't thought about it, but now that he's said it, I think he's on to something.

"Yes, actually. I think I might have been. You don't black out from root beer."

My older brother narrows his eyes like he's contemplating his next move. Then he rakes a hand through his hair, spins in place, and lands a punch into the drywall next to the door.

"Get dressed. Emory will take a blood sample, but you've left me with no choice here, Colt. I have to put you on administrative leave, effective immediately. The media has already surrounded your building. The girls are saying you forced them here, and until we can prove otherwise, you need to lay low. The chopper will be here in an hour, and Ash is expecting you. I'm sure the gossip columns will track you to Vermont, but no one is getting past Ashton's security. You're on lockdown until we can sort this shit out."

"But I didn't fucking do anything, Preston."

His expression softens but doesn't lessen the blow. "You put yourself in this position, Colt. Maybe not intentionally, but you know that you have to be aware of your surroundings as well as we do. We've literally been taught to watch out for those that will try to take us down since we were kids. Now my hands are tied. I have to keep our ship afloat, and as CEO, the only option is to suspend you. As your brother, it's the last thing I want to do. As the CEO, it's my only choice."

"So … what? You want me to go into hiding like I'm guilty?"

"I'll have Ash pull security footage from The Loft and start interviewing anyone that was there last night, but until we have concrete evidence, yes. You're to stay out of sight. We cannot handle another scandal right now, Colt. This will devastate Mom, too, so we need to get you out of here before she shows up."

I cringe at the knowledge she's about to see pictures of me naked as the day I was born. But the only thing that matters to me right now is that my brothers believe me. I may be the fuck up as of late, but I love them and this family with all that I am.

"Fine," I agree. "But I need to know something first. Do you believe me?"

Preston and Halt share a look that hits like a lead weight to my gut.

"Yeah, Colty. We believe you," Halton says softly. "But you make it really fucking hard sometimes."

≈

You can pre-order One Little Kiss here!

≈

Want to know who Colton's heroine will be? Join my reader group, The Luv Club, on Facebook for exclusive sneak peeks…coming soon!

≈

One Little Kiss Blurb:

My name is Colton Westbrook, and life just threw me into a dumpster fire. I like to have fun. I like to go out, but when one wrong decision puts me in the spotlight with a less than favorable glare, my family puts me on lockdown.

Vermont has become a second home to me, but every time I'm here, I find myself searching for *that* girl around every corner. One little kiss that happened three years ago in a deserted airport terminal. One little kiss that branded me, scared me, could even ruin me if I were *that* guy looking for a happily ever after.

But that's not me. I'm not hiding out in my brother's home secretly searching for the one that got away. I'm not wearing stupid disguises to fool the paparazzi, hoping she'll turn up. And I'm definitely not that guy relying on a crazy old lady and her tarot cards to find a girl. Nope. Not me.

I'll stay a lost boy in Neverland...until the day I realize some people are worth growing up for.

Hello Luvs,

You didn't think I managed to get this book out on my own did you? I can barely remember to brush my hair everyday, so let me introduce you to the people who help me succeed in life:

First and foremost, my husband. Mr. Maxwell will probably never read this, but it is his love and support that truly makes this possible. *Thank you for being believing in me, even when I'm hiding under the covers crying.*

To my children. I know you hate that mommy works now but thank you for being the best part of every day.

Beth: My word finder, first reader, supporter, and encourager, thank you for being awesome. *Thank you for reminding me that twatwaffles don't matter and for being my fiercest protector,* especially when I can't see the rainbow through the storm. xoxo

Rhon: What would I do without you? *Thank you for being my support system 24/7.* You build me up on my darkest days, and I'll forever be grateful. Thank you for working tirelessly to get me organized and for keeping #teamavery on track.

Marie & Carissa: *Thank you for being my cheerleaders,* especially when I'm doubting myself, and for keeping The Luv Club the happy, kind place it is. I appreciate you both so much.

Kia, Michelle & Melissa: My made up SPARC Team. *Thank you for being my front line.* For reading my stories and making them better. For offering encouragement and friendship when the Imposter takes over. I value your opinions and your friendship so very much.

Street Team: Seriously! You guys are rock stars! *Thank you for pimping me tirelessly.* Your efforts never go unnoticed, and every boost I get is because of you. I appreciate you all sticking with me, pushing me, and loving my stories the way you do.

ARC Team: *Thank you for continuing to read my stories.*

Your feedback is what makes me a better author. Without you, my nerves would get the better of me and I'd be curled up in the fetal position instead of hitting publish. Your support is a huge part of any success I have and I am beyond grateful for you all.

My small network of Author and PA friends: *Thank you for holding my hand.* Thank you for encouraging me when I was at my lowest. Thank you for reaching out, pushing me, and mostly, thank you for believing in me. I luv you all.

Finally, YOU, my readers. Where would I be without you? *Thank you for taking a chance on an indie author.* Thank you for loving my characters and supporting me every step of the way. Thank you for encouraging me when I wanted to quit. Thank you for investing your time in this crazy, chaotic family that keeps growing in my head. It's your enthusiasm and belief in me that keeps me moving through the chaos to bring you these crazy brothers. I LUV you all.

Imposter syndrome hits me hard. Every. Single. Time. It's because of you I'm able to continue, so thank you all from the bottom of my heart.

Dark City Designs: Jodi, you are amazing! *Thank you for designing all the things!* Your support and help with all things author-ish is appreciated more than you know. Xoxo

There For You Editing: Melissa, *thank you for your patience.* I'm trying to learn, but let's be real...there are just some things I'm never going to get. That's why I have you. Thank you for always delivering.

All my luvs,
Avery

GET TO KNOW AVERY!

A New-England girl born and raised, Avery now lives in North Carolina with her husband, their four kids, and two dogs.

A romantic at heart, Avery writes sweet and sexy Contemporary Romance and Romantic Comedy. Her stories are of friendship and trust, heartbreak, and redemption. She brings her characters to life for you and will make you feel every emotion she writes.

Avery is a fan of the happily-ever-after and the stories that make them. Her heroines have sass, her heroes have steam, and together they bring the tales you won't want to put down.

Avery writes a soulmate for us all.

Want to get to know Avery? She hangs out in her reader group, The Luv Club, every day! See her chaos, her crazy, and her luv. We hope to see you there!

HATTY'S COOKIE RECIPE

*R*ylans Coconut Heaven
- 2 ¼ cup all purpose flour
- 1 tsp salt
- 1 tsp baking soda
- ¾ cup sugar
- ¾ cup light brown sugar
- 2 room temperature eggs
- 2 sticks room temperature butter
- 1 ½ tsp Mexican Vanilla
- Dash of cinnamon
- 1 bag of chocolate chips (use the good ones, you'll thank me; I use Ghirardelli milk chocolate)
- 1-14oz bag of shredded/flaked sweetened coconut
- Chocolate for melting/dipping (I use Ghirardelli Dark Chocolate wafers)

1) Preheat oven to 350.

2) Using an electric mixer, beat butter and sugars until smooth.

3) Add in one egg at a time.

4) Add in vanilla (if you can't find Mexican Vanilla, just use the best vanilla extract you can find.)

5) Scrap down the sides of the bowl, then mix again for 30 seconds.

6) In a separate bowl, mix the flour, salt, baking soda, and cinnamon together until combined.

7) Add dry ingredients to you butter mixture in three batches.

8) Once combined, add chocolate chips.

9) Add the entire bag of coconut and get ready to use some muscle. This batter is thick.

10) One thoroughly combined (make sure there are no big chunks of coconut hiding out) use an ice cream scooper to measure out the batter. Place scooped batter onto a cookie sheet lined with parchment paper.

11) Bake for six minutes. Rotate your pan and bake for another 5 minutes. They're done when the edges are slightly brown and the center looks a little soft.

12) Cool for at least an hour.

13) Melt your chocolate for dipping according to the package instructions. Moving quickly, dip ½ of each cookie into the chocolate mixture. Place on parchment paper to cool and harden.

Now, try not to eat them all!

Luvs,

Avery

BOOKS BY AVERY MAXWELL

The Westbrooks: Broken Hearts Series:

Book 1- Cross My Heart

Book 2- The Beat of My Heart

Book 3- Saving His Heart

Book 4- Romancing His Heart

The Westbrooks: Family Ties Series:

Book .5- One Little Heartbreak- A Westbrook Novella

Book 1- One Little Mistake

Book 2- One Little Lie

Book 3- One Little Kiss (Pre-Order Now)

Book 4- One Little Secret (Coming Soon)